The Madman
and the Medusa

by Tchicaya U Tam'Si

*translated by Sonja Haussmann Smith
and William Jay Smith*

Introduction by Eric Sellin

CARAF BOOKS

D1527383

The University Press of Virginia

CHARLOTTESVILLE

This is a title in the CARAF BOOKS series

THE UNIVERSITY PRESS OF VIRGINIA

Originally published as *Les meduses, ou les orties de la mer*
© Editions Albin Michel S. A. Paris, 1982

This translation and edition Copyright © 1989
by the Rector and Visitors of the University of Virginia

First published 1989
Library of Congress Cataloging-in-Publication Data

Tchicaya U Tam'si, 1931–
The madman and the medusa.

(CARAF books)
I. Title.   II. Series.
PQ3989.2.T35M4413   1989   843   88-26086
ISBN 0-8139-1205-9

Printed in the
United States of America

To Robert Sabatier
and
Christiane Lesparre

Contents

Glossary

aya: A term of respect.

bilanda laï: Those who followed the railroad.

Chargeurs Réunis: United Freight Haulers.

Chemin de Fer Congo-Océan (C.F.C.O.): An important rail link built by the French at considerable loss of African lives. It connected Brazzaville, the capital of the colony, to the port at Pointe-Noire.

Compagnie Générale du Bas-Congo: Commercial monopoly in the French Congo.

Djindji: A section of Pointe-Noire.

foufou: Mashed cassava made into dumplings.

Laris: Ethnic group of the Lower Congo.

mami-ouatas: sirens.

Mayombe: A mountain range between Brazzaville and Pointe-Noire.

mboulou mboulou: Deprecatory term for African militiamen identified by their red cylindrical cap, or chechia.

Native Village: In regions of Africa colonized by France the Native Village was distinguished from the City, which was reserved for Europeans.

saka-saka: A dish made from cassava.

Scieries Réunies: United Sawmills.

Sergeant Malamine: Sergeant Mamadou Lamine (1840–87), leader of a rebellion against the French.

so-ouassi: A pidginization of the French word *sauvage.*

tchilanda laï: Singular form of *bilanda laï; laï* is a pidginization of French *rail:* railroad.

zambi abkulu: A treacherous situation or problem.

Introduction

The second novel by Congolese poet, novelist, and dramatist Tchicaya U Tam'Si, first published in French in 1982 by the prestigious Parisian house Albin Michel under the title *Les méduses ou les orties de la mer* —(here translated as *The Madman and the Medusa*)—is a fascinating and brilliant, but most puzzling, fictional work.

The elusiveness of this novel will not surprise those familiar with earlier publications by the author of *The Madman and the Medusa*, for they would not really expect a work by Tchicaya—whether in prose or poetry—to be anything but enigmatic. His creative works, from the very outset of his career, established him as a major writer and yet something like an index of difficulty in his work may be gauged by the relative paucity of substantive criticism about his writing over the past thirty-odd years.

Tchicaya's highly refracted style, privately encoded references, and recurrent use of symbols whose meanings easily elude us contribute in most of his works to what amounts, at first glance, to a forbidding discourse. His work has always been difficult to penetrate, and remains so even in recent years, when a generation of readers and scholars exposed to contemporary trends in fiction and critical theory has been weaned on the appreciation of fragmentation and the tolerance of lack of closure.

The Madman and the Medusa, which can, of course, be read as an individual work in its own right, also functions as an integral part of a sequence of novels consisting of four books—*Les cancrelats* (The roaches), 1980; *Les méduses ou les orties de la mer* (The madman and the medusa), 1982; *Les phalènes* (The moths), 1984; and *Ces fruits si doux de l'arbre à pain* (Those sweet, sweet fruits of the breadfruit tree), 1987— in which Tchicaya paints in very broad strokes the historical mural of the stereotypical African adventure in the twentieth century, beginning with a fully colonized Equatorial African country—the French Moyen-Congo, or Middle Congo—in the first half of the twentieth century and proceeding through several generations up to the 1960s in what was by then an independent Congo republic.

We shall return to these other novels and to a direct discussion of *The Madman and the Medusa,* but first it seems appropriate to situate the novel and its author in what may be said to constitute something approaching a literary canon; or perhaps we might better speak of several overlapping canons, including that of literature written in French by Africans, that of Third-World authors, and that of diglossic or bilingual writing involving an acquired creative tongue that is different from the mother tongue. We shall also tarry a moment on Tchicaya's country, the People's Republic of Congo, which provides the important visual, social, and historical setting for *The Madman and the Medusa.*

The African novel of French expression—or what some critics prefer to term *de graphie française,* or "written in French," reserving *expression* or *francophone* for those who speak the language as their first tongue—is a most interesting, rich, and varied corpus of fiction, embracing as it does places as disparate as Algeria, Cameroon, Zaïre, Senegal, and, of course, Congo. Naturally, there are regional differences, as there might be between a novel by an American southerner and one by a northerner, but the African novels of French expression from various areas do have a number of traits in common.

African writers of French expression belong to a tradition of hybrid, or mixed, lingua-ontology. Under this rubric, we place writers who were born to a mother tongue and then went on to write in another language, one that was usually first acquired when the child went to a French school. The de-

Introduction

gree of linguistic acumen varies substantially among the many Africans in francophone countries who aspire to publication in French, from what amounts to little more than schoolboy French as a foreign language to a dazzling mastery of the language. Tchicaya's command of the language is, of course, at the extreme latter end of the spectrum, for aside from having such prerequisites as great talent and dedication, he spent most of his life in France. Tchicaya U Tam'Si's control of French is total: not only does he possess a vast vocabulary and a sophisticated style, but he also embarks effortlessly on such linguistic adventures as word coinage, punning, and the like.

To some degree, however, every francophone writer brings to his or her writing a hybrid lingua-ontology, and Tchicaya is, of course, no exception. The particular African culture, mores, customs, and rhetorical predilections—for example, the use of proverbs to convey instruction and to preserve tradition that we find in writers as remote from one another as Tchicaya of Congo, Ahmadou Kourouma of Ivory Coast, and Chinua Achebe of Nigeria—are the birthright of the writer, whereas the customs and traditions of the culture *behind* the acquired language (in Tchicaya's instance, French) are foreign, belonging rather to those for whom the language in which they write is the maternal tongue. The writer is, in sum, of one ontology, but uses a language proper to another ontology. As we shall see when discussing the affinity Tchicaya had for Rimbaud, this ontological dislocation is a discernible and significant factor in his work.

In general, a hybrid lingua-ontology poses some problems for the author, but it also presents him or her with a number of opportunities and benefits. The literature resulting from an author's bilingual background is often infused with original creative features as a result of the "interference" between his culture and elements in the adopted language. Linguistic creative development and interaction occur in different ways in the bilingual or plurilingual experience. Sometimes one can detect and analyze the workings of bilingualism (in which the system reverts by default to alternative solutions and associations within the *same* language whenever a communication glitch occurs) or diglossia (in which the system defaults to another system, from one language to another, in a neural short circuit of sorts, when difficulties are encountered or interference occurs). This phenomenon has been described by the Moroccan poet Abdelkebir Khatibi in a number of his essays and lectures, as in, say, the following passage from *Amour bilingue:*

> In French—his foreign language—the word [*mot*] is close to death [*mort*], with only one letter missing. . . . Why did he believe that language is more beautiful, more terrible for a foreigner?
>
> Suddenly he grew calm [*se calma*], when there appeared to him the Arabic "word" [*mot*] "kalma" with its learned equivalent "kalima" and whole gamut of diminutives, the puns of his childhood: "klima". . . . The diglossia "kal-(i)ma" came back without the word "word" disappearing or being erased. They wearily watched over one another in him, preceding the sudden and rapid emergence of memories, word fragments, onomatopoeic sounds, festooned sentences, entwined to the death: indecipherable.[1]

The possibilities of aesthetic enrichment through such "interference" are obvious. The writer will certainly adopt, along with the second language, a good bit of its attendant literary and cultural patrimony; but he or she will also bring to the literature in the second language a host of new concepts and new impulses, new aesthetic blood, so to speak. This enrichment will be true to some degree among Québecois writers, but it is much more applicable in an African, Antillean, or Vietnamese writer because the Québecois, despite his unique environment, shares the same ethnic background—the ontology—as inheres in the *lingua*, whereas the others operate according to hybrid lingua-ontological principles.

We shall not go over the history of the francophone African novel in detail, but it is necessary to review a few salient fea-

---

1. Abdelkebir Khatibi, *Amour bilingue* (n.p. [Montpellier]: Fata Morgana, 1983), p. 10. My translation.

tures of that history if we are to appreciate Tchicaya's sensibility as a novelist, for if he was in many ways an avantgarde poet, he was even more of an innovator in fiction and only failed to receive his full historical due because of the difficulties he initially encountered in finding a publisher for his brilliant first novel, *Les cancrelats.*

The history of the African francophone novel dates back to before World War II and such works as Paul Hazoumé's *Doguicimi* (1938), but it really began to develop an identity, a canon, with the publication in 1953 of *L'enfant noir* (The African child) by the Guinean Camara Laye (1928–80). There followed, in the 1950s, a number of books by such writers as Ferdinand Oyono (b. 1929) of Cameroon, Bernard Dadié (b. 1916) of Ivory Coast, Olympe Bhêly-Quénum (b. 1928) of Benin (ex-Dahomey), and others that tended, like Camara's *L'enfant noir,* to be autobiographical and/or "ethnographic." The novelists, though worthy stylists, seemed timid when it came to adjusting the French language to their African weltanschauung, preferring to use existing metropolitan literary patterns that they found suitable to their outlook and that were closest to the structures appropriate to orature: namely, those entailing directness of style, episodic formatting of narrative, and a preference for the autobiography, diary, chronicle, and so forth.

True, there had been one work by Camara Laye, *Le regard du roi* (The radiance of the king), published in 1954, that seemed to possess oneiric and cinematographic effects that were far ahead of their time in the African francophone canon. A number of people, notably Lilyan Kesteloot, claim that someone else wrote the novel for Camara Laye, but these claims are based on flimsy arguments. The recovery of a "lost" story by Camara, "Le prince," which was composed about the same time as *Le regard du roi* and which seems to be a variation on the theme of the ending of *Le regard du roi* and yet also in a style reminiscent of Camara's story, "Les yeux de la statue," generally acknowledged to be by the Guinean, would seem to support his claim to authorship of the novel as well.

Introduction

Aside from that novel—and, of course, *Nedjma* (1956) by Kateb Yacine of Algeria—one had to wait until 1968, a pivotal political and cultural year in France and her ex-colonies, for a turning point: one that would find sub-Saharan African writers no longer paying slavish obeisance to European forms and diction but instead manhandling the French language, molding it to conform to and to express structures and impulses true to their own cultural identity.

Two novels published in 1968, *Le devoir de violence* (Bound to violence) by Malian Yambo Ouologuem and *Les soleils des indépendances* (The suns of Independence) by Ahmadou Kourouma of Ivory Coast, undermined—each in its own way—the European preeminence in francophone discourse and revolutionized the canon.

What is interesting here is that Tchicaya U Tam'Si's first novel, *Les cancrelats*, published in 1980, was actually begun in 1954. He has recounted in an interview how he had a rough plan in his head for the trilogy of *Les cancrelats, Les méduses,* and *Les phalènes* and had actually written the first book, but wanted to see if it were publishable before he wrote the next two works. *Les cancrelats* was turned down in 1958 by four publishers and in 1979 by six publishers. Finally, Tchicaya showed the manuscript to his friend Robert Sabatier while on a visit to the latter's country house in southern France with the intention of giving up on it if, in Sabatier's frank opinion, it was not worthy of publication. Sabatier saw the clear merit of *Les cancrelats* and Albin Michel became Tchicaya's publisher.[2] It is no wonder, then, that the subsequent novel, *The Madman and the Medusa*, was dedicated to Tchicaya's friend Robert Sabatier and his painter-writer wife Christiane Lesparre.

Two facts emerge from this little contretemps: first, Tchicaya was ostensibly a visionary and a forerunner in African francophone fiction but simply did not have the revolutionary impact he might have had on the canon because his book had remained in manuscript for twenty-two years and was thus

2. Unpublished interview with Tchicaya U Tam'Si, Paris, 24 July 1987.

unavailable to readers at large; second, one can discern a difference in tone between *Les cancrelats* and the ensuing novels that becomes more understandable when one considers that the first book was written many years before *Les méduses* and *Les phalènes,* which had been roughed out in Tchicaya's mind but not actually written until after *Les cancrelats* was placed with a publisher. As Tchicaya said: "I wanted to write a trilogy that would accompany the poetry because between the poetry and the novel the themes are more or less the same. . . . And then when *Les cancrelats* was finally accepted . . . and I didn't even believe it, I thought they were making fun of me . . . when it came out all sorts of things were liberated, and I continued and I was able to finish that trilogy. . . . I had stopped after the first volume."[3]

The Moyen-Congo and its capital Brazzaville were at the center of the French cultural, political, and intellectual activity of French Equatorial Africa, just as Dakar and Senegal were the focal point of French West Africa. The Congolese had a high literacy rate, and today the visitor to Congo is still struck by the high number of writers and intellectuals in the country. Tchicaya is, without doubt, the foremost Congolese writer, but other names come to mind, including those of Jean Malongo, Guy Menga, Sylvain Bemba, Martial Sinda, Henri Lopès, Théophile Obenga, Jean-Baptiste Tati-Loutard, E. B. Dongola, and Sony Labou Tansi, whose robust novels appear to be, in part, inspired by Tchicaya's work.

The Congo has been a witness to important moments in the recent history of the continent, perhaps none more important than the Brazzaville conference in June 1944, when de Gaulle and others convened to discuss the future of Free France and the overseas territories. Brazzaville is also the neighbor of Congo-Kinshasa across the river, where so many political dramas were to be played out in the 1960s. Congo-Brazzaville, like many other new African entities, had an uncertain, violent beginning in the years following independence as it groped to-

3. Ibid.

wards political identity. The period saw a parade of names like Fulbert Youlou (present under an alias, l'Abbé Lokou, in *Ces fruits si doux de l'arbre à pain*), Henri Lopès, Marien Ngouabi, and Denis Sassou Nguesso, not to mention such preindependence figures as Governor-General Félix Eboué, René Pléven, and Charles de Gaulle.

A major enterprise in Congolese history was the building from 1922 to 1934 of the Congo-Ocean railroad, which like the cutting of the Suez Canal or the Panama Canal, was measured in backbreaking toil and many lost lives. Even as the railroad opened up the interior to export (a spur would, for example, be built in 1962 to bring minerals down from the northern region and Gabon to the main east-west line), it also became the vehicle of political and labor tensions. The railroad also brought with it European commodities and new values that threatened the old. In addition, it provided a broad-based forum for labor agitation and strike action with consequent violence.

Railroads figure prominently in a number of works by Africans, notably in Camara Laye's *L'enfant noir* as an intrusion that scatters sparks and fire in the child's village and whose warm ballast provides hiding places for dangerous snakes and in Ousmane Sembène's 1960 novel *Les bouts de bois de dieu* (God's bits of wood) as the center of syndicalist job action on the Ocean-Niger line. Finally, the railroad holds a central role in *The Madman and the Medusa*, as we shall see below.

Gérald Félix Tchicaya (U Tam'Si) was born in 1931 in M'Pili, Moyen-Congo (today the People's Republic of the Congo). His was a privileged family in what was in some ways a privileged country. His father, Félix Tchicaya, was named a deputy to the French National Assembly in 1946. Thus, much of Tchicaya's youth was spent in Paris, where he attended the Lycée Janson-de-Sailly. In 1960, after several years working at various jobs, Tchicaya joined UNESCO, where he was employed for some twenty years, until 1985, when he began to devote all his time to his writing. Tchicaya died suddenly of cardiac arrest during the night of 21–22 April, 1988.

Introduction

Tchicaya composed prose at an early age along with his poetic production; he also wrote plays and retold traditional African legends. He had essentially two successful careers: first as a poet, then as a novelist. He adopted the nom de plume U Tam'Si: and over the years his name appeared under different forms and spellings, from Gérald Félix Tchicaya U Tamsi to Tchicaya U Tam'si and U Tam'Si. I once tried to pin him down as to which spelling of the several that appeared on his books he preferred, but he maintained that it did not matter, and he would not choose.

In 1955, Caractères Editions in Paris published Tchicaya's first collection of poems, *Le mauvais sang* (Bad blood) and Hautefeuille of Paris followed, in 1957, with *Feu de brousse* (Brush fire). This latter collection, which was awarded the Grand Prix de Littérature de L'Afrique Equatoriale Française, established Tchicaya's international reputation. Mbari Publications of Ibadan, Nigeria, brought out *Brush Fire*, translated into English by Sangodare Akanji (Ulli Beier's nom de plume) in 1964.

Several collections of poetry followed: *A triche-cœur* (A game of cheat-heart) was published in 1960 by P. J. Oswald in its J'exige la parole series; *Epitomé* (Epitome) by Oswald in its L'aube dissout les monstres series in 1962); and *Le ventre* (The belly) by Présence Africaine in 1964.

Some of these early works were no longer available in 1970 when P. J. Oswald reprinted *Le mauvais sang, Feu de brousse,* and *A triche-cœur* as one volume and a new work, *L'Arc musical* (The bow harp), preceded by a new edition of *Epitomé*. After a period of relative silence, *La veste d'intérieur suivi de Notes de veille* (The indoor coat followed by Waking notes) was published by Nubia in 1978.

Tchicaya turned to theater with *Le Zulu, suivi de Vwène le fondateur* (The Zulu, followed by Vwene the founding father) (Nubia, 1978) and *Le destin glorieux du maréchal Nnikon Nniku* (The glorious destiny of Marshal Nnikon Nniku) (Présence Africaine, 1979), and in 1980 his first major prose fiction appeared.

Tchicaya had published a collection of African legends, but

the publication of his first, boldly conceived novel, *Les cancrelats*, in 1980 by Albin Michel must be considered a literary event of some magnitude. That same year Robert Laffont published in its Chemins d'identité series, a collection of short prose pieces—they are not what we would call traditional short stories but rather like some of Samuel Beckett's briefer prose texts—under the title *La main sèche* (The withered hand). These stories are interesting primarily as spinoffs or footnotes to Tchicaya's longer prose works.

Despite failing health, Tchicaya published in the 1980s the novels that continue and develop the themes inherent in the first: *Les méduses ou les orties de la mer* (Albin Michel, 1982), *Les phalènes* (Albin Michel, 1984), and *Ces fruits si doux de l'arbre à pain* (Seghers, 1987). In our interview on 24 July 1987, Tchicaya U Tam'Si spoke of his first three novels as a trilogy, but then agreed that the fourth novel, *Ces fruits si doux de l'arbre à pain*, which had just come out, was a contextual sequel to *Les phalènes* and that the four books do constitute something of a tetralogy.

Tchicaya's four published novels are linked in a number of ways. They all discuss events occurring in the Congo. They are all written in approximately the same style, especially after *Les cancrelats*. Their overarching narrative thrust is in chronological order. The first novel covers the first half of the twentieth century up to the eve of World War II and the three other novels cover roughly a decade each. *The Madman and the Medusa* focuses on the war years, *Les phalènes* takes place in the 1950s, and the plot of *Ces fruits si doux de l'arbre à pain* unfolds in the first half of the 1960s.

The novels are linked in other ways as well. There are actually small references, or *renvois*, to the earlier books in several of the novels. For example, near the end of the original text of *The Madman and the Medusa*, there is a somewhat jarring authorial intervention that the translators have properly omitted in their text, a parenthetical *renvoi* sending the reader back to the author's previous book and the events of the period it covers: "'You had a cousin . . . wait a minute! Prosper

Introduction

Mpoba.' 'He is still my cousin.' 'And one of your relatives was Ndehlou Damien, whom I took to Diosso in the ambulance.' 'Well, it all happened a long time ago!' [See *Les cancrelats*.] 'Fifteen years maybe. That's right, that's right.'"

In a corollary to this procedure, Tchicaya likes to pick up anew and elaborate on images in his earlier novels, such as the image of the short-lived mayflies (*éphémères*) that he mentions in *The Madman and the Medusa:* "But our madman who could have been one of the preachers of those many sects who behave like mayflies springing from the ground in the rainy season, flying clumsily before losing their wings and crashing into the mud, the muck in which they suffer a sordid death . . ." and that Tchicaya elevates from metaphor to full-fledged symbol in the third part of *Ces fruits si doux de l'arbre à pain,* which bears the title "Les Ephémères" and contains the following description involving the little seeress Mouissou:

> When, in that year, at the beginning of the October rainy season, for a whole week clouds of mayflies never stopped coming out of the ground, flying low, losing their fragile wings, and crashing to the ground squirming like caterpillars, Mouissou—the little storyteller—went into a trance, rolled on the ground, spread spumes of spittle, uttered cries of unheard-of violence that would freeze the bravest of souls with fright. She recovered and announced: "There, that's a very bad omen. A sign of death! Alas, nothing can conjure it!"[4]

Furthermore, there is a uniformity of style among the novels, although the last three rely less for their impact on the narrative content and more on paracontextual effects; they are slightly more oneiric and symbolic than *Les cancrelats,* presumably in part because of the above-mentioned manuscript history.

---

4. Tchicaya U Tam'Si, *Ces fruits si doux de l'arbre à pain* (Paris: Seghers, 1987), p. 164. My translation. (The English quotations that follow in the text of the Introduction are from the present edition of *The Madman and the Medusa,* and no page references will be cited.)

Les cancrelats possesses a labyrinthine plot with subplots that need not detain us unduly here. Essentially, it deals with the affairs of two generations in a colonialist French family and in the family of the elder colonialist's servant, Ndundu, in the half-century before World War II. Ndundu's children, whom he has named Sophie and Prosper with the hopes of propitiating the forces of wisdom and wealth, live through the years of rising nationalist awareness and will reappear in *Les phalènes,* in which Prosper Pobard (Frenchified form of Mpoba) has become a political militant in the years between the cancellation of the infamous double-standard set of laws known as the "Indigénat" in February 1946 and Congo's independence in 1960.

Between these two novels, we have *The Madman and the Medusa,* whose main characters are three Congolese men—two skilled workers and a clerk—and their relatives and colleagues. But behind the mysterious goings-on in this novel two major historical phenomena loom almost as characters in the book: (1) the world war, which has brought troops and ships and the ban against strikes that might undermine the war effort, and (2) the railroad, with its own saga of prestige (Elenga is proud to drive the engines), dangerous wrecks, economic importance, labor disputes, and so forth.

Ces fruits si doux de l'arbre à pain unfolds in Brazzaville in the early 1960s, in the period during and immediately after the presidency of Abbé Fulbert Youlou (here called Lokou), perhaps best remembered for his wardrobe of splendrous cassocks. The protagonists are Judge Raymond Poaty and his wife, Mathilde, a school director, and their children and Prosper's children. Once again, what is tantamount to a character role in the narrative redounds to the cultural and political system in effect at the time. The system is rampant with corruption, venality, and the loss of traditional values with attendant moral decadence, and it victimizes people like the Poatys. The judge and his wife place honor above ambition and pay the price.

Tchicaya's first collection of poetry, *Le mauvais sang,* provides us with a fascinating instance of intertextuality. The collection is composed primarily of rhymed metrical or near-metrical poems that are postsymbolist in style, yet possess a highly charged and dense syntax that not only reminds one of Arthur Rimbaud's metrical poems—the title of Tchicaya's collection, *Le mauvais sang,* would in itself warrant our seeking a parallel in them—but brings to mind as well the poems of the Martinican poet Aimé Césaire, who was in turn inspired by Rimbaud, among others.

It is not difficult to understand the appeal of Rimbaud to an African writer who could empathize with the French youth's rebellious spirit, but an even clearer link is established between Tchicaya and Rimbaud in the final poem of *Le mauvais sang.* This text, "Le signe du mauvais sang" (The sign of the bad blood), is a prose poem reminiscent of Rimbaud's "Mauvais sang" (Bad blood), in *Une saison en enfer* (A season in Hell).

Mere resemblance would not cause us to linger over this poem, for such intertextual similarities can be found in virtually any work of art; but Tchicaya's poem is not mere imitation or derivation. It is a reply, the second *voice* in a dialogue, or *contrasto,* across the decades and geographical distances separating the two poets. Furthermore, "Le signe du mauvais sang" contains the seeds of many of the characteristics of Tchicaya's later prose style. Just as the seeds of Algerian Kateb Yacine's novels lay, by his own admission, in his very early poem "Nedjma ou le poème ou le couteau" (Nedjma or the poem or the knife), the essence of Tchicaya's novelistic style is perceptible in "Le signe du mauvais sang."

Rimbaud's "Mauvais sang" is a stunning, if occasionally infantile, vituperation. Its somewhat formless structure and its invective reflect changes in style that were occurring in French literature around 1870. In a span of a few years, we encounter the productions of Rimbaud's *Une saison en enfer* and *Les illuminations,* Lautréamont's *Les chants de Maldoror,* and Corbière's *Les amours jaunes,* not to mention Baudelaire's prose poems, inspired by Aloysius Bertrand's *Gaspard de la nuit,* published a generation earlier (1842).

What interests us here about "Mauvais sang" is not only its structure but also certain stylistic and contextual elements that Tchicaya adopts in his 1955 reply "Le signe du mauvais sang," which is a brotherly acknowledgment of Rimbaud. And, as has been mentioned, the text contains in embryonic form many of the elements that were later to surface, fully developed, in Tchicaya's novels.

African intellectuals like to cite the ludicrous practice, under the French policy of *assimilation,* of exporting lock, stock, and barrel to the colonies the educational attitudes and rote-learning material of the metropolitan scholastic system. They point out as particularly ridiculous the necessity for young African schoolboys to recite such phrases as "Our ancestors, the Gauls, were blue-eyed and blond and valiant."

Rimbaud's "Mauvais sang" opens with a debunking of the virtuous portrait of these ancestors:

> I get from my Gallic ancestors my pale blue eye, my small brain, and my awkwardness in fighting. I find my clothes as barbaric as theirs. But I do not butter my hair.
>
> The Gauls were the most inept flayers of beasts and scorchers of grass of their time.
>
> From them I get: idolatry and the love of sacrilege;—oh! all the vices, wrath, lust,—magnificent, the lust;—above all, falsehood and sloth.

> J'ai de mes ancêtres gaulois l'œil bleu blanc, la cervelle étroite, et la maladresse dans la lutte. Je trouve mon habillement aussi barbare que le leur. Mais je ne beurre pas ma chevelure.
>
> Les Gaulois étaient les écorcheurs de bêtes, les brûleurs d'herbes les plus ineptes de leur temps.
>
> D'eux, j'ai: l'idolâtrie et l'amour du sacrilège;—oh! tous les vices, colère, luxure,—magnifique, la luxure;—surtout mensonge et paresse.[5]

5. Arthur Rimbaud, "Mauvais sang," in *Une saison en enfer* (1873). (p. 108). There are numerous editions. I have before me Arthur Rimbaud, *Poésies, Une saison en enfer, Illuminations et autres textes,* ed. P. Pia (Paris: Le Livre de Poche, 1963), pp. 108–13. The translation from "Bad Blood" is from Arthur Rimbaud, *Une saison en enfer, Les illuminations: A Season in Hell, The Illuminations,* trans. Enid Rhodes Peschel (New York, London, and Toronto: Oxford University Press, 1973), p. 45. Subsequent page references will be cited in the text.

Introduction

Rimbaud continues to demean himself and his "race," which he avers has always been inferior:

> I have always been of an inferior race. I cannot understand revolt. My race never rose in rebellion except to plunder: like wolves with the beast they have not killed. . . . I am of a race inferior for all eternity. (pp. 45–47)

> J'ai toujour été de race inférieure. Je ne puis comprendre la révolte. Ma race ne se souleva jamais que pour piller: tels les loups à la bête qu'ils n'ont pas tuée. . . . Je suis de race inférieure de toute éternité. (p. 108).

Rimbaud's prose poem grows vindictive and promises action with the acknowledgment and assumption of his status:

> Here I am on the Breton shore. Let the towns sparkle in the evening. My day is done; I am leaving Europe. The sea air will scorch my lungs; odd climates will tan me. To swim, to trample the grass, to hunt, above all, to smoke; to drink liquors strong as boiling metal,—as my dear ancestors did around their fires. (p. 49)

> Me voici sur la plage armoricaine. Que les villes s'allument dans le soir. Ma journée est faite; je quitte l'Europe. L'air marin brûlera mes poumons; les climats perdus me tanneront. Nager, broyer l'herbe, chasser, fumer surtout; boire des liqueurs fortes comme du métal bouillant,— comme faisaient les chers ancêtres autour des feux. (p. 109)

Rimbaud then goes on to describe his return from a flight to the tropics, his "return from torrid countries" ("retour des pays chauds"), as a metamorphosed being, an angry-eyed, dark-skinned man of iron:

> I shall come back, with limbs of iron, my skin dark, my eye furious: from my mask, people will judge me a member of a powerful race. I shall have gold: I shall be idle and brutal. (p. 49)

> Je reviendrai, avec des membres de fer, la peau sombre, l'œil furieux: sur mon masque, on me jugera d'une race forte. J'aurai de l'or: je serai oisif et brutal. (pp. 109–10)

Finally, in the last third of the poem, Rimbaud identifies directly with the black man ("Je suis une bête, un nègre. . . . J'entre au vrai royaume des enfants de Cham" [p. 111]. / "I am a beast, a Negro. . . . I am entering the true kingdom of the children of Ham." [p. 53]) and reviews the abuses of the colonial adventure:

> The whites disembark. The cannon! It is necessary to submit to baptism, to wear clothes, to toil.
> I have received in my heart the coup de grâce. (p. 55)

> Les blancs débarquent. Le canon! Il faut se soumettre au baptême, s'habiller, travailler.
> J'ai reçu au cœur le coup de grâce. (p. 111)

It is only natural for Tchicaya to express sympathy for this fellow self-proclaimed Caliban. In Tchicaya's "Le signe du mauvais sang," we find reprises and replies alike. The poem's structural characteristics owe their inspiration to Rimbaud and, possibly, to Lautréamont and others, and Tchicaya has also orchestrated his imagery on the basis of images in "Mauvais sang." A full analysis of these two poems would require a book-length discussion, so suffice it to point out here one or two replies.

The first several versets of Tchicaya's poem read as follows:

> I am Bronze the alloy of the strong blood which squirts
> when the wind of the surging tides blows
>   Is the destiny of the old divinities athwart my destiny
> reason enough always to dance the song against its grain?
>   I was a lover frolicking with dragonflies; that was
> my past—my mother put a verbena blossom on my brown
> eye . . .
>   I felt my alloyed blood rumbling raucous cadences.

> Je suis le Bronze l'alliage du sang fort qui gicle quand
> souffle le vent des marées saillantes
>   Le destin des divinités anciennes en travers du mien est-
> ce raison de danser toujours à rebours la chanson?
>   J'étais amant à folâtrer avec les libellules; c'était mon

Introduction

passé—ma mère me mit une fleur de verveine sur ma prunelle brune . . .

Je sentis mon sang allié sourdre des cadences rauques.[6]

Tchicaya has, of course, directed our intertextual sensors at
Rimbaud's text with the words *bad blood* ("mauvais sang")
contained in his title. There are, then, possible literary gloss-
ings for a number of the images in Tchicaya's text. For example, the words *Bronze, alloy* ("l'alliage"), and *alloyed
blood* ("sang allié") in our quotation above, echo Rimbaud's
references to iron, boiling metals, and gold as well as to "tanning" ("tannage") and "dark skin" ("peau sombre"). The
"strong blood" ("sang fort") is evocative of Rimbaud's discussion of both the "inferior race" ("race inférieure") and its
opposite, the "strong race" ("race forte"). Rimbaud's reference to the "pale blue eye" ("œil bleu blanc") of his ancestors
and the "furious eye" ("l'œil furieux") of his would-be new
identity are intimated in Tchicaya's image of the "brown eye"
("prunelle brune").

Tchicaya is, then, empathizing with Rimbaud for the French-
man's empathy with the African, but he also has riposted in
kind, for in "Le signe du mauvais sang" Tchicaya debases his
race, too, in a way not unlike Rimbaud's debasing his own
race and in a way that cannot help but remind the apprised
reader of a celebrated passage in Aimé Césaire's *Cahier d'un
retour au pays natal* (Notebook of a return to the native land)
in which the poet/narrator feels contempt for a down-trodden
black man in a tram. Tchicaya writes: "I am a man I am a
black why does this take on a feeling of disappointment?"
("Je suis homme je suis nègre pourquoi cela prend-il le sens
d'une déception?" [p. 45]) and he concludes his poem with
the words: "No it's my blood in my veins! / What bad blood!"
("Non c'est mon sang dans mes veines! / Quel mauvais sang!"
[p. 48]).

6. Tchicaya U Tam'Si, "Le signe du mauvais sang," in *Le mauvais sang,
suivi de Feu de brousse et A triche-cœur* (Honfleur and Paris: P. J. Oswald,
1970), p. 45. My translation. Subsequent page references will be cited in
the text.

It is appropriate to make several further comments about the similarlity between these two texts and the notion that in Tchicaya's prose poem—inspired by Rimbaud's—lies the seed of his later prose works. First, Tchicaya has telescoped—in an elliptical manner characteristic of both his poetry and his prose—the various images that he has derived from Rimbaud. Thus, Tchicaya's word *Bronze* brings together several images in Rimbaud, notably the three images of liquors (like boiling metal), iron (as a metal, but also through the secondary linguistic linkage of the iron and bronze ages), and tanning and darkened skin (through secondary meanings of the French words *bronzer* and *bronzé* (to tan, tanned). Such ellipses, or eliminations of logical transitional material, along with a disregard for conventional chronological narrative order in the evocation of events, are common procedures in Tchicaya's poetic and prose styles alike and make their deciphering somewhat challenging to the reader.

Second, there are a number of sentences in Rimbaud's "Mauvais sang" that are couched in the interrogative, including one entire paragraph:

> To whom hire myself out? Which beast must be worshiped? What sacred image is being attacked? What hearts shall I shatter? What falsehood must I maintain?—In what blood wade? (p. 51)

> A qui me louer? Quelle bête faut-il adorer? Quelle sainte image attaque-t-on? Quels cœurs briserai-je? Quel mensonge dois-je tenir?—Dans quel sang marcher? (p. 110)

There are not an inordinate number of interrogatives in Tchicaya's "Le signe du mauvis sang," but in his novels, Tchicaya makes extensive use of the interrogative sentence as a mode of discourse. We shall address this question again in our discussion of *The Madman and the Medusa*.

Finally, we should briefly mention Rimbaud's importance in another context. Tchicaya has often been called a surrealist author, and yet he denied being a surrealist or being particu-

Introduction

larly influenced by the surrealist movement.[7] Since there are, in his poetry and prose, elements that are undeniably supernatural and oneiric, perhaps we would do better to see in his works a "surreal" dimension inherent in traditional African religious and cosmological beliefs and, perhaps, in the type of "pure hallucination" ("hallucination simple") that Rimbaud admired in "The Alchemy of the Word" ("L'alchimie du verbe").

There are other stylistic elements of significance in Tchicaya's novels, but these may just as well be taken up in the context of a single novel, in this instance *The Madman and the Medusa*.

The plot is rather simple. Tchicaya does not intend it otherwise, for he reveals the basic elements of the story from the very beginning when, after an anecdote that illustrates the power of superstition and rumor, Tchicaya's narrator describes the events that will form the nucleus of the entire novel:

"Two men died the last week of June 1944." "Actually three died. . . ." But the third one didn't die, miraculously perhaps. Who knows?

The three men were, of course, acquainted. . . . When I say that the third one didn't die, I mean not the same week. How and why? If I told you now, you wouldn't understand this strange case any better. . . .

Two men, both in perfect health, suddenly die the same week. The case is suspect; people are what they are and don't believe what seems obvious. Too true to be believed. They knew each other and were bound together by real friendship, I might even say a strange friendship. Then just like that, one dies after the other, the same week, within twenty-four hours of each other. Thursday, Friday, Saturday. Saturday, or more precisely, Saturday night, the third one escapes death in the strangest way. Where does it all happen?

7. Interview, 24 July 1987.

Death struck down the first two men at their workplace. But where do you think they found the third one almost dead? In the graveyard! Yes, lying between the tombs of his friends.

In the course of the novel we will learn the identity of these three mysteriously doomed men: Elenga, a train engineer with the Chemin de Fer Congo-Océan (C.F.C.O.), who will be shot by strikebreaking troops; Muendo, an employee at the lumber mill of the Scieries Réunies, who is killed by the circular saw while sawing boards for Elenga's coffin; and Luambu, a clerk at the Compagnie Générale du Bas-Congo (C.G.B.C.), whose dark past seems to be in some way linked to his final accident in the graveyard.

Among the numerous secondary, supporting roles are those of André Sola, who acts as sometime narrator, Elenga's sister, Mazola, their uncle Malonga, Monsieur Martin of the C.G.B.C., who embroils Luambu in a conspiracy, and a mad prophet who delivers sermons and prophecies on the beach and seems to exert magical influence on the other characters.

There is no suspense in the traditional sense in the main plot of the novel, for we know the end result from the outset, although we do find suspense in some of the subplots: Who is Juliette? What caused her drowning? What dark crime had Luambu been an accomplice to in Gabon? Are we to take some of the oneiric moments—such as the appearance and disappearance of the characters before a speaker's eyes—as dream visions, figments of a distraught mind, a novelistic device, or genuine magic? We are held enthralled, on the one hand, by the enigmatic odds and ends of information with which Tchicaya gradually reveals and elaborates on the events whose broad outline has been given in the beginning pages and, on the other, by the raw lyric energy and various rhetorical devices that Tchicaya deploys in the telling of the story.

As with the other novels, the personal dramas are set against the sweep of the recent history of Africa, specifically the events of World War II and of June 1944. There are a number of references to the war, Felix Eboué, Charles de Gaulle, and to warships in the harbor at Pointe-Noire, where the novel's events unfold, as well as to the soldiers who put down the ill-fated three-day strike, but the events are blurred and sketchily understood by the characters. The story truly unfolds *against* the backdrop of those events and does not reflect any conscious involvement in them or awareness of their worldwide significance. The accuracy of history is of minimal significance here, and we are reminded once again of the opening page of *Les phalènes* and Prosper's remarks: "Are you sure of the year of the end of the *indigénat?*—What do the archives say? And what are archives anyway?" ("Vous êtes sûr de l'année de la suppression du régime de l'indigénat?—Que disent les archives? Des archives, c'est quoi même?").

The optics are, simply put, Afrocentric in a period of transition. It would be illogical to be astonished that the Brazzaville conference that took place in the same month as the major events of the plot is only obliquely referred to, for Africans like Elenga, Muendo, and Luambu could hardly be expected to espouse a Eurocentric weltanschauung.

In this context it is interesting that, over the span of the tetralogy from *Les cancrelats* to *Ces fruits si doux de l'arbre à pain,* the point of view and the amount and vividness of the history and politics introduced specifically into the narrative change, shifting from a Eurocentric viewpoint during large parts of *Les cancrelats,* to a rather timeless or ahistorical Afrocentric viewpoint in *The Madman and the Medusa,* to the awakening involvement by Africans in contemporary African politics and the miniaturization of the colonial paradigm and its defeat represented by Prosper's alternately triumphant and humiliating liaison with a European woman described in *Les phalènes,* to the very close and cynical, yet Afrocentric, scrutiny of African postindependence politics in *Ces fruits si doux le l'arbre à pain.*

There are a few rhetorical elements in *The Madman and the Medusa* that are so characteristic as almost to constitute the very fabric of Tchicaya's prose style in all of his novels. As we have seen, some of the elements, such as an elliptical poetic prose style, were already in evidence in the early prose poem "Le signe du mauvais sang." Others that we have mentioned in passing but that warrant closer attention are the use of the interrogative, the use of the proverb, the use of the symbol, the use of contradiction or paradox, and the development of textual structure as expressions of a mode of thought.

Can one think of another author who makes more extensive use of questions than does Tchicaya? Just as the first person singular can be used as a surrogate third person—saying *I* when we are in no way making autobiographical remarks, or vice versa (Henry Adams wrote his autobiography in the third person singular)—so can the interrogative either be used repeatedly or expressed in such a manner as to lose its conventional grammatical purpose and to become simply an alternate mode of discourse. I have already mentioned Rimbaud's use of the interrogative in "Le mauvais sang."

The interrogative functions on at least five levels in this and the other prose works of Tchicaya. First, there are real solicitations of information in the dialogue. Second, there are questions in the narrative that express the desire to have an answer but may, on the other hand, only be meant to reinforce bewilderment about the mysteries at hand. Third, there are some questions that are mere conventions ("Etonnant, non?"). Fourth, this rhetorical convention involving a phantom interlocutor/reader sometimes becomes extended to passages of several sentences or to entire paragraphs. Fifth, the question mark is even introduced as having the weight, not of punctuation, but of vocabulary: "Luambu dit Lufwa Lumbu né ? à ?" (which is here translated as "Luambu, known as Lufwa Lumbu, born when? where?" whereas the pertinent portion would more literally read ". . . born ? at ?" in which the question mark both poses the questions and stands for the concepts entailed in the words *quand* and *où*).

In many instances, the interrogative becomes a manner of discourse that acts as a pausal element, adding no information to the fundamental proposition. The following passage—given in the original as well as in translation because of the repetition of the original interrogative "où":

Introduction

Death struck down the first two men at their workplace. But where do you think they found the third one
almost dead? In the graveyard! Yes, lying between the
tombs of his friends.

Les deux premiers, c'est sur leur lieu de travail que la mort
s'empare d'eux. Mais où, où crois-tu que l'on trouve le
troisième quasi mort? Au cimetière! Oh! Entre les tombes
des deux autres.

One might well argue that the interrogative adds nothing to
the contextual proposition of this passage, but some addi-
tional things are certainly conveyed by this style. The echoic
"où, où"—reinforced by the near echo of "Oh!"—is onomato-
poetically appropriate to the ghostly atmosphere of the graveyard, just as elsewhere in the novel *mbou* is said to echo the
sound of the sea. Furthermore, the use of the redundant interrogative, especially after instances of it begin to accumulate in
the reader's mind, is appropriate in a novel whose central
theme is an enigma. Finally, elsewhere, as in this example, the
contextually superfluous interrogative serves as a rhetorical
device to bring the reader into the narrative as addressee, as
interlocutor, and even, by extension, as accomplice, in that he
(the reader) is ultimately as privy to the meaning of the riddles
in the book as is the narrator/author.

In traditional African society, the proverb is the repository
of the collective wisdom and teaching of the society. Proverbs,
as well as such variants as the riddle and such elaborations of
the proverb as the folktale, provide a popular pedagogical
tool. If storytelling and chronicling of nobility's deeds has
fallen traditionally to specialists, the griots, the proverb has
been accessible to the average person and handed down from
parent to child and from elder to neophyte. The proverb is,
then, a privileged form of exchange in African discourse; it is,
as Achebe says, "the palm-oil with which words are eaten."[8]
Critics have maintained that in various traditional societies

---

8. Chinua Achebe, *Things Fall Apart* (Greenwich, Conn.: Fawcett Publications, 1959), p. 10. Subsequent page references will be cited in the text.

thoughout the world the proverb constitutes a miniature myth, sometimes barely more than a mytheme, and that myths are, conversely, extended proverbs.

Virtually all sub-Saharan African writers make some use of the proverb, but some make greater use of it than others. Perhaps the best-known example is Chinua Achebe's *Things Fall Apart,* in which the narrator and his characters make generous use of proverbs throughout the novel, as in the following:

Our elders say that the sun will shine on those who stand before it shines on those who kneel under them. (p. 11)

As the elders said, if a child washed his hands he could eat with kings. (p. 12)

As the Ibo say: "When the moon is shining the cripple becomes hungry for a walk." (p. 14)

Everybody laughed heartily except Okonkwo, who laughed uneasily because, as the saying goes, an old woman is always uneasy when dry bones are mentioned in a proverb. Okonkwo remembered his own father. (p. 23)

For the African, proverbs, which one Sierra Leonean example describes as the "daughters of experience," are not, then, merely elegant turns of phrase or witticisms, but rather what the authors of the book *Littérature camerounaise* term "a veritable petrified philosophy, remarkable for its concrete observation, its prudence, and its functional character" ("une véritable philosophie pétrifiée, remarquable par son observation concrète, sa prudence et son caractère fonctionnel").[9]

The best example of the proverb as the basis for discourse in the francophone novel is probably Ahmadou Kourouma's *Les soleils des indépendances.* In this fine novel, not only is the proverb exploited directly, but the chapters seem to be built up as embroidered, accumulated, or extended proverbs.

Tchicaya also uses the proverb extensively, in *The Madman and the Medusa* as well as in his other books. The most ob-

9. Basile-Juléat Fouda, Henry de Julliot, and Roger Lagrave, *Littérature camerounaise* (Cannes: Club du Livre Camerounais, 1961), p. 20.

vious use of the technique is in the title of his first novel, based on an African proverb quoted as an epigraph to the novel: "Le cancrelat alla plaider une cause au tribunal des poules!" ("The roach went to plead his case before a tribunal of hens!") However, the most extended use of the proverb occurs in the first paragraph of chapter 14 of *Les phalènes*. This paragraph, which covers a page and a half, consists entirely of aphorisms, which are presented without prior explanation. The second paragraph explains that these are aphoristic highlights in a speech by the intellectual Pierre Tchiloangou on the values of traditional African culture. The theme of his lecture is "Yesterday in the Steps of Tomorrow" and the talk is peppered with aphorisms, some of which are "etched in Prosper's memory."

There is proverbial discourse in *The Madman and the Medusa*, as when Malonga chastizes Elenga for trying to sabotage his plans to marry off Elenga's sister Mazola to Massengo—an older man—by bringing Luambu to the house. Elenga replies: "You thunder and you make rain for naught; you want others to sow seeds when it is not yet the season."

This exchange is followed, a few pages later, by a delightfully direct aphorism in which Malonga, furious at Elenga's rudeness to Massengo in his uncle's house, accuses him of biting the hand that feeds him, but in these rather more picturesque terms: "A duck shits where it eats."

Some other examples of proverbial discourse are: the reflection during the shooting of the striker Elenga that "one rarely stops one's ears without also closing one's eyes"; the aphoristic remark near the end of the novel that "the night is no stronger than the word of a dead man"; and, finally, a passage containing an interesting multicultural use of aphorism:

It is said: "Face life and it will watch you live; if you don't face life, it will not take care of you!" Had he forgotten that? He could also say it in Christian terms. Without your guardian angel, death will push you and your steps will lead to the threshold of the abyss. In the language of the past the guardian angel is replaced by manna.

Introduction

In his preface to the collection of short fictional pieces entitled *La main sèche*, Tchicaya discusses the implications of the number of stories in the collection:

> Does the number eleven contain a legend? An esoteric meaning? I don't know. I ask this question because I resisted the urge to include other texts in this book. The first impulse of refusal assumed the character of superstition (I am superstitious, I mean by that: I believe in symbols), so here are eleven texts.[10]

The symbol has been defined variously as a figure of speech whose meanings cannot be exhausted, as an emblem that has acquired a collectively recognized meaning over time, and as an image whose meaning surpasses the total of its rational parts; but perhaps it is necessary to redefine it each time one speaks of it. Clearly the above statement by Tchicaya equates symbol with numerology even as it suggests, indeed, that a collective evaluation is inherent in the symbol, since he speaks of superstition. Traditionally superstition is handed down from generation to generation.

D. H. Lawrence has written:

> The images of myth are symbols. They don't "mean something." They stand for units of human *feeling*, human experience. A complex of emotional experience is a symbol. And the power of the symbol is to arouse the deep emotional self, and the dynamic self, beyond comprehension. Many ages of accumulated experience still throb within a symbol. And we throb in response. It takes centuries to create a really significant symbol: even the symbol of the Cross, or of the horseshoe, or the horns. No man can invent symbols. He can invent an emblem, made up of images: or metaphors: or images: but not symbols. Some images, in the course of many generations of men, become symbols, embedded in the soul and ready to start alive

10. Tchicaya U Tam'Si, *La main sèche* (Paris: Robert Laffont, 1980), p. 7.

Introduction

when touched, carried on in the human consciousness for centuries. And again, when men become unresponsive and half dead, symbols die.[11]

One might argue, however, that the symbol must, at some point, find its genesis in an invented image or set of images. Perhaps, indeed, the ultimate poetic gift is that of coining imagery that has a chance of someday becoming symbol. However that may be, Tchicaya uses symbols that appeal to accumulative, timeless interpretations and throb with collective memories, as well as images that we might best describe as private images possessing the superficial attributes of symbols. We can, then, for expediency, speak of private and universal symbols. Furthermore, as Lawrence points out, myth shares with symbol the ability to outlive explicit meaning.[12] Tchicaya's work is loaded with both, and the line of distinction between them is not always clear. Let us consider several of the most important symbols, aside from those mythemes inherent in the collective wisdom of the proverb that we have already discussed.

Tchicaya's first three novels bear as their titles names of roaches, jellyfish, and moths. When asked why he had picked such animals for his titles, he replied:

Perhaps to strike the imagination of my readers, but also they are essentially symbols. . . . In the second volume *The Madman and the Medusa,* the medusas—jellyfish—well, they sting and they are very beautiful. For me they represent fascination, yes, fascination: one forgets that this very beautiful thing can give you a burn. . . . The people don't understand . . . They understand the myth but they go around

11. D. H. Lawrence, "The Dragon of the Apocalypse," quoted in Maurice Beebe, ed., *Literary Symbolism: An Introduction to the Interpretation of Literature* (San Francisco: Wadsworth Publishing Company, 1960), pp. 31–32.

12. Ibid., p. 31.

xxxviii

Introduction

seeking the precise details elsewhere. . . . André Sola could very well explain the story of what happens to Luambu, but it would be too easy to give that explanation.[13]

We might, however, break down the different creatures into different categories. The roaches of *Les cancrelats* function primarily in the context of the proverb about the folly of a roach pleading his case before a hen. The moths of *Les phalènes* appear in the book in the form of a metaphor—that of insects flying around a hurricane lamp whose heat burns their wings—that parallels the lives of the protagonists fluttering blindly around the central glare of rapidly changing political events. And the jellyfish, or medusas, of *The Madman and the Medusa* qualify either as universal symbols or at least as private symbols that have the initial appearance of being universal.

Indeed, Lawrence does not take into account the possibility of transferal, by which an author's presentation of a private symbol might in some way provide a matrix and ambience into which a reader might insert a symbol, private or universal, of his own.

The jellyfish of Tchicaya's novel are mysterious. They appear, not randomly, but in an apparently significant manner as adjuncts to a number of enigmatic narrative moments, notably when they sting and create the strange wound in Elenga's foot, when they appear in the surf and on the beach during the mad prophet's sermon, when they are described as a panacea in a bowl in the marketplace, when they are associated with the deaths of Elenga and Muendo, and, finally, in the closing lines of the book, when they are metaphorically invoked in the description of the ground where Luambu falls into a coma between the graves of Elenga and Muendo:

> Luambu turned around so fast that he lost his balance
> very oddly and fell. His head hit something soft, recently
> upturned earth that had little more consistency than a pile

13. Interview, 24 July 1987.

---

of medusas, but though it was rather acid, it didn't give one a rash.

If the creatures discussed above are metaphors or private symbols—possibly elevated by virtue of Tchicaya's treatment to the rank of universal symbol—there is one symbol that truly functions as a universal. The sea, which has been used as a symbol by Camara Laye in *Le regard du roi,* "Les yeux de la statue," and "Le prince," is replete with meaning. Aside from the obvious universal associations that we can attribute to the sea as the source of life on land and as the primal mother image (with its monthly tidal fluctuations), there are a number of associations that Africans traditionally make with the sea. Africans often say that a loved one in Europe is "on the sea" ("sur la mer"), since the last "real" image a person—for instance, the mother in Ousmane Sembène's *Le docker noir* (Black docker)—has of a relative who has gone to France is that of a ship disappearing over the horizon.

In *The Madman and the Medusa,* the sea functions not only as this image in reverse—the warships out in the roads that wink their Morse codes at each other have come from Europe and never seem to land—but also as a vast, mysterious, area full of the forces of life and death:

> The empty beach looks as if the world had come to
> an end. The sand is dull and unblemished by human
> footsteps. Luambu looks back, sees footprints and con-
> vinces himself that they are his. He fights the overwhelm-
> ing feeling that the end of the world is close and that his
> ultimate torture will be, as the last one remaining, to see
> the earth open wide and engulf the sea in wide whirlpools,
> pulling him down, farther and farther, to the bottom of
> the earth.

The beach—where Elenga, Muendo, and Luambu often meet, where the prophet of doom gives his prophecies—is the juncture of the apocalyptic world of the mysterious sea and the solid earth. There are rivers, lagoons, and marigots, or inlets, that blur the line between the sea and earth, and it is in these areas that much of the unspecified violence of the book seems to have taken place, such as the drowning of Julienne.

The railroad plays an important role in the novel, not unlike that held by the Mississippi River in Mark Twain's *Huckleberry Finn.* As mentioned above, the railroad symbolizes European civilization, progress, opportunity, and corruption. One of the principal African settlement areas in the novel is Kilometer 4 along the railroad, and in the following passage the normally pejorative term for those who follow the railroad, *Bilanda Laï* (*laï* is a corruption of the French word *rail* according to Tchicaya), is uttered with some pride:

> Our entire family is from Kinkala. As the Vilis say: I am a real *Tchilanda Laï,* I have followed the railroad here. . . .
> Old beliefs have nothing to do with civilization. He said that for the teacher, who, like him, was closer to civilization. To learn to read and to make money were steps toward civilization and progress. His brother who drove the express train also wanted progress.

There is one brief passage that encapsulates the way in which the lives of Elenga's family are intimately intertwined with the railroad. In it, derailment is presented on two planes, first as a literal explanation for Elenga's father's death and then as a metaphor for the "derailing" of Elenga's life in his untimely and absurd murder:

> No, they had expected him to die like his father, who was also an engineer and who had died in an accident when his train went off the track. Elenga also died in an accident, in a derailment. It was to be expected.

There are a number of passages in which Tchicaya presents contradictory information. In some instances, it is merely a matter of the simple reversal of expectations, as when André Sola "saw himself the prisoner of a circle of white magic drawn around him by Monsieur Martin and Luambu." In this passage, the apt reference to "white magic" is reminiscent of the humorous reversals found in Bertène Juminer's *La revanche de Bozambo* (Bozambo's revenge).

Elsewhere, there are contradictory versions of dress; for example, the body found in the cemetery is described variously as dressed in black and completely naked, and as lying between the graves and on Muendo's grave.

Such variations abound in the novel and may be a device by which Tchicaya defines hearsay, distraction, hallucination, and dream. Another explanation, however, is that Tchicaya is consciously seeking to establish an opaque rather than a transparent style of writing, which is not amazing for a writer who lived in Paris during the most fashionable years of the New Novel. We have tried to show that Tchicaya's novels are profoundly African, not just in their choice of setting and their use of such components as African words and proverbs but in their entire way of grasping reality; and yet it is possible that Tchicaya's style owes something to writers of the 1950s and 1960s like Alain Robbe-Grillet. There come to mind such scenes as the sudden changes in dress color in Robbe-Grillet's movie *Last Year at Marienbad* and the deliberately varied facts and spelling of names (Johnson, Jonestone; Marchat, Marchand; Ava, Eva) in Robbe-Grillet's novel *La maison de rendez-vous*, both of which render the style opaque and bring the viewer-reader's attention back to the surface of the screen (even back conceptually into the celluloid of the film) or back to the surface of the book page.

Tchicaya has said that he is not a surrealist but a symbolist, in that he is concerned with the "quest for the symbol" and interested in expressing in his African novels the Manicheism and the underlying surreality, or what Tchicaya has termed the "unreality" ("irréel"), that are inherent in African culture. He has opted, the better to do this, to interweave the worlds of dream and reality, of night and day, for, as he has expressed it: "There is the fundamental truth that one interrogates the night as much to understand the day as to understand the night, and vice versa." To illustrate his creative vision, Tchicaya drew on the analogy of a statue that a friend from Ivory Coast had recently shown him, which depicted two connected bodies, or Siamese twins, that, according to Tchicaya, represented the opposing forces of good and evil in one body; and Tchicaya averred that that was what he was trying to do in his novels.[14]

The brilliance of Tchicaya's novels, and perhaps most specifically *The Madman and the Medusa,* lies in the dazzling impressionistic style resulting from his vision of the African consciousness (he has said that he probably would not use the "unreal" style of his other novels if he were to write one set in Europe or Russia or America). There are pages where sublime poetry and the banal phrase abut without transition. And the use of symbols surpassing ready comprehension and of information that permits interpretation either as contradiction or as input from both realms of a dichotomous weltanschauung leads the reader ultimately to appreciate the aesthetic impact of Tchicaya's style through an abandonment akin to that which one brings to music or poetry appreciation. The fragmented style, the interfusion of rationally remote or incompatible elements, the blurred outline of discourse resulting from so many interrogatives, all contribute to an impression that *The Madman and the Medusa,* like the poetry—though grounded in a very personal reality—appeals directly to the sentience, the feelings, of the reader. We are afforded a direct glimpse of the inner workings of the writer and his cultural acumen, a *tranche d'âme,* or cross-section of his being, so to speak.

Tchicaya's *The Madman and the Medusa* is a novel that may properly be read in the context of several overlapping traditions: the African novel, the francophone novel, the symbolist novel, the lyrical novel of direct psychical expression, and the Nouveau Roman. Finally, it is an excellent introduc-

14. Ibid.

tion to the work of an important poet and novelist whose work was for years admired by specialists but somewhat neglected by wider audiences because of its difficult, elliptical nature.

We are grateful to Sonja and William Jay Smith for having provided the first major English translation of Tchicaya's work since Gerald Moore's *Selected Poems* (1970).[15] They have done a fine job, especially in several highly poetic passages, such as the "wake scene," without whose beauty the novel would be underrepresented. In the interest of achieving fluidity of style and an idiomatic diction, they had to make some hard decisions about omitting tricky material, such as the titles of respect and devotion, *ta, ma, ya*, which immediately precede names of family members or older people, as well as the parenthetical reference to the earlier novel, *Les cancrelats*, mentioned above. These concessions are not the proverbial treason but necessary adjustments that the translator must make in wrestling with his or her material. Sonja Smith mentioned to me that she thought *The Madman and the Medusa* was a magnificent and highly poetic novel; the sentiment shows through in this translation.

Finally, a word of caution to the reader. In discussing the interrogative as mode of discourse, we did not mention the fact—saving it for this conclusion—that the entire novel, *The Madman and the Medusa*, is a question, an enigma. It leaves the reader with many questions unanswered. To paraphrase Tchicaya's remark about André Sola: The author could have brought in a deus ex machina or tied together all his loose ends in a rational answer to the enigmas in the book, but that would have been too easy a solution. Take courage and seek out the answers to the many unanswered questions involving Luambu, the madman, the medusas, the little boy in the marketplace, Julienne's fate, supernatural happenings, the length of the coma, where Luambu was found and what he

15. Tchicaya U Tam'Si, *Selected Poems*, trans. G. Moore (London: Heinemann, 1970).

Introduction

was wearing, and so forth. As far as Tchicaya is concerned, the aesthetic reward lies not so much in the answers as in the asking.

Eric Sellin
Temple University

Bibliography

PRINCIPAL WORKS BY
TCHICAYA U TAM'SI

Poetry

Le mauvais sang. Paris: Caractères, 1955.

Feu de brousse. Paris: Hautefeuille, 1957.

A triche-cœur. Paris: Hautefeuille, 1958; Paris: Pierre Jean Oswald, 1960.

Epitomé. Tunis: S.N.E.D., 1961.

Le ventre. Paris: Présence Africaine, 1964.

Le mauvais sang, Feu de brousse, A triche-cœur, new, revised ed. Honfleur and Paris: Pierre Jean Oswald, 1970.

Arc musical précédé de Epitomé. Honfleur: Pierre Jean Oswald, 1970.

La veste d'intérieur, suivi de Notes de veille. Paris: Nubia, 1977.

Le pain et la cendre, Le ventre. Paris: Présence Africaine, 1978.

Fiction

Les cancrelats. Paris: Albin Michel, 1980. (novel)

La main sèche. Collection "Chemin d'Identité." Paris: Robert Laffont, 1980. (stories)

Les méduses ou les orties de la mer. Paris: Albin Michel, 1982. (novel)

Les phalènes. Paris: Albin Michel, 1984. (novel)

Ces fruits si doux de l'arbre à pain. Paris: Seghers, 1987. (novel)

Theater

Le Zulu, suivi de Vwène le fondateur. Paris: Nubia, 1978.
*Le destin glorieux du maréchal Nnikon Nniku, prince qu'on
sort.* Paris: Présence Africaine, 1979.

Anthology

Légendes africaines. New edition. Paris: Seghers, 1979.

WORKS BY TCHICAYA U TAM'SI IN
ENGLISH TRANSLATION

Brush Fire. Trans. Sangodare Akanji. Ibadan: Mbari Publications, 1964.
Selected Poems. Trans. Gerald Moore. London: Heinemann,
1970.
The Glorious Destiny of Marshal Nnikon Nniku. Trans.
Timothy Johns. New York: Ubu Repertory Theater,
1986.

The Madman
and the Medusa

This story took place about the time when, so they said, a white man used to wander at night through the Native Village of Pointe-Noire and with a magic wand turn men, women, children, and dogs into corned beef, which people called monkey meat. Although most inhabitants had no aversion for the meat of the macaque, which was delicious when cured, a total boycott of canned meat took place.

The merchants, wholesalers, and retailers united in a defense plan but fortunately did not resort to violent countermeasures. A war was on, and the authorities did not want law and order upset simply because the sale of canned meat had slumped. "When they get tired of munching on greens, they'll be back. . . ."

Corned beef in particular was shunned, and the sad expression of the ox on the can was rather pitiful to contemplate. Masses of cans started to accumulate in butcher shops displaying an astonishing variety of meats—supposedly human flesh, but how can anyone be so naive?—which, thanks to the unrelenting tropical humidity, quickly turned into a monstrous, foul-smelling heap of rusted metal.

Rather astonishing behavior for a people said to be maneaters! Still, eager not to fall or to fall again into cannibalistic habits of ill repute—they were civilized, what the hell—the people withstood curses and insults: "Filthy superstitious niggers, uneducated and stupid." What was really funny was that they could not be called cannibals any longer, since eating human flesh was precisely what they were refusing to do. A sign, no doubt, of the advance of civilization!

Meanwhile, at night the inhabitants hid out at home, in

their cabins, in their houses if they owned houses, or in their huts of straw and dried mud if that was all they had. The nights were darker and more suffocating than one had ever known—imagine, no nightlife at all! To awaken after an exaggeratedly long sleep is known to be bad for one, so you could see dazed people drifting about all day long, prisoners of the hazy landscape of peat bogs and swamps that still held out against the burgeoning development of an encroaching civilization.

Warships, real metal monsters whose terrifying aspect was barely hidden under their camouflage nets, were anchored in the bay instead of berthed at the pier in the harbor, which was not equipped to accommodate them. From one of them a white man disembarked at dusk and came ashore near the Songolo, the river of bad spirits, where an accomplice, a black man, a number-one sorcerer, awaited him.

Whoever remembers this event will undoubtedly find a certain similarity with the story that will unfold in the following pages.

"Two men died the last week of June 1944." "Actually three died. . . ." But the third one didn't die, miraculously perhaps. Who knows?

The three men were, of course, acquainted. . . . When I say that the third one didn't die, I mean not the same week. How and why? If I told you now, you wouldn't understand this strange case any better. . . .

Two men, both in perfect health, suddenly die the same week. The case is suspect; people are what they are and don't believe what seems obvious. Too true to be believed. They knew each other and were bound together by real friendship, I might even say a strange friendship. Then just like that, one dies after the other, the same week, within twenty-four hours of each other. Thursday, Friday, Saturday. Saturday, or more precisely, Saturday night, the third one escapes death in the strangest way. Where does it all happen?

Death struck down the first two men at their workplace. But where do you think they found the third one almost dead? In the graveyard! Yes, lying between the tombs of his friends.

When they found out that the three men knew one another, they were totally mystified. Note that they readily accepted the fact that the third man, wearing a white T-shirt, white canvas shorts, white socks, and espadrilles, was found lying on the ground between the graves of the two others. There was a good reason for that, which they quickly discovered, as you will see! When his full name came to light, they said it was unnecessary to look further for a motive for the inexplicable deaths that had occurred one after the other at the end of the week. Quite a coincidence apparently! What obvious facts were being suppressed?

Luambu, known as Lufwa-Lumbu, as he lay in a coma, was identified by Jean-Pierre Mpita, a guard at the C.G.B.C. (Compagnie Générale du Bas-Congo) and by Mazola, the sister of Christophe Elenga, who had been buried the same day, Sunday, June 25, 1944.

Christophe Elenga, born June 24, 1922. His baptismal certificate states that he was born sometime in 1922. But the exact date of his birth was established in the following manner: André Sola had consulted a seer who had expressed his astonishment that Elenga had been buried the day following the day of his birth, hence a Saturday, and that the month of his death had also been the month of his birth. Furthermore, he stated that the day of his death would have been the beginning of a new year for Elenga if he had not died. Therefore, he had been born on Saturday, June 24, because in the twenties there is only one Saturday, June 24, and it is June 24, 1922. Moreover, his baptismal certificate, dated April 13, 1924, shows that the priest of the Linzolo Mission had baptized a child about two years old, born in 1922.

"No doubt he was too young to die, but in any case Luambu was not responsible for his death, although this man seems never to have existed because there were so many lives involved in his one life. . . . When I look at the water over there, my eyes see a great deal, but not what I am supposed to see. . . . Elenga died by himself without anybody's having pushed him. But I can't say more. He got in the way. . . ." But Sola had formed his own opinion of Luambu. As for Omar Muendo, he was born in 1919 in Mouila, was foreman at the Scieries Réunies. A whole crowd of people mourned him. Like the rest of his family, he had been a neighbor of Sola's.

Luambu, known as Lufwa Lumbu, born when? where? There were many unanswered questions in the life of this man. People looked at one another wondering, but no one came forward to claim him, to say, he is ours, he is mine. Was he self-sufficient? Writer, meaning clerk at the C.G.B.C. (Compagnie Générale du Bas Congo), import-export trading company. That was all.

Elenga was a railroad engineer at the C.F.C.O. (Chemin de Fer Congo Océan). Isn't that strange? What was surely strange was not that the three men knew one another, but that a sawmill employee, a railroad engineer, and a writer were friends. Why had a writer become buddy-buddy with a railroad engineer and a sawmill employee?

As a matter of fact—and it should be stressed again and again—the obvious reasons didn't reveal . . . but rather hid the guilty one. Luambu's coma was proof of the crime, his crime! It was the opinion of his colleagues who now understood why the fellow had worked all the time right beside them without ever giving anyone the opportunity to learn anything about him. His self-effacement, his modesty hid something that became clear later. We now know . . .

Jean-Pierre Mpita stressed the fact in the office when he said briefly and mysteriously, pointing to Luambu's desk, that was still empty at that late hour: "He won't come today, maybe not tomorrow either."

"Who?"

"What do you mean, who? Do you see him there at his desk?"

Obviously the others had not noticed Luambu's absence. He was indeed not at his desk. They looked at one another. No, they hadn't noticed. At this moment Monsieur Martin arrived. As usual he looked around the clerk's office. The head clerk conveyed to him the hazy information that he had had from the guard, who took the opportunity to show off and explain that most probably Luambu would not come to the office because he had been found comatose Sunday morning in the Vounvou cemetery and that it was doubtful that he would recover.

"What are you talking about?"

André Sola, who was always upset in the presence of Monsieur Martin, at a loss for an answer, began to stammer and looked helplessly toward the guard. Monsieur Martin cut him

short: "When you find out why he's absent, let me know."
And he went into his office.

André Sola and his colleagues seemed to have difficulty facing the fact that one of their group was missing. Although Luambu had been with them such a long time, they seemed to wonder what he had actually looked like.

"Tell me, what were you doing in the cemetery Sunday?"

Mpita did not condescend to answer and left the office quickly.

They knew each other. The proof is that Muendo and Luambu were both at Elenga's wake. And what a wake! In living memory never had a body been watched thus in total silence, while the cries of mourners rose from the depths of the terrifying night! Furthermore, the three men had been seen several times after work on the seaside path. It was absolutely certain that they had been together quite often, always by the sea, going from one group of fishermen to another. Jean-Pierre Mpita was even astonished one day to see Elenga in his work clothes waiting for Luambu at 5:00 P.M. in front of the C.G.B.C. It was probably one of those days when Luambu finished working at the freight station just across from the C.G.B.C. Mpita watched them walk once more toward the company of the Chargeurs Réunis, which is what you have to do if you go back to the Native Village by the seaside path. As if this man had had the gift to render invisible anyone or anything close to him, it is only after the tragic events that people made the following connection, namely, that it was Mazola, Elenga's sister, who had identified as the clerk Luambu the man lying unconscious in the Vounvou cemetery, for she used to bring him lunch regularly. That's how people had noticed her and admired her: "Who is that beautiful girl? To whom is she bringing lunch?"

They didn't know that it was to Luambu, a strange fellow, you must admit. . . . In the cemetery, when she bent over the body lying on the ground and recognized him, being already deeply affected by the death of her brother, she completely lost control of herself. She expressed her heartbreaking despair by shouting above the cries of the mourning women: "No, no, not him too!" She fainted, and Malonga caught his niece in his arms. Mazola, who had torn her cheeks and bruised her limbs on hearing of her brother's death, could only faint for a man she loved, a man who had been her lover. Malonga clenched his teeth, fearing that dishonor would be added to the calamity of death. . . . Good heavens, what trouble his brother's children were. He knew all the men who came to the hospital to visit him, the medical supervisor, in his lodge late at night under various pretexts, none of which fooled him. One wanted a tablet of quinine, another some permanganate, and another an enema, but not one of them failed to ask about Mazola. Some even offered their services. Muendo said that if his wife wanted some sawdust, she should send Mazola, who would bring as much as she wanted. But he had no idea who the fellow was for whom his niece had fainted and couldn't even remember having met him. How devious these skirt-chasers are! But who knew who he was?

Only Mazola, Elenga, and Muendo knew Luambu. Perhaps, perhaps. What kind of man dares fall into a coma in the middle of the night deep in a graveyard—as had been reported by witnesses, although with this kind of fellow, you never know, as you will see later. . . . Some people had seen him earlier in the evening at Camdanto's, the dance hall of the Popos. Who has known him? Who knows him? One day or another the most intricate knots of the secret will be untied.

André Sola felt his throat tighten: he had to find a clue; he had to unravel this affair, which was not only an enigma, a mystery, but a dangerous threat to him and to others.

Apparently Luambu's six coworkers were so familiar with him and his strange behavior of seeming to be absent when he was present that none of them had noticed his real absence. To tell the truth he had never been chummy with any of them, and since he took his orders directly from Monsieur Martin, they pretended that he wasn't one of them. Although André

Sola was officially his supervisor, he didn't consider him one of the employees for whom he was directly responsible. But that Monday, because he had been asked by Monsieur Martin to report on Luambu, André Sola suddenly remembered that he was the one who had been instrumental in Luambu's appointment in the first place. When the latter was still a warehouse employee, about one or two years earlier, André Sola had come upon him, a guard at the time, writing on a sheet of paper with such elegance that he had asked him: "Sh . . . Show me! Isss . . . it you who . . . who . . . can . . . wr . . . write like that?"

Instead of answering orally, Luambu went on writing, changing his style slightly: "Yes, dear Monsieur André Sola, I have a whole array of pens which . . . etc., I, the undersigned, Luambu, known as Lufwa Lumbu, guard at the C.G.B.C., Pointe-Noire, Middle Congo. He added as a postscript: "I can do better. . . ."

Obviously André Sola didn't grasp the implication of the postscript. Flabbergasted, and forgetting to stutter, he asked: "Why are you only a guard?"

Luambu took the page from André Sola's hands and wrote: "When I applied for work, the only opening was for a guard. A bird in the hand is worth two in the bush. That is why I've been a guard ever since." He signed with a flourish and handed the sheet of paper to André, who had already read the answer over his shoulder. André Sola thanked him with such unexpected enthusiasm that it brought a smile to Luambu's lips. . . .

At first Monsieur Martin didn't understand why his stockkeeper had such a conspiratorial air when he showed him a handwritten sheet of paper.

"What is it?" he asked.

"It'ss . . . b-b . . . beautiful . . . h-h . . . handwriting, sir."

André Sola always talked with his head turned sideways, not facing the person to whom he spoke because he spluttered a lot. Monsieur Martin examined the sheet of paper and read Luambu's answers to André Sola's questions.

The Madman and the Medusa

"It's the guard who wrote this?" he asked, his hand already on the bell, which he rang once. Luambu appeared: "Okay, André, go back to the warehouse. . . ."

André Sola remembered that Luambu had thanked him in a strange manner. He had given him a handwritten page of a Latin text, the Credo written in Gothic script with different inks, red, green, violet-blue, Indian black, set off by gold, a veritable painting! It was an enchantment for the eye, the senses, the heart, and the soul. For him who had been a seminary student this present was at the same time a kind of *Jubilate* and a *De Profundis*. An excellent seminarist, he had been prevented from becoming a priest because of his terrible stutter, an ordeal that the Lord had set for him, no doubt. His wife, Victorine, who had seen his mood change suddenly from joy to despair, asked with concern:

"Bad news?"

"No, no, not bad news."

"Somebody also brought us a chicken."

He then explained: "It's about a guard for whom I got the position of clerk."

He remembered that for one week he didn't stutter. A miracle! *Deo gratias!* To express his gratitude to God, he made a novena, but, poor fellow, his stuttering then resumed.

This is how Luambu had become a clerk thanks to him, André Sola. And now he had to explain to Monsieur Martin the reason for the absence of Luambu, who had been in a coma since Saturday night, and who might die, who was his coworker, and about whom he knew nothing, not even if he had a wife and children. If his name had been Liambu instead of Luambu, André would have recognized his Vili origin, but a name like Luambu gave no information whatever about the tribe of his ancestors. André spoke of him in the past tense, as if he had already died. . . . Luambu was the friend of two men who had died a violent death, one after the other, then he himself had fallen into a coma in the middle of the night. Why?

How can we find out? Luambu had presented him with a prayer, thus alluding to their common religious belief. But he, André, had not responded in a Christian way; he had not offered his friendship. He shuddered. But his Christian faith was so genuine that he said to himself, "What did Elenga and Muendo gain from their friendship with this man?" The Lord had kept him away from a man possessed by the devil. He thanked the Lord!

His coma lasted fifty years. He lay bedridden in a shack exposed to the elements, to bugs, in a cul-de-sac lost in weeds and brambles, which also bordered his plot to the north and east. In the middle rose the miserable and disheartening shack that sheltered a body, his body.

The hedge forming a right angle on the street side was of an astonishingly bright green that did not fade, the green of the lantana, the hibiscus, the bougainvillea. A luxuriant vegetation with no flowers. This diabolical coma discouraged and frightened away any visitor rash enough to think of dropping by. Not that the place itself was gloomy. Here peace and resignation reigned. An oasis suspected of malevolence, engendered by an illusion or by the delirious imagination of those who swore on the head of the most venerable of their ancestors, or even in the name of the Lord, that this coma may already have lasted a hundred years, a not surprising possibility, because this man could very well defy death, considering. . . .

When they found him lying on Muendo's grave, all dressed in black, in his sport shirt, trousers, socks, and espadrilles (others swore that he was wearing patent-leather shoes), he was holding a knife with a golden blade in his left hand. The knife had an inch-wide blade that ended in a needle similar to the needles doctors use to give injections. With such a needle you can introduce something into a body just as you can remove something from it. However, nothing was surprising: sometimes in his office Luambu had made himself invisible so that his colleagues were so accustomed to not seeing him that they had forgotten how he looked. Was he big, little, thin, tall? Moreover, when his supervisor came to see him in the hospital, he had said, "What, that's him?" or "Maybe that's him!"

He didn't know anymore. All he did was enter and leave the room, and when he came back, let's say three or four seconds later, the body had disappeared from the bed. Or it might still have been there, but nobody could see it. What I know comes straight from the son of his supervisor who told me what he heard his father say. Now, don't forget that it's definitely his fault that Elenga and Muendo died. The flagrant proof is his coma. You don't have to be a sorcerer to understand that!

Where was his shack? Can we locate the plot of ground on which it stood? Over there. Near the cemetery. No, in Vounvou. . . . Not at all, in Ntiétié! In the street where the clinic is. Yakoma Street. In . . . What was his first name again? "Paul, Paulin, Pascal, Pierre? Or maybe it started with a J (Zay): Jean, Jules, José, Joseph, Justin, Julien?"—"So you know all the names on the calendar by heart. That's what you wanted to show us, isn't it? But what matters is not his Christian name that nobody ever heard. You have to examine the origin of his family name if you want to understand anything about this affair."

The whole population of Pointe-Noire, shocked by the news of those deaths that last weekend in June, had fastened on that coma and had let its imagination wander deliriously in order to hide an unspeakable terror. All Pointe-Noire, the Native Village, the people of Kilometer 4 (where Elenga had fallen, killed by the soldiers' bullets), Pita, Tchibamba, Ngoyo, everybody, the Vilis, the Popos, the Mpounous, the Mbochis, the Bayandjis, the Mkotas, the Tékés, the Laris, the Baskongos, everybody, perhaps even the city of Brazzaville, spoke of only one thing, the coma of the man who had been found "sitting, completely naked, leaning against the cross on the grave of Elenga, whom he had caused to die because he did not want someone of another tribe marrying his sister; he could accept him as a friend but never as a brother-in-law." Therefore, Luambu had said: "Ah! Is that so? We shall see, and there it is." Elenga is dead and Luambu in a coma. It proves how

The Madman and the Medusa

clever he was. . . . A man of the Lari tribe is not to be trifled with, he's like a headless sardine that fucks its mother just to show that it has no head. Muendo had Senegalese ancestors who can cast a spell over you in no time, but Luambu had caught him off guard, played palsy-walsy with him, and then wham! He had ripped him up, literally ripped him up.

When time seems endless, fifty or sixty years appear to be the right length of time for people's memories to come to some kind of acceptance of a story. After all, it wasn't such an exaggeration, they could have said a hundred years just as well. . . . Strange things happen. Wonders, miracles that we don't always notice because we don't pay enough attention. Miracles, mirages, wonders, so why get excited over a coma?

The event, it is clear, took place in June 1944. That could well be a hundred years ago. . . . "Do you mean that there was this man in this shack in Pointe-Noire, or rather before Pointe-Noire existed, before the train, I mean the railroad, before Kilometer 4, before the Ntiétié train station was built, before? . . ." "Before what?" Look how far fantasy can take you! The truth was hidden deep in people's anxiety and later in their imagination.

Perhaps there had only been fifty or sixty round-trips, if you counted one a day, even though that wasn't her count, a woman's count, or more precisely a young woman's count. But the girl's aunt, who was prone to exaggeration, her eyes blurred with tears as is usual in a period of mourning, had noticed the comings and goings of her niece. She seemed at certain times to be absent from her body and out of her mind. It always happened at nightfall and started by her muttering words that her aunt and uncle could not understand: "Lord, take my heart; mourning ashes and my feet. It is as if they were coming twice with the sad news, as if my own body, my own heart . . ." The aunt explains: "It breaks her body and her heart each time. When she gets up again, her arms fall, her face turns into a mask! . . . When she gets up, she leaves for a long time! . . . She returns in her grief, more dead than alive! . . . Then she is freed of this inner call and returns to her senses; she is like us again."

It was assumed that at dusk Mazola went to visit the man in the coma, the man—it makes me shudder to think of it—who walked around in a coma! They saw him here, they met him there. A blind man had recovered his eyesight just by passing him. People swore to it. The blind man had suddenly felt great heat on his eyes. "Who is there?" he had asked. "Look where you are going." He looked; he could see. He saw the things around him but there was no one there—anywhere. He saw the houses, the coconut palms, the mango trees and was so overjoyed that he didn't care what had happened and who had spoken to him. He had had the sensation of burning coals in his eyes and his blind eyes could see again. . . .

Malonga remembered that his niece had fainted in the grave-yard during Elenga's funeral. . . . The reason for her fainting spell, the terror that befell her when she was already stricken had all been swept away to allow mourning to take its proper course. For the male nurse comatose people were, if not common, nothing extraordinary. . . . So he couldn't quite understand what his wife was talking about and to which comatose man she was referring. Therefore to change the subject, he asked quite naturally in the loud voice with which he usually addressed a room full of sick people who always imagined they were much sicker than they were: "Didn't Elenga have a friend who was after Mazola?"

"Ask your niece."

"I'm not asking anybody anything!" he shouted.

That was when Mazola had stopped her coming and going.

When an event is reported, each person in turn adds an unlikely detail to make it more truthful.

Let's go over the facts again, one by one, calmly, without panic. One must remain calm. It's understandable to be upset when one's coworker falls into a coma. However, when the circumstances look rather murky, the calm that one seeks vanishes. André suddenly remembered the visit of Etienne Ling'si of the railroad company C.F.C.O. (they were vaguely related through their grandparents). . . . When was it? That's it . . . no . . . wait a minute! That's right, it was Wednesday. No, Thursday, the well-known Thursday, the day the engineer died. Etienne hadn't come to ask advice. He wanted to discuss the event, have his opinion perhaps. Actually he didn't say anything, or very little. Did he know himself why he wasn't in the mood to listen to anyone, even to a relative?

When you know what happened to him and to the others it's understandable that he was struck dumb. . . . He was deported. Shh! One shouldn't say these things out loud. André recalled what Etienne kept repeating: "It's terribly serious, it goes far beyond the death of that poor fellow!" One cannot pretend that the death of the engineer had upset him deeply, especially since any action that would seem to lead to disorder made him distrustful to the *Bilanda Laï,* those hotheads who stepped off the train each time that it arrived at the station.

He had come to talk. But either he couldn't find the right words or he was afraid to articulate them. "This strike is bad, very bad." He was ducking the issue when events were taking a turn for the worse. Hadn't he been one of the employees who reacted against the sound advice of the authorities? Inwardly, like several of his colleagues, André had made fun of his young relative. "These crazy young men, they think their fathers are just old fuddy-duddies, but they are as stubborn as those backward people who we know will be the last to be civilized. The white man will get washed out in the process.

The next day, which was Friday, in the late afternoon, Rosalie, Etienne's wife, came to Victorine. The poor woman was in tears, as if it were her own husband who had died. She was crying so much that she could barely speak. How can you help someone who can't even tell you what is wrong? Victorine was losing patience: "Now, tell me, what happened?" She thought that her husband had perhaps misbehaved. These young women assume that their husbands are as homebound as a door that never leaves its threshold. No, that was not the case, what did she imagine . . . a husband sleeping with other women! "They took him away!" she finally managed to say. . . . That was it! And . . . André believed that he had come seeking advice! All he wanted was help, to be hidden away or in case he was arrested for André to take care of his family, his wife and children. "Is he in jail?" asked Victorine. . . . She wanted the answer repeated. "In Ubangi-Shari . . . but where is that?" "The faraway land of the Saras, the ferocious people with cat's teeth. . . ." André had explained to her later.

Friday night after work, when André arrived home around 5:30, he rushed into his house without noticing Etienne Ling'si's wife, who was sitting, or more precisely, was slumped on a mat, totally distraught, silent whereas she had always been so lively and amusing when she came to visit.

He didn't take the trouble to put his bicycle away, as he usually did, but rushed into the house and in a panic-stricken voice called out: "Victorine, Victorine! . . ."

Victorine came out of the kitchen to meet him, frightened by the note of panic she detected in her husband's voice. Looking at her imploringly, meek and dismayed, he begged her to sit down. He knew how to be pathetic even for a trifle, but in this case it was definitely not a trifle: "Sit down!" "What's happening?" Victorine asked. "What's happening is that you don't know what's happening." Just last night Etienne told us: "It's serious!" "Well, he said more than he realized." Victorine rose abruptly, shuddered as if she had mistakenly and absentmindedly sat on a snake.

"Muendo is dead, Muendo is dead. We saw him alive this morning. . . . Tonight he's a corpse."

Victorine was filled with a strange feeling of relief for Rosalie, whom she had made comfortable on the porch. Therefore she asked quite spontaneously: "Do you have any news from Etienne?" If she had planned to startle her husband, she couldn't have done it better. Undemonstrative, which she usually wasn't, she strained her ears, trying to find out what was happening at the Sows. André wondered what had prompted his wife to ask about Etienne, when he was giving her such astonishing news. Anticipating his questions, she said: "He was arrested and is going to be deported to Ubangi-Shari."

It was mind-boggling! Were they falling into an abyss or what? The surprise prevented him from closing his mouth as if he had no control over his jaw muscles or probably because his mind was slow in registering both calamities one after the other, before he could make a statement. He was totally bewildered.

"Rosalie is here. Didn't you see her when you came in?" How could Victorine be so composed! But it's like that with her, the shock will hit her much later. She crossed herself, then cried out: "Rosalie, Rosalie! . . . Did you hear, Muendo, Laurent Sow's brother . . . well, we saw him this morning as he went to work. . . . André says he's dead."

"André confirms that Muendo is dead. But how did it happen? How? This morning he was in perfect health when he left for work to make money and feed his wife and children. Last night your husband came, he said . . . André, what did he say exactly? You, Rosalie, you say that he was arrested and deported, that he's being held by soldiers, he isn't in jail at the militia camp like the others. Of course, we don't know what he's guilty of. And Muendo, what was his guilt that caused him to die? André, you did say that Muendo is dead? Rosalie, Rosalie! Misfortunes never come singly, and one doesn't replace the other!" She left Rosalie abruptly to go to add her tears to those of the other mourners of the funeral procession who at dusk were following the path taken by Muendo in the morning and who were now carrying his mangled body. Rosalie kept staring at André, but he turned his eyes away. "Go home to your children" he said solemnly in order to hide his confusion and to show some authority.

André knew that he had to unravel the tangled threads of these successive deaths. He would be cursed if he did not try. Of course, he was concerned with the deaths, though not so much with Etienne's deportation. He was particularly interested in the comatose man who fell into a coma right in step—one might say—with the other two men who died, this Luambu who had worked right under his eyes and who had probably already invaded his life. Surely he had. And how, indeed! He felt threatened, for who could say that it was all over? Etienne's deportation could not be overlooked either, because it seemed that an evil spell was on him, André, on his dependents and on his distant relatives (Etienne). Poor, poor Rosalie! But she wasn't the worst off. What about Muendo's wife, a widow now, whose child had been born in the throes of her grief. Don't tell me that it isn't an evil omen on which no light can be shed. But where is the light? Oh, Lord, pity our wretchedness. André, find out, you must find out. And then there is this stranger . . . whatever his name is. Yes, supposedly the nephew of Malonga, the medic. Where is the heart of the whole matter? Where the heart is, arms reach out for help. You must find out, André, you must consult seers and marabouts. How did we get where we are? You know people or rather you think that you know people, and when you examine them carefully, you realize that you don't know them. And suddenly André becomes aware that he actually doesn't know much about the neighbor he saw leaving his house in the morning, walking on short, robust legs, plump and healthy, the brother of the honorable Sow.

We let ourselves be taken unawares. We say, Why surprise us? No, nothing ever surprises us! We are so inattentive. He knew, André, that he was guilty of absentmindedness. God is

The Madman and the Medusa

not responsible for all the evil that occurs. Guilty of absent-mindedness. Nevertheless, it doesn't help to beat one's breast. We must pull ourselves together and find out what has happened. We must search our memories, and if that's not enough, we must consult seers and marabouts. We must also go to church and confess. His fright came from a dream that he didn't understand and that grew blurred each time he tried to translate the message from the language of the night. Then there was the panic that overwhelmed him when Monsieur Martin reminded him of his duties (but didn't he go a bit too far?). He was to investigate and report on the man and his coma. In his dream the bogs of the Tchinouka were covering the town and the houses, whether made of straw, mud, or concrete, when not built on piles, all had slimy black water on the ground floor. Monsieur Martin was pointing to a sand pile that could have been salt. . . . André couldn't understand the order that was shouted at him. The jail surrounded by a high wall crowned with broken glass was at the center of the drainage operation of the vast swamp. What worried him most was the total lack of vegetation.

Where did he come from, this nephew of the medical supervisor who insisted on being called Elenga when his real name was Kodia? Muendo's joviality must have hidden something— and then what kind of name is Luambu? What is hidden behind the nickname, Lufwa Lumbu? You ask yourself that, as if you hadn't heard what it meant.

It was on his way back from the hospital where he went to comply with Monsieur Martin's order and inquire about the absent employee that panic took over completely: "I see him, I close my eyes and search my memory, I open my eyes and the body isn't there any more." Where is the body? At what moment were his eyes fooled? And why?

I.
Elenga

This is what the soothsayer saw in the life of Kodia, known as
Elenga, the real nephew of the hospital supervisor who worked
and lived at the A.-Cissé General Hospital. He revealed it to
André.

———

"Ho, a child!"

The sun reigns, an absolute monarch. The light is blinding, the eyes squint. The steaming heat suffocates. The thatched roofs crackle. Elenga is playing his favorite game. Stretched out at the end of the courtyard, his head close to the ground, he watches the quivering sheet of water and enjoys the illusion of coolness. He gets up slowly, pouting. He sees now, instead of the cool water, the washed-out floor of the courtyard. Then he lies down again and admires the beautiful clear pond, imagining a school of fish with glittering silvery fins. He smiles at the work of his imagination. He touches the water, moves forward with a breaststroke—what delight! The pond is wide and deep, and the water clear and pleasant. Ouch! He has kicked too hard and the wound on his instep bleeds again, hurting terribly. No more swimming. He limps toward the shade of the porch. His naked body is covered with dust. His finger searches the navel just under his protruding belly. He leans against the wall, his head resting in the mouth of the cayman drawn in red ochre on the whitewashed wall. He forces back his tears. His self-confidence returns when he confronts the painted reptile: "Come on, come on, eat, eat." He punches the head of the beast, which remains motionless, stunned by the boy's blow. Isn't that cayman ridiculous with its double row of sharp teeth? "Is that just for show or what? Come on, bite, bite!" He puts his arm in the animal's open mouth. "You good-for-nothing beast!" He didn't go fishing with his father. He looks toward the field where his mother went with Mazola. He recalls Mazola fastening two water bottles on her back with a show of motherly care, setting a small cushion on her head and a bundle of cuttings and a hoe on top of it. She looked like the miniature of a grown-up. In fact the bottles are empty. There is water in the lower field near the river bend, before the reeds and the papyrus. There is a spring to which he loves to go, because when it's slightly windy the fibers of the papyrus sing softly. In the evening she will bring water in her bottles.

He is not afraid, even though he is all alone in the village. But what could happen to him? The neighbors are away on a trip to the Lower Congo. "Let them stay down there. They put on airs when they leave and again when they return." His resentment goes back to Solola's first trip; when she came back, she didn't want to be called Solola any more. "From now on Marie is my name!" She didn't want to run in the savanna with him any more either, she didn't want to soil and tear her skirt and vest. "I have three skirts and three vests. In town people are covered from head to toe!" Anyhow he couldn't care less, Solola or Marie, Lemba is the one he likes best. Kodia, the chief's son, also went to the Lower Congo, to Brazzaville. But he couldn't care less. "See, now you don't know what to say. . . . Kodia is a boy who doesn't cover himself from head to toe like a girl." Seeing no other way to silence the cackling little bitch, he raised his clenched fists. And the little bitch got her hackles up and taunted him: "You limp along, you can't even run to catch me, so how can you beat me up? Watch out, what if I told Kodia? . . . You are afraid of Kodia, aren't you? Don't tell me you're not." She added a word that Elenga didn't know: *So-ouassi*—which she translated as *mossendji* (savage). Did he know if he had relatives in the Lower Congo? There were many families in Kinkala. He had been in Kinkala. "Kinkala is just like here!" he shouted. He could have punched her or strangled her. If he could only run, but he had been limping for months because of a wound that wouldn't heal. In his heart of hearts he had to admit that it was not Lemba he loved best, but Solola. Psst, Marie. But why did she make eyes at the *so-ouassi* if it's Kodia she likes? . . . You stole my friend, damn you! There you are, a woman gets between two men and they fight. Anybody can

The Madman and the Medusa

put on airs. So he pretended not to notice her seductive glances. Still, how mortifying it was never to have been to the Lower Congo. Another scene came to mind. Once when Elenga had avoided the amorous glances of the little seductress, she had resorted to another trick, either to annoy him or to attract him. She had come to the fence and chanted: "Bye-bye-bicycle! Handy-handy-handlebar! Luggage-rick-rick-rack!" What did she think? That she had aroused his interest like that? He had ridden a bicycle in Kinkala, so what?

There were no other children left in the village except him, his sister, and a few tiny tots, either babies still carried on their mothers' backs or toddlers crawling on the floor! Kodia, Singa, Lemba had all left for the Lower Congo. Once his foot has healed, he'll surely be off to join them in the Lower Congo. He thinks of all that. His heart is heavy, and his eyes grow heavy under the ever-increasing pressure of the blinding light. The flies buzz around his wound and defy the hand that tries to catch them. It would be ridiculous to use a slingshot to kill them! He plays with his ammunition, his pebbles and flints. He remembers his hunting expeditions. Flints for big game, crows, cuckoos. For turtledoves and quail, a pebble is enough. It's difficult to surprise quail, moorhens too. Once, bent on revenge, he decided to shoot Solola's father's rooster, but he had to do it without being seen. The opportunity presented itself one day when he was alone in the village. There was the rooster in the fork of his slingshot, bold, swaggering, blazing like a flamboyant branch in December. Elenga spends so much time heaping abuse on him that his enemy trembles and visibly loses his arrogance, his puffed-up neck is plucked of its feathers, his dazzling plumage turns into a miserable old mourning coat. "The son of a bitch trembles so much that he doesn't know which way to turn. But he's not going to fool me." He shoots, bang! He calls himself every nasty name he can think of, even a no-good *so-ouassi*. A chief's rooster is a sorcerer like the chief and turns into a vulture when a *so-ouassi* like Elenga holds him in the line of his slingshot and shoots, not with a rock but with a tiny pebble. He looks everywhere, but can't find the damned rooster. He has been tricked by his female foe who is proud of her triumph, for now the rooster is crowing loudly like a public announcer who laughs at the humiliating and bitter defeat of a fair-playing enemy. This is a cruel lesson that he won't forget easily. First bewitch an enemy, then knock him down with a deadly punch. If he forgets that, he will never be a good hunter.

On the other side of the door are pictures of hartebeest, okapi, racoons, bustards painted in the same dark color of dried blood. These are not pictures of trophies but of game taken each time it came within range of his father's flintlock.

He will remember the lesson. Drowsiness overwhelms him, and he falls asleep, his daring head resting in the contemptuous mouth of the cayman.

He is engulfed by flames. Half his body is on fire. The right side of his face is burning, and he is astonished to see smoke rising from it. What did he do? He is unable to remove from the flames the part of his body that is most exposed. Women, some crouching, with partly denuded breasts, are holding out their hands. Where do they come from? Why do they all have his mother's face? And to add insult to injury, they all beg him: "Forgive us, papa!" Instead of remaining crouched on the ground, wailing, why can't they pull him out of the flames that engulf him? If you can't help, turn away, so I can pee to extinguish the fire. The lamentations become cries and the cries end in a mourning song. In despair he shows his heart and cries out that there will be no forgiveness because he never thought of revenge. With the eye that is away from the fire, he gazes in all directions, especially toward where the women who are standing and raising their arms are now staring. He could open wider the eye that is not in the fire, but he doesn't want to because he could hurt himself. The women seem to pray to a post set up like a totem pole, charred with patches of fluffy ashes. "I don't understand anything that is going on." He sees the pole writhing. He is going to die. On the path leading to the fields he sees his father coming, and with him the other men of the village. All the men have his father's face. A soldier with a red chechia on his head, boots on his feet, but nothing on his body, swings a hemp rope thicker than his neck or his calves. His eyes are stung by the ropes that whip the men along. The soldier, who with his fat and his baldness turns out to be his uncle Malonga, brings the gasoline. Another soldier drags something between his legs, a hernia or a gas can, he can't make out. Good Lord, he is pouring the gasoline all over my father, and here I am, stuck in this fire, if only I could aim my slingshot with one hand. I would kill him, kill him. . . . Stop, stop. Never mind, no reason to be ashamed. He pees. Good. The flames have dissolved into black mud. Now we can get going. But it's too late. A huge flame consumes both the totem pole and his father, mingling the sting of the rope with the smell of burnt wood and charred flesh and filling his lungs with its choking irritant.

The shade had receded and half his body lay in the sun. He opens his eyes and sees his mother sitting beside him. The bottom of his loincloth is wet. Can't you wake up? Look, one of his eyes is swollen, he can't open it. What's wrong with your eye?

"A bad dream," said his father, who was sitting with a man wearing clothes like those he had seen in Kinkala, worn by people who had perhaps come from the Lower Congo. It was his uncle Malonga. Kodia said: "He has dreamed the story that you were telling."

A dream as hot as all the fires of hell. A belly that drinks a whole demijohn of water as if it were a drop. It's terrifying and exciting at the same time. He had this dream, lived it and died from it. Like father, like son. Like his father, he lived it and died from it, in spite of all the warnings. His father's sisters drove him out of Brazzaville when they found the little fellow possessed by horrible monsters and in good faith sent him by train to their younger brother. They were hoping that Elenga would decide to become a medic like his uncle, who had power. But with the uncle's power went the bandages, the wounds, the nauseating death rattles, ugh! The young man was so disgusted that he started loafing around Kilometer 4, near the workshops of the C.F.C.O. He was swallowed up by the thirst of the engines, guzzled by their ferocious hunger. He drew deep pleasure from their long-drawn sighs, whined when they whined, and went home late at night smelling of fire, water, and soot, and so drunk that he was ready for the abuse heaped on him by his uncle who, at his wits' end, would shout at him: "Don't you know that your father? . . . You'll die like your father! . . ." He didn't realize that . . . In a strange way he began to resemble a locomotive; his complexion, his bearing, everything about him took on the look of one. The warnings and anxiety that others felt for him only strengthened his faith in a job for which he felt a special calling and in which any man, even a little whipper-snapper, could exercise an incredible power over a machine that, once gorged with fire and water, could reduce time to nothing and could knock down woods and savannas in its path and hurl men, women, and children out beyond life!

He got himself hired and soothed his uncle's rage with his first paycheck. The uncle discoursed at length on all the jobs people had to take nowadays, some that destroyed the body, others that pounded the soul in the head. . . . And why shouldn't the soul have a head and a body like anything else? What on earth had come over him?

He never took a day off, even when a member of his own tribe died, one who had to be mourned by all his kinfolk. He spent his days feeding coal to voracious fireboxes, quenching the bottomless thirst of those monsters one would have all the difficulty in the world imagining, if one hadn't seen them, right out of some terrifying nightmare. Besides, how many unlucky men had been sacrificed to them, his own father among them. Before and after, tribute had always to be paid, funerals were innumerable, several members of the same family were thrown in the abyss where the spirits of the Mayombe who were violated night and day . . .

What uncle Malonga didn't say . . . what he could have told was that, while he moved up in his job, he witnessed many smashed-in chests, lacerated bellies, feet, arms, and heads crushed to a pulp. . . . But he never told about any of that. The aunts had gone to the sorcerers and had potions and fetishes prepared, and had prayed in church for the protection of the child. After all, the father of the orphan was in a good position, wherever he was, to know what his child was doing and how to protect him. The rope with seven knots that Elenga always wore around his waist would protect him. Provided that he never took it off. Better to lose his life first.

In 1934 Malonga arrived in Pointe-Noire with the entire Batignolles medical staff and had never since taken the train back to Brazzaville. He had had quite a few nightmares for a long time afterwards, for many years afterwards. And yet he is one of those who remember hell with nostalgia. "I was there." He wondered how so many people could still be alive on this planet. It means that in spite of all the calamities, all the famines that kill people off like flies, there will be over and over again men, and women too, doomed to a hard and difficult life. Sorcerers will be busy for centuries to come. . . .

The money of Elenga's first two weeks of work appeased his uncle's wrath. He recognized that from then on it was necessary to make money. Money means progress. The following week he invited a few old Laris and offered them drinks paid for from his nephew's wages. He steadied himself, trying to control his voice when he asked the old men if they had had enough to drink. He gave them some tobacco and a few kola nuts and explained in the same restrained voice that the wine was paid for with his money, the tobacco with mine. Please sniff, I mean not the wine, not the tobacco, but him. This boy is my son, my brother's son. He himself chose the work that he chose. His father had the same job before him. He is following in his father's footsteps, of his own free will. I wanted you to know. One never knows. For me, he's my son. Let him pour you some more wine. . . . Here, pour some more! That's it, now you know everything. His aunts in Brazzaville also know. You know what happened to his father. He also knows. One of them said in conclusion: "There are more people underground than there are living above it. How can the living avoid walking on the dead?" Perhaps he wanted to say that you can't recreate the world or something else that nobody understood. Elenga lowered his eyes and touched the rope at his waist with its seven knots.

The seer could not see or tell what had happened these last days. In vain he held his hands above the water of the divining gourd, but nothing appeared on the surface. The exceptionally clear water, on the contrary, darkened suddenly and became as black as the blackest soot. A strange thing happened: acrid smoke like the smoke of train engines arose from the gourd. The seer said that one shouldn't try to find out more, and that this death could be explained by what one already knew.

2.
Luambu-Lufwa Lumbu

What André discovered about Luambu was a web of mysteries. There had been a woman in his life, a young woman. "A young woman carrying a child on her back. They are walking toward a stream, they are hurrying." Suddenly the surface of the water in the gourd divides into two parts, sunlight and dark. The parts are equal. There is soot on the path in front of them, more in front of the woman. . . . They are fugitives, they are running away. "He had a serious problem with a white man named Martin!" André didn't take in the sense of the seer's pronouncement. His mind was elsewhere, trying to make the features of the fugitive seen in the water fit those of the man who had worked in his office. "Good heavens!" He sees again at the moment he remembers it Luambu giving him a sheet of paper. The smell of incense invades his nostrils. The soothsayer watches him sniff and shakes his head.

From time to time the man turns around, showing his impatience at having to slow down because of the grass on the path. . . . They would soon have to leave the path. His wife is trailing behind, and he begs her to walk a bit faster. In addition to the child on her back, she carries a bundle on her head. . . . They had to leave so many things behind! They are not moving out. She had wanted to give this and that to this one or that one of her friends. But he had scolded her, because if you give things away, you have to explain why. . . . Do you really want to? . . . No, she doesn't want to. She can't stay behind with the child. It wouldn't be home for her like that—all alone with the child. . . . Then it's settled, anyhow, what you leave behind will be taken by whoever wants it.

He bustles about, holding in his hand all the while a small parcel no bigger than his open hand. She glances furtively at the parcel, but doesn't ask any questions. Hurry up! Turn down this lamp . . . please! She busies herself, going from the bedroom to the living room a few more times, while he goes out to see if the way is clear. Ready? Let's go. Fortunately, the child is sound asleep, though only a sorcerer would detect something amiss in the cries of a child at night. Light sleep is easily disturbed and one hurries out to enjoy the cool of the night. . . . The night is dark. He could knock over the lamp and start a fire. The thought goes in and out of his mind, any diversion would betray them. From under the eaves he grabs a stick the length of a man's stride. He puts the end of the stick in his wife's hand, telling her not to let go of it.

They had left the village for some time when the first rooster crowed. "Don't go so fast." "All right!" He adjusts his pace so that he doesn't have to pull on the stick. The stick maintains the right distance between them. "Better now?" "Yes!" How gentle a woman is. He has been married to her for some time now. His memory turns to the past.

He hears the voice of his father. They had realized that one "stopper" wasn't enough for the big bottle that his family represented. Count: More than one mouth, more than one body. Of course, we have always been prolific. So one "stopper" for so many mouths, so many bodies wouldn't do. . . . (He then gave his usual long list of complaints.) What is the count? How many are there? He, the great-uncle possessed the blood that . . . he is the master of the family blood . . . that is so fertile. He is silent, because the time hasn't yet come for him to speak. She, the mother, bore the girl that you want to take for your son. . . . They are all behind her, the next to last seed of the ear of grain—the seed for sowing. All those behind her have a body, a mouth. Myself and all of them. All those behind me. Isn't it for those who are at my side and at her side that I say: "This head has scabies, this body is cold, this belly is hungry, this mouth is thirsty. We, she with her hoe, she with all she is that you want for your son, for us she is our mother and now our chance of survival. She is going to take everything and leave. Are we going to be left high and dry? You gave only a small "stopper." . . . Of course you weren't stingy with the wine, but what will happen if one of us grabs this little "stopper?" Doesn't that scare you? Don't you think about the suffering of others?"

He gives his word when the father looks at him. Manners. Necessity has the force of law. He promises to work hard, cent after cent, to enlarge the "stopper" until it fits the family bottle. The father slaps the shoulder of his son, chuckling as he always does when he is embarrassed, because he can then express himself only with a long chuckle followed by a rasping of the throat. He makes a gesture that allows the son to guess what is coming. Always surprising the way the father shakes his hands. "We see the world as it advances, but where does it go? We need new mouths, new teeth, and new tongues to say what needs to be said." He speaks in riddles. In the secret words of a ritual. The noble gesture and the pompous words said with a cracked voice allow the son to prophesy. A father like him who catches on easily, when he has a son, that son will be blessed. Blessed. This is my father, this is my son. The stopper. One, two and three stoppers and more and more stoppers. The solemn agreement is sealed. Life goes on, in search of what excess?

He found happiness. Shortly before sowing time and after the fires to clear the land had died down. He found happiness in marrying the daughter of Landu Tchitembu. Julienne, with strong arms and legs. With a forehead as pure as her heart, she was so gentle that her smile always had a touch of humility and gentleness. Her body and her breast were so pleasantly warm. She was a treasure, and for her he wanted more treasures, all the treasures of modesty and immodesty, of luxury and lust.

Modesty led him to say "stopper," brazenness led him, feet firmly planted on the ground, to say: MONEY. It is to money that the world opened up with all its miracles and all its evils.

Julienne is modest. Her wealth is in her blood and in her smile. She doesn't smile to show off, but because she knows that her smile is a source of joy.

She says: "All right!" This response that he has so often solicited is as refreshing as a kola nut. He checks the folds of the rolled blanket that he carries on his shoulder. The parcel is still there. She sees what he does, but immediately lowers her eyes to the nursing baby. Soon, after the hill, they will have to leave the road. Julienne hadn't asked why they had to flee. To leave. That's the word she would have used. So suddenly to leave everything behind, without even saying goodbye to anyone.

Did she wonder about the reason for this sudden departure in the middle of the night?

The child babbles on, patting its mother's nipple. The father looks away: "We must go." He gives Julienne time to fasten the baby on her back. She doesn't expect any explanation. But he says: "I was compelled to take this decision to leave."

In the past they had also left M . . ., and lots of other places where he had worked, in the same way. As a former student of the Catholic Mission, he spoke the whites' language so well that he never lacked opportunities to work. They had been all over the country, by boat, by truck, on foot. They settled down with barely enough time to arrange a home, then, after her first deep sleep, she had to wake up, take just a few necessary things, and walk off into the night. She followed him without a wrinkle on her forehead, without a shadow on her heart.

This isn't a woman I have here. If he had had a child right away, it would now be a slip of a boy—or girl. You should be sorry only for what you can't do. Don't be sorry for what you can do but don't until the right moment.

He was right, otherwise her eyes would have been sad and her heart heavy. She knew that he was not degrading her because he made love to her only when she was menstruating. It was the justification for this strange behavior, this rejection of all taboos. He wanted to belong to a world he had made himself, not to a world made by others. That was his argument. But what did she understand about that? What did it mean to belong to a world one had made oneself?

But he would have been the best of men were it not for his habit of leaving in the middle of the night. She didn't detect any arrogance in him. He was a well-educated man who put his brain to work.

They had wandered off the road, still keeping the same direction. His hands were not calloused, the inside was smooth. "Your work is not hard, is it?" That was the one and only time she had inquired about his work. "I drive, or I write, or I count, or I supervise the work of others," he had said. These had been his various jobs. Jokingly she counted them on his fingers, starting with the ring finger, and this one (the thumb) does nothing then? He had laughed. This one will accomplish great things, he had said, and then he had placed his forefinger on her lips: "Hush!" The world one makes oneself is a mystery that should be kept secret . . . otherwise it might stab you and knock you down. Life is a strangler! How somber he was when he said that.

They were sitting outside in the shade enjoying the cool of the day, his head resting on her lap. It was a Sunday afternoon. His "Hush" hadn't kept her quiet about a secret he didn't want to reveal. A secret is a thing, an object, but there was no secret object in the house she spent all her time cleaning, since he had forbidden her to hoe in the field. A secret is also a word over which one passes, over which one sighs. He had taught her to read at the beginning of their marriage, and from time to time to shut him up she would say in French, raising her eyelashes and imitating some woman she had seen: "Mr. Husband of mine work all week. The month was tough." She exaggerated the movement of her lips when she came down hard on "tough." But business is good! "Ah, you want me to behave like a lady, do you, but I am a black woman. Leave me alone," she used to tell him when he wanted her to take up her primer and read. He argued: "If ever I became somebody, white people might come to visit me for a drink or a meal." "He is mad, mad! Anyhow my father respects you and that's enough for me." They were teasing each other. And then all of a sudden, bang-crash, they were up before dawn and leaving everything behind.

In L . . ., where they had last been, there were at least ten white couples. The president of the club, the manager of a company, an engineer, a physician, who were all addressed by their titles. The others had names: Messieurs Potier, Berger, Van Hut, and so on. The doctor had asked Julienne: "Wouldn't you like to become a nurse?" The doctor always came up to her all smiles as soon as he saw her. The doctor is very nice! "I think, doctor, tomorrow maybe, I say yes!" "And you answered him: 'Tomorrow maybe I say yes!' Isn't that right?"

"What a beautiful baby."

He wasn't thinking of the compliment paid the baby, but of the doctor's suggestion. Indeed, she could learn. . . .

It was not a good sign that snatches of his life kept coming back to him like that, each one reminding him of something that had happened before their abrupt departure. She puts the food on the table. He is alarmed at the way she mocks him by repeating: "Monsieur Martin, may I introduce our future nurse?" Whether from surprise or astonishment, he makes a movement that she interprets as an enthusiastic response to her new position. He takes hold of himself. When it's definitely the turn of the thumb to act. . . . So close to the great hope of his life . . . Monsieur Martin: and bang-crash! He feels in his throat a knot as big as his fist. How can he eat? The more he tries to eat to hide his sudden panic, the less he can swallow. The baby starts to cry and allows him to avoid Julienne's vigilant eyes. A secret is heavier to carry than life itself. What crime does it hide? Monsieur Martin, the assumed though not confirmed witness, is the reason for his flight, whenever he appears, whenever his name is pronounced, that name which only he seems to bear.

Along the way, they walk on the shady part of the path. The trail is like a wide wound cut across the forest and the savanna that avoids the low terrain and the swampy areas. Pitted with potholes and ruts, it indeed looks like a wound that won't heal easily. In spite of its bright shades of yellow pus and pink flesh, the road is as dreary as the baked and rebaked green mass that festoons trees, shrubs and bushes. Deprived of human presence, devoid of human care and love, it is indifferent to the flight of this man and the woman following him, as they head for heaven knows what disasters. The palms of his hands are wet. He wipes them on his thighs. He rubs his forearms. The child babbles on, trying out sounds new to the mother. The child breaks off with: "Ah, ah, ah" and then resumes its babbling. The mother is happy with the child who hasn't cried since they left the night before. Julienne watches Luambu gazing at the child, who is chirping and laughing. Her glance doesn't necessarily mean: "Why?" She still remembers hearing him say: "Now we can have a child." It happened when they settled in L . . . and lived in a house belonging to the Compagnie des Mines, reserved, along with ten others, for the educated natives. Now we can have a child! He no longer waited for her period to have sex with her. She was impregnated and the baby was born, a baby boy. In the maternity ward of a hospital, yes in a maternity ward. Not the way she and her husband had been born. The way one was born had changed just as the way one lived one's life had changed. It was his choice, and he knew why it had to be like that. . . . He teases the child. She smiles and abandons her memories, which she can't drag along on their trip and add to her burden. Nothing is more exhausting than memories on a trip, especially when the trip is on foot. She is doing well. "Let's go!" Julienne gets up as soon as he does; she fastens the baby on her back and follows on her husband's heels. Since they left, Julienne hasn't said a word. He has watched her to find out if she was making an effort to remain silent. At every stop, she showed him the same ever-so-trustful face. How can she not expect an explanation from him? She keeps silent. Her silence, this complete silence overwhelms him. What are the right words to make her understand? He doesn't search for them. He gathers all his strength to find a solution to their flight. He had been the supervisor of the natives at the mine as well as at the workers' camp. They were going to hire an assistant book-keeper. He was born counting on his fingers, which means that if. . . . But what crime is it on which his eyes are closed, as if a rock had been thrown on a grave? He turns around. Now Julienne shows signs of weariness. The previous flight had lasted one week. They went alone, the two of them, through the forest, the savanna, the forest again, along the streams looking for a way to ford the dark and treacherous waters.

She is trailing behind. Where is he taking them? "The village is still far, if we follow the road. Let's take the shortcut by the stream over there, shall we?" There is a plain but no village in sight, just a dark green corridor crossing it from right to left. A strip of forest on both sides of a stream. Her back is aching. He looks up: "We'll arrive before the rain." In front of them the landscape was darkening with black clouds blown by the wind. The clearing didn't offer any protection. The trees and the stream were awaiting them. . . . The stream was awaiting Julienne and her child.

Luambu-Lufwa Lumbu

As in Elenga's case, a complete uncertainty manifested itself when André tried to find out what happened these last few days, the reason for Luambu's coma and his disappearance. For Luambu had certainly disappeared right before his eyes, although a few moments earlier he had seen him lying in bed on his back, his arms alongside his body, his eyes open. Eyes open and with no expression. It's impossible to recognize a face with lifeless eyes. . . . But why lifeless eyes?

"This man is not a relative of yours, any more than the other man," the soothsayer had said. "No, no!" he had exclaimed, his whole body horror-stricken. André put an abrupt end to the consultation.

Further investigation would only bring a few more images of Muendo's life that wouldn't explain anything. He would again strike against a wall of soot, and these successive shocks were more than he could take. "This is the realm of the dead, no living being can enter it at will," explained the soothsayer, who clearly had sized him up and had found him too superficial to confront that realm. This wall of soot had appeared twice, a third time could be his doom. Therefore he had best accept the torment of the threat he felt hanging over him. In reality there was one question he couldn't face: Had he sold himself to Luambu in exchange for losing his stutter? The only way to know for sure was to find out if Luambu had anything at all to do with the deaths of Elenga and Muendo, his two friends, and to find out if they hadn't been bought for the price of a prayer like . . .

3.
Muendo

Muendo and women, women, women! He wants them all! They all fall for him! What do they find so special about him? What does he have that others haven't? He is a fool, therefore funny. If I wanted to be vulgar like some—I am not thinking of anyone in particular—I would say that he puts their you-know-what on fire! Anyhow with all the sawdust he can let them have, it's an appreciated saving and a lot less work for them. Moreover, if you go somewhere and the mistress of the house tells you she uses sawdust for cooking, you bet that she has offered herself to the guy. Wood is expensive, but thanks to sawdust the fellow keeps his underbelly warm and his belly also. I think myself that one attributes to him many more conquests than he has racked up, poor fellow! You can pity him, you whose face a woman dare not contemplate for fear of one day bearing a son with a hilarious hippopotamus head. If you have a bone, a dog runs after you. If you have money, women won't turn away. This fellow had the dough, the sawdust, and the talent to entertain. You like to spread scandal, don't you? I tell you that a husband . . . Well, you think Muendo is a vigorous type, handsome, with domineering eyes and a forehead impressive enough to convince you he's no dummy. Nah! he's just a puny little guy with a twisted mouth hanging on one side where a tooth protrudes like an elephant tusk. But he smells of wood, and women detect that right away! When I listen to you, I really wonder. . . . Aren't you running him down to take some kind of revenge? Some people are like that, the woman who rejects him is a whore and his lucky rival is a nonentity, a nut! Yeah . . . but don't forget it, Muendo will come to a bad end.

The Madman and the Medusa

When André Sola found out the truth about Muendo's well-publicized womanizing, it appeared quite different and far less glamorous than he had believed. As far as women were concerned, he behaved quite normally. He was a ladies' man for sure, but being gallant, he was also helpful. He had made more married couples happy than he had made cuckolds. He won them over, the women of course, gained their respect and in fact very seldom seduced them. His talent for suggestive talk provoked a great deal of jealousy and spite, especially from those who thanks to him had the best-cooked food. There isn't much wood for cooking in the big savanna of Pointe-Noire. There is plenty of grass, but what is missing is wood, and one has to get up early and hurry to market before the least little faggot is snatched up. He might easily give a woman a small bucket of sawdust out of generosity and not with seduction in mind, yes sir! A bachelor is a man who cannot place one woman above another, with the exception of his own mother. Well, he's a kind of egalitarian. Oh, yeah! He did run into some trouble . . . they say. . . . There we are, hearsay again.

Muendo is a married man with one wife only and three children, with a fourth on the way, and if the fourth turns out to be twins, that would make five. But there have never been twins in his family. Of course, that's not a reason. Yes, I agree, that's not a reason. I, for one, was not aware that he . . . I didn't know him under that name. Just picture the situation: He was my neighbor and not only was he my neighbor, I knew his entire family, his eldest brother, Sow, whom everyone knows, who is in the public works. Oh, him! Right, he's the eldest brother; we also know the other brother, Nguèye. But how come these Sencgalese are your neighbors? It's the grandfather or the father who was Senegalese, the mother is an authentic Vili. Oh, so that's it. Well, since they were born here and raised by their maternal uncle, that explains the name Muendo. I get it. I get it. Wait a minute, isn't it the grandfather or father who is said to have been a companion of Malamine! Who? Forget it, that's the scholar speaking. Don't you see that he doesn't miss any opportunity to show off all he knows. Sergeant Malamine . . . Savorgnan de Brazza. You don't have to shrug your shoulders, even if you are not an ignoramus, you can't be expected to know everything. Do you see how pleased he is? So you were saying that this Muendo was a most respectable man . . . but what I still don't understand is what in the hell he was doing with a fellow of whom we still know nothing. "*I know in my heart it's a mad dream.*" "*Let me love you.*" Hey, shut up, Tino Rossi! Go sing somewhere else. Why are you still hanging around a corpse who really isn't one! Like vultures! There is something in the wind. . . . Everybody is frightened. We were speaking of Muendo, well let me tell you . . . No, nothing. Let André speak; come on, André, speak. What is surprising indeed is that the other fellow was never intimate with the family. Neither Sow nor Nguèye knew that their younger brother was acquainted with him. As far as Elenga, Malonga's nephew, is concerned, they must have known him, everybody knows the family of the medical supervisor at the A. Cissé hospital. "What's that, A. Cissé?" "Oh, you too! Don't try to be smart, we have enough to worry about." They knew Elenga, at least by sight and name, but they had never heard Muendo mention him. Nor had his wife, who had never been to their house for a visit or a drink. See . . . now listen . . . it could be that Malonga's family had no idea of the fellow's existence. No, no, I am mistaken. On the contrary, our guard, Jean-Pierre Mpita, saw them together; Elenga's sister knew the fellow. Nevertheless, neither the medical supervisor, nor his wife . . . But go on André, tell us about it. "Well, it's very simple, I went to offer my condolences, wondering what the calamity meant. There are three friends, two of them die and the third one falls into a coma and doesn't recover, isn't it strange?" Of course, he remembered this man found comatose in the cemetery—he also remembered the fainting of his niece—but he couldn't figure out who he was. "A friend of my nephew? And you know what I found out later about the sister? Just one or two days before her brother's death, there had been talk of a marriage to a suitor chosen by the uncle but rejected by the brother and the sister. . . . Ah, orphans are sometimes more difficult to raise than twins. . . . You can imagine that because of his dangerous work the family had not been stingy and had gone all out for every possible fetish! They were armed and armorplated, you can be sure. And you know who Mazola turned down? . . . A relative of the medical supervisor's wife, Massengo, the teacher." "Oh! I thought he was already married. Do you know him?" "He's the teacher of my eldest who is in the tenth grade." "Look how proud he is! Look at him, he can't help boasting!" "It's natural to be proud of one's kids when they are good students, right?" "All right, be proud!"

"I tell you the fellow who really interests me is Muendo!" "We already told you, he was a nice guy who was supposed to have seduced many women, but, as you know, my friends, our wives are all faithful, and Muendo was probably tenderhearted. A good man! When women know that a man is weak, they enjoy making eyes at him." "A real expert, believe me. If I had been told that Tchilala was a good judge of female behavior, I would have said, you've got the wrong guy, buddy!" "That's right, go on laughing!" "What are we all doing? Joking when evil is threatening. I am going to tell you what has happened and what is happening. Have you seen all those ships off the coast? Have you never seen them? Well, this is war, and the French want to win the war there also. Actually we don't want them to lose it, but what do we have to gain by working faster and faster. . . . That's what's happening. Elenga, Muendo, all of us are, willy-nilly, on the battlefield." "Luambu also! Then he is AWOL, isn't he?" "Do you know what martial law is? It's in force only during wartime, and we are at war. At war, not on strike. In wartime one works hard, one works oneself to death, one is confused, frightened. . . ." "Enough, let me speak, we are afraid that the same thing will happen to us, so we assume that Luambu bewitched both his friends. . . . And you, André, are spreading that story, are you?" (Superstitious bigot!) "What story? What story?" "Come on, you're not going to fight, are you? Better go to bed and not talk any more about all that."

Because of Muendo's popularity, because of the good reputation and the respectability of his family—especially that of his older brother, because of the generosity of Muendo himself—because of Muendo then, people found out how the aforesaid Luambu and the aforesaid Elenga and Muendo had met and become acquainted. (There had been witnesses to the scene that brought them together.) It had happened approximately six or eight months earlier, before the event that had upset everyone and had everyone's imagination in such a frenzy. From the testimony of eyewitnesses it had been possible to unravel the story—a very mysterious one indeed—of their encounter during a fight provoked by a mad preacher who had appeared on the beach at about that time. Nobody knew where this strange preacher had come from, this preacher, this fisher in muddy waters—which beats all because our water is so clear and tonic and the swimming so good that it lives up to its name Tchikungula, or the swimming beach. The story of the meeting was very strange indeed. André with his repressed religious vocation could easily imagine the madman preaching like a slightly batty priest who painfully utters the words of the Gospel that he gets all screwed up. What a hopeless situation it was, if the Devil was using the word of God.

4.
The Meeting

———————

"I speak of things that you see, of things that you don't understand. As does the sea. You don't wash your mouth, you eat and your hunger is insatiable. Who made you the way you are? The sea doesn't laugh. But you, you laugh at my words. You say: he has no brains because what he says does not make sense. Who taught you to lie to yourselves? You lock your hearts against life. You hold a handful of water out to the fire and extinguish it. You are not afraid that the fire dies. You look at woman and turn your back on life. What kind of life do you want to live, putting so much smoke between your eyes and your heart? You, for instance. Don't be surprised, don't look around, it's of you that I speak. Are you going to disavow every day of your life? And pay for it with what kind of death?"

The man looking around was in the crowd with two other men who didn't know each other. At that moment they looked at each other for the first time. With their eyes they asked each other of whom the madman had been speaking, the madman who was standing up to his hips in the waves. The madman could have pointed at anyone in the crowd, at any one of the men, women, boys, girls, fishermen waiting for the return of the fishing boats. More and more people were rushing up to see what was happening. Children came hopping, shouting, jostling one another. The man was standing alone in the water. When he stopped talking, his whole torso, from which his ribs protruded, began to shiver; his jaws, his eyes, and his apparently toothless mouth started to shake.

The waves were so tame and the rustle they made was so weak that they couldn't drown out the cries of the squabbling children.

"The angels are coming. Don't leave any trash in their path. I'll tell you where the path is. But you don't know any longer where your heart is. How can you find your path in the dark? Why are you coveting what you already have? If only you wouldn't forget. You, what have you done to your father? You there, what have you done to your father? And you to your mother? And you, to your wife?"

Voices rose from the crowd shouting: "They are coming!" Three or four canoes indeed were landing at different points on the beach. The crowd broke up and the people went back to the different fishing places they had left. Only three men stayed on. One was tall and strong and his name was Luambu; another one had big arms, big calves, and a big head and was called Muendo; the third one, Elenga, who looked younger, was puny and about as tall as the fattest of the three. Besides the odor of their sweating bodies, two of these three men had another distinctive smell. The skinny one smelled of grease, the one with fat calves of wood. Perhaps, besides the smell of sweat, one could have detected the odor of ink and pencil on the long fingers of the third one. But nobody sniffed them, not even the most insolent of the brats who shouted obscenities and made nasty gestures at the madman. The men looked at one another, said hello, and introduced themselves. Luambu. My name is Elenga. And I am Muendo.

"If he weren't slightly batty, he would make a good priest," said Muendo.

"Do you know him?" asked Elenga.

"You can see him often like this, in the evening, saying things that frighten people, but that they soon forget."

"Look!" Muendo was pointing at the people who were busy around the canoes, one of which had put ashore not far from where they were standing.

"What do you think of him?" Elenga inquired of Luambu, whose eyes were still fixed on the madman.

"You have nothing left but your belly, and your belly is an abyss. Seek out the path, seek out your heart. Don't say that you didn't know, that I didn't speak." He became more and more agitated when he saw that people were not listening any more and were busy pulling the nets out of the water. With greedy eyes they looked forward, some to a fish soup, others to grilled sardines. . . . Was he going to keep silent now? But our madman who could have been one of the preachers of those many sects who behave like mayflies springing from the ground in the rainy season, flying clumsily before losing their wings and crashing into the mud, the muck in which they suffer a sordid death . . . Our madman—was he really mad?— was not yet resigned to silence. How could he possibly be silent when the fire of his message still burned his mouth? "Lord, let me baptize them in spite of themselves, for their hunger must be appeased."

He approached the fishermen and started throwing water on them, yelling at the same time: "I baptize you in the name of the Lord, I baptize you in the name of the Lord." He scooped up water with his hands and flung it at the fishermen who were pulling the nets. Along with the salt water, some of them received medusas, jellyfish, in their faces and on the bare part of their bodies. All the kids, spurred on by the commotion the madman had created, threw themselves into the water. Imitating the madman, they gamboled about, splashing water and medusas with it, for the sea happened at the moment to be full of them. Some of the fishermen, knee-deep in water, knew at once what they had stepped on when they felt the stinging pain. The children sprang out of the water as fast as they had plunged in, shrieking more from pain than from joy. They rolled over in the sand, bawling. People were stunned. Mothers cursed obscenely, calling down the wrath of God on whoever was responsible for this horror. The madman was triumphant: "I told you so, I told you so!" He was so wrapped up in his righteousness that he didn't see the chief fisherman advancing toward him, so enraged that he ignored the jellyfish that were sticking to him. He caught the madman by the neck and plunged his head and his whole torso, one, two, three times, into the water, and pulled him out and gave him a thrashing. The madman wasn't raving mad, because he took the punishment—the violent blows given by fist and foot that would have crushed any other man's chest—without unleashing the evil forces usually harbored by the insane. . . . Luambu said calmly and firmly to the fisherman: "That's enough, you don't want to kill him." But the fisherman was so incensed that he turned his rage against Luambu. Muendo and Elenga stepped in to separate them, but with the other fishermen siding with their chief, a general fight ensued that sealed the friendship of the three men who had never met before, neither the previous day, nor the morning of that day. They had not known one another before they found themselves in the crowd listening to the madman. There is no mistake about it: a madman was instrumental in their meeting. . . . Farther along was another group of fishermen, and some of them could be seen running out of the water. They were scanning the sea with anxious eyes. "Come out!" they cried. "Watch out!" "Over there also?" "What's happening?" The waves were slow and heavy. "That's all we'll get in the net." "Don't speak of disaster!" "Didn't he say, you think only of your bellies?"

How could one quiet all those kids? Shut them up. Calm them down.

Muendo and Elenga went from one group of fishermen to another. But Luambu, standing firmly in the sand, didn't move. His eyes were examining the sea, the crowd. . . . Just as had been predicted, there were largely jellyfish at the bottom of the net, more jellyfish than fish: three swordfish no bigger than your hand, one skate, two dogfish, and some small fry that had to be separated from the gluey mass of jellyfish. Someone ventured a prophecy: "It looks like an evil omen!" Muendo was right; people heard what the madman had said but forgot it immediately afterward. Perhaps he had told them what the prophecy was all about. After having beaten him up, now they were looking for him, probably to question him. But he had disappeared. How could it be, after all those blows that could have killed him? He was no longer there. Had he joined another group of fishermen to get beaten up again? "It's not likely after such a thrashing!" Elenga was telling himself that in Loango country two eyes were not sufficient. But he didn't know what else you should have. His uncle Malonga used to say that two eyes were not enough in Loango country to see that one is deep in total mystery. No use trying to understand. "They slip the night into your eyes and you don't see anything!" But what he had seen was not just nothing. The Laris might not have beaten up a man who spoke as he did. Luambu had saved the madman from being beaten to death. Perhaps he was not completely Loango. He didn't dare ask him outright. One thing was certain: "We'll always remember how we met," said Muendo. "That's right, we'll say that when we met there were medusas everywhere, and the words of a madman, a would-be preacher, brought us together."

Did the circumstances of this meeting explain Luambu's coma? Let's assume that Luambu found this opportunity to make friends with Elenga and Muendo. . . . The madman, or this strange character, who some people thought was a priest with a screw loose—might he have been a ghost like him? Was one the master of the other? Were they accomplices? But have you ever heard of a ghost falling into a coma? That's mind-boggling! Unheard of! And why one rather than the other? We can imagine anything. It appears that Luambu attacked a foe stronger than he thought, having overrated his strength against the son of a Lari and the grandson of a Senegalese. (You know that the Laris and Senegalese are equally talented in dealing with spirits and black magic. Nobody can stop them!) In spite of his Vili name, Muendo is the grandson of a Senegalese. *He* had practiced his talent on him, André, when he had taken advantage of his weakness (his profound faith in Christ and his angels) and had given him a prayer, though not the devil's prayer, for the Credo is certainly not the devil's prayer. He was wondering what would have happened to him now, if he hadn't made a novena, after his stutter had miraculously disappeared. But the threat remained.

André listened carefully to the animated discussions around him, but they all offered the same explanation. The apparent causes of the deaths of Elenga and Muendo were not the real ones. The guilty man: Luambu. His strange coma was of a kind that could only alarm anyone who had seen it. You couldn't get around it. André knew how to end his dilemma: trust in his religious faith, make as many novenas as necessary, not consult soothsayers or marabouts anymore, sleep soundly, and not listen to the gossip that was so bad for his nerves. He suddenly remembered the words attributed to the idiot who had presided over the meeting of Elenga and Muendo with their . . . He had mentioned angels. . . . Could a ghost, a manifestation of evil, speak of the coming of angels? Something wasn't quite right. . . . A few clever people even pretended that Muendo and Elenga had died in the war, as if the front line against the Germans weren't far away in suffering France. It is outrageous to twist facts to that extent. "The front is also in Africa." "I am speaking of the real front. In war there are lots of people killed and where are the ruins?" "The ruins were just an image, that's all!" "Don't think that because we are surrounded by swamps, we are in the mud of the trenches." "Death in the war is very much like Elenga's death and even more like Muendo's. I repeat, they are similar, but I won't say more, because over there people are dying by the thousands under the bombs. I know what I am talking about; I am a veteran." "What a set for a film!" someone joked. "In the meantime, at Kilometer 4, death and deportation have taken place." The deported had already been forgotten. André had forgotten Etienne Ling'Si and lost track of Rosalie. . . . He promised himself to ask Victorine if she had news of Rosalie. Poor woman! People were losing their minds. . . .

Perhaps there were men in the war who also fell into comas, but no bomb had fallen near Luambu in the Vounvou cemetery, where he had been found, and that was what made all the difference. André detected in this difference the mysterious danger that threatened him. When the young men who had gathered at Tchilala's started to speak of "chance," he listened without interfering, pretending even not to take the slightest interest in what was said, but in fact he didn't miss a word.

5.
Rumors

Chance

Chance, chance! Chance explains nothing, nothing at all. It doesn't explain anything. Whatever you say, nothing at all. Most probably there were other deaths that same week, that same month—that very same week. It happens that people die at the same time, people who knew each other, who lived more or less together. What does more or less really mean? Ah, you see now? Don't give me the reasons for your reasons. It isn't fair. No, it isn't fair. Me not fair? No, that's not what he means. He should make himself clear then and not get tangled up in his words. Let me get a word in. . . . Yes, let him speak. Speak, who prevents him from speaking? Shut up! Come on, speak, make your point, don't beat around the bush. Are you going to let him speak? I was saying that chance . . . Yes, we know. You, too, leave him alone! "*Love is a star*! . . ." There he is, there he is, the one who started all the trouble. If you don't want to listen, take your love song somewhere else! A corpse rots away, but the flesh of a comatose man remains fresh a long time. It sets people's tongues wagging and whets their appetites, their cannibalistic, morbid appetites, right? He's mad or what? Go on, go on! I want to get to the bottom of this story. I want to understand it, understand it thoroughly, because the more we talk about it, the more . . . Actually who really wants to understand it? Nobody, nobody, I can assure you. People are afraid, people are cowards! The death of that young guy at the C.F.C.O. (he was in his early twenties, wasn't he?), the death of the man of the Chemin de Fer Congo-Océan, this death calls for rebellion. Re-bel-lion, I tell you! And what do we do? We tell stories! We are involved in the coma of the other guy because it's of no consequence for all of us. You, why aren't you rebelling? Gee, let him speak, will you? You never let anybody speak. The one with his chance theory is silent now, disgusted with your habit of never listening. But you, you never shut up, you just go on talking, so go on. Rebellion, indeed! We already have war, we don't need another slaughterhouse. Now listen to this stupid windbag! Are you fighting the war? You haven't even lost a battle, so how do you know how to win a war? So he has you flabbergasted, stymied! I want our friend to speak about the rebellion, I want to know all about it! Never mind, forget it. He's going to do like the other guy, he'll look for reasons to explain his reasons and he'll end up explaining nothing. . . . Okay, sorry, go ahead! Let him think before he speaks. Oh, what a joker you can be! Ha, ha, ha, ha! And you said that it was chance. Don't listen to him. Muendo's death (well, there were quite a few cuckolds who wanted it. . . . What? You are one of them? Who is the motherfucker who dared ask the question?), his death was like Elenga's. That's right. The war killed them, why didn't it kill you? The men behind the lines kill themselves working. You make me laugh!. . . Not everybody dies in the war, otherwise there wouldn't be any veterans. By the way, do you know what Churchill said? . . . We don't give a damn! You hurt his feelings; look, he is leaving. You didn't let him speak. You never want anyone else to speak and you never want to listen to anyone else. We have listened enough to the others who have so little to say anyhow. What they say is like a grain of salt thrown in the kettle that leaves the fish tasteless! Whistle with admiration, don't shrug your shoulders! . . .

I must say, I like your idea of rebellion; can you elaborate on it? Man! I am impressed by what you said. Do you mean that the entire Native Village with their fists bigger than their hollow and empty heads should face as one man the submachine guns, tatata, tatata: a rotting heap of bodies! That's the rebellion? For what? For . . . Enough. We know, you speak French well! If we are interested in what he is saying, it's because he's not an empty parrot, a polly like you, but a man of intelligence! It's his idea, let him speak out. . . . First, I am not a polly; second, anyone can have an idea. Perhaps, but he is the one who had the idea first, nobody had it before him, so shut up. Don't shout, big mouth! No, no, no fight! No more blood. No more blood. How can you witness such a great event and all you think of doing is . . . is . . . I can't even find the word, it's simply outrageous. "O Gaul, our motherland." Here comes our singer again. Hey, singer . . . For my part, I'm convinced it's all in the name, when a man with such a name falls into a coma and his body disappears mysteriously . . . well, for me the name explains it all, period! You can't get around it. Just to think of it gives me the willies. . . . Are you sure you were not born with it? Motherfucker! Here we are, we can't discuss anything calmly anymore. . . . How would you translate his name into French, the other part of his name, Lufwa Lumbu? "Death, chant!" Death is a chant, a song. . . . It's easy enough to raise your fist, but a gun appears and you pee in your pants. Hey man, that's good thinking, but how did we do before the white man made us wear pants? Ha, ha, ha, ha, hee, hee, hee! Don't make such a long face, you've really got to laugh, because laughing is like breathing. You breathe more deeply. But of course with your turned-up nose you miss all the good smells and you must strain to catch them. . . . Ha, ha, ha! Let's face it, we are not serious, we are not taking life seriously! Sure, so what, we won't start all over again. Let's go. Are you coming? And you? One moment! Okay, we'll wait, but hurry up.

Now that you and I are alone, we can speak calmly of your idea: rebellion. You know, you aren't wrong, but the other fellow was right also to be against it. My older brother, who is a clerk at the C.F.C.O. and who was against the work stoppage on Wednesday and against the strike on Thursday, told me that high up, the commander in chief, the manager, the engineer, all spoke of martial law. In wartime a strike is considered a rebellion and in no time you are up against the wall—bang. The whole Native Village would be in danger at the first move—you know where the village is, you know where the army camp is, where Kilometer 4 and the militia camp are, so you know your idea might be interesting, but really it stinks.

Lufwa Lumbu gave us his coma and disappeared, that's clever, because it gives us the opportunity to think of something else. I wish I had known the man, quite a guy! We are stuck with Luambu Lufwa Lumbu, we let the relatives of Elenga and Muendo deal with . . . Obviously, everybody understood that, because even the mourning families will join us later. They will speak of the coma and undoubtedly there will be a sorcerer, a soothsayer, a marabout to explain that it all happened because of the coma, or rather because of Luambu, and they will try as we do to understand how it happened. It is possible that right now they feel avenged because the man responsible for their grief has been punished and is the prisoner of a coma. He won't come out of it. They don't even know where he is, but he must be somewhere. Those with only two eyes didn't see anymore. Who took him back to the hospital? Elenga's uncle. When he realized that they were looking for him, he had the body disappear. . . . The head clerk of his office was present when the body vanished from the hospital bed. Now, what do you think of that? Vanished from the sight of those who have only two eyes, but those who have four eyes, two plus two, have met him. Perhaps we could ask their help to find him, for as they say, it takes a sorcerer to know a sorcerer.

André Sola seemed to be always present wherever the conversation was about the dead and the coma that happened the next to last week in June. He was gathering every detail that might allow him to understand what had happened. Who were these men, Muendo, Elenga? That was fairly easy, for they had families. Actually he knew Muendo's relatives, for they were his neighbors. He even knew Muendo, who used to come to his house for a chat or for a beer, when there was any. Come to think of it, lately he hadn't seen much of him.

6.
Tuesday, June 20

The day you die, you have a bitter taste in your mouth. He swallowed, it wasn't bitter. Death can happen at any moment. It's marked down somewhere. Your morning is merry, your evening sad. From one moment to another. Death is in me somewhere. In me, in all of us. Here, so to speak, or there. In a wound that doesn't heal, a wound of mine that doesn't heal, and bang! He was speaking to himself in a stubborn way. He was loosening up for the first time. Elenga looked at Luambu's set face. Luambu said: "Stop looking at me like that! Your glance scratches my face. It's like a fly biting the tip of my nose, an arrogant fly. A fly full of arrogance. Everything it touches reeks of arrogance. But you are not going to infect me." Elenga looked puzzled.

To forget the unpleasantness of that look, to avoid being aware of it, he faced the sea. His eyes swept over the sea from the lighthouse to the tip of the pier. On the other side, Cape Yoyo had disappeared in the warm haze.

Warships were anchored in the bay: a battleship, a destroyer, a . . . A whole squadron. Strange words like war meant, not dead bodies, but that life terrified of itself was going through a dark and uncontrollable agony. The sea is unconcerned, it has its own war. At the end of the pier you could watch the sea fighting the rocks torn from the Mayombe and brought in by the trainload, in order to tame it and break the waves of the bar. The battleships seemed to be making eyes at one another.

"It's Morse code," said Elenga, "I know it."

Luambu looked at him incredulously.

The Madman and the Medusa

We say: "Salt water." The Vilis say: "Mbou," defining the sea by its noise. It's a sound that repeats itself for all eternity, perhaps since the beginning of time. Time comes out of the night. One morning, night gave birth to time, as well as to the stars and the moon. The sun and time came out of the night.

After the creation of time, man came out of the hole in the ground. He blinked. His hair was as stiff as the warthog's. He stepped into the water to wash his eyes and his body. Then he understood that the animals, the turtle, the rooster, would obey him and he entered the woods to eat the fruit and the leaves.

Man is small. Particularly inside his skin. Inside and outside. Shit! What are you talking about? He couldn't help asking. But once launched, Luambu couldn't stop. Perhaps, he was talking to himself: man is really small in his skin. Elenga didn't agree; Luambu inspired such awe in him that he had to be full of weighty ideas. Where did he get lost without his skin? Small, maybe, because of all the ideas bubbling within him that finally made him fragile. The sea is the night of time. The sea, the night, death. Impervious, permanent. There are two nights. The first is the devious sister of the one that created time, the stars, the moon, the sun. The first, a secret part of the second, *ab absurdo* engendered life that was stillborn. He was looking at the sea thinking that he taught Elenga these things he was supposed not to know. "How does one look, in order to understand?" A strange question!

Looking is important. "I'm not scatterbrained . . . but I don't know what I'm thinking about when I think," confided Elenga.

"When you look the way you have learned to look, you'll understand what I mean." Elenga rubbed his head. Luambu glanced toward the land. The land was flat. Standing on the beach, one could catch sight of the hill called the love woods (the town's first park), which was covered with *passe-pallum*, a grass that weaves a thick mat over the ground and doesn't accept the presence of any other grass on the same ground. Remembering it, Luambu thought: "Soon we'll be like that."

Tuesday, June 20

Walking to the beach from the Chargeurs Réunis, you were allowed to walk only on the far side of the dirt road that went by the European club. You can't slow down, or you'll irritate the militia men on duty in front of their sentry boxes painted with large diagonal stripes of red, white, and blue.

Children were allowed to catch fish in the mud of the neighboring swamps that were being drained. Swamps were everywhere, on both sides of the road that connected Djindji to the plateau, passing both railroad stations, the new and the old one, which is now the freight station. The Normandy, that's its name. "I shall see my Normandy again, the country where I was born." Gelair de Baltazar, also known as Pambu, a nice chap, sings with his deep voice, the pain of nostalgia in his eyes.

The year before, the fishermen had been driven away beyond the Songolo. Where they used to fish and where they had been authorized to come back, opposite the tip of the pier, bunkers had been built and buried in the sand, under camouflage bristling with cannon, rifles, and machine guns. Prisoners had helped the soldiers construct them.

The Germans with their submarines . . . one had been sighted in the distance and chased by the squadron that had just called in the harbor, or more precisely, in the bay. People still remember a telegraph operator who became popular in the Native Village, because he secretly sold little pieces of paper at five cents each. Schoolchildren boasted that they could communicate with one another in Morse code. But they didn't understand a word of the ships' communication with one another or with the harbor. Naturally, all the warships were French. Gelair used to say: "My skin is only an accident." He was French, so were the schoolchildren, when they sang: "O Gaul, O Motherland, brave as of old! . . ." But he . . . he went on: "Don't you remember?" No, Elenga didn't remember. "You know, for us the locomotives are the problem. We have to keep them running. The soldiers. The equipment."

For a while, the bunkers were used by the fishermen, but only after they had been abandoned by the soldiers of the infantry battalion of Chad. "That I remember," said Elenga, "I saw them get on the train; I worked on the engine of their train." Later, after the departure of the soldiers, much later, a cannon was fired from one of the bunkers and started a real panic along the seaboard and in the town. In reality it wasn't a cannon shot, but a fisherman who had set fire inadvertently to a shell or a bunch of hand grenades. Fortunately, it was raining that day and he was alone on the beach. We thought: "That's it. Here comes the war that until now had only been the fantastic legend told by the cooks and the servants who kept adding their own horrifying details." We all went to examine the large crater caused by the explosion. We called it the hole of the "Veteran of Pointe-Noire."

It might have been a fisherman, but nobody knew to whom the remains belonged. One arm, one leg, and I don't remember what else were found in the lagoon nearby and everywhere around. People were still talking about it until quite recently. . . .

"Let's walk!" They got up. Waves inched forward to lick their feet. They didn't go very far. They sat down again on the beach. Muendo had not yet arrived. No flaw, no crack. Not even some harshness that might have made him unpleasant. It was impossible to see through him. Elenga thought: "He has put me in his pocket!" But he felt comfortable snuggling into it. A talisman is an object that doesn't reveal its power. Neither fish nor fowl. It is inside you and protects you against all the bad blows of the evil eye and of fate. Gives you more breathing space. Nevertheless, he felt somewhat shaken by what Luambu had just said: "Man is small inside his skin." The modesty of superior men makes them say strange things. . . . If he was talking about himself, he was perhaps trying to put himself at Elenga's level. Or it might be his overall judgment of mankind. These words, perhaps a flaw. No, there was nothing to cheer Elenga up. There was the flaw.

"A man like you . . . I mean you must have no flaw!"

"No flaw, why?"

Sure, he had more than one flaw; he had many. If you knew the reasons for my silences, you would understand.

"People must say how good you are from morning to evening, every day of the month, every month of the year and for centuries to come!"

"Why?"

"I don't know, but that's what I think. Am I embarrassing you?"

"No, why?"

"You see, I ask questions and you answer, well at least you say, No, why? but it doesn't bother me. I hope my questions don't bother you either." . . . (Changing the subject.) "What is Muendo doing? He should have been here by now!"

"Look, no, behind you. People can also approach you from the back."

Muendo, fatter than ever, was walking toward them, swinging in his stride, because of the loose sand of the upper beach. He held in his hands the sandals he had made from an old tire. Luambu pretended not to notice Elenga's surprise.

"He saw you come, he saw you without turning around."

"So what? Do you want me to claim he's a sorcerer?"

"But he is a sorcerer. I knew it, I knew it."

"Do you know that he has a better sense of humor than I?"

Luambu didn't say anything but simply extended his hand.

Muendo asked: "How is our dear writer? Show me your hand, not very calloused, hey? Pen, paper, are all very light. By the way, you who write, do you know that paper is made from wood? If only I had been told that paper is wood! . . ."

"Couldn't you stop him, you who work like a white man, it gives you the authority to stop a stinking savage."

"Stinking? You know a dog without fleas is rare, so what about your smell of grease. No comment!"

"Now you two, come on!"

"Ah, listen to the wise man. How wise you are!"

The three men burst out laughing and resumed their walk, three abreast and trying to keep in step, but they gave up because of the loose sand. Elenga was the first to quit. He entered the sea and splashed about in the waves. They were alone on that part of the beach, but further away were groups of people waiting for the return of the fishing boats. Taking advantage of Elenga's moving off, Muendo asked Luambu in confidence if he could help him with a secret matter. But since he was at the same time gesturing emphatically, writing in the air what he was saying under his breath, Elenga guessed what it was about.

"Couldn't you write those damned letters yourself? You know, they might not be able to read!"

"You better believe that nowadays most women have a little brother who can read."

"And you dare ask a priest to write sinful letters?"

"He must have diarrhea from the fat he has eaten. Besides, is he a sorcerer or a priest?"

"It's the same, hey, asshole! The proof is that just before your arrival, he said: 'Man is small in his skin.' A priest says things like that. So, first, he is a priest. Second, he sees you coming from behind without turning around. So, second, he's a sorcerer. Third, he says nothing, he is silent, he thinks: 'They are children, you and I, children!' So, third, he is wise. But you bastard, you can't leave women alone. . . ."

"I know people who start joking and end up quarreling, therefore, let's try to be serious. . . ."

Elenga, Muendo, and Luambu repeated together "therefore" and laughed heartily.

"Hey, look, there's the guy we saw last time, a 'prophet' according to Elenga."

The last time had been six months earlier, the day of their first meeting. The man was again up to his waist in the water.

"Shit, he's preaching again. You, wise man, do you think that he might have been a priest once and that his priesthood has gone bad?"

"How should I know?"

"Don't disappoint him, the poor boy, he thinks that you are a sorcerer!"

They ran breathlessly to the spot where the prophet was shouting: "The day will come when the wave won't stop at your feet, it will go beyond you, and the father will weep, the mother will weep, the brother will weep. . . ."

At some distance from the fishermen people were listening. A few in the crowd were moving their lips, as if they were silently repeating the words of the prophet, as Elenga had called him. His voice, at once anxious and violent, bore down: "The sister will weep, and who will comfort those overwhelmed by grief? One rotten apple in a barrel spoils all the rest, which one will be good enough to eat? I give you my word, take it, eat it, keep it in your heart."

"See how they listen," said Elenga.

"You, too, are listening, maybe you are afraid, do you want me to comfort you?"

Luambu seemed about to say something, but the other two carried on: "Now, let's be serious!"

"Okay, but this time let's stick to it," concluded Luambu.

Elenga insisted: "Don't you think he is mad?"

Luambu was staring at the prophet, as if he was trying to find out who he really was. The tone of his speech had changed. More relaxed. He was no longer addressing the crowd, on which he had turned his back to face the sun that was slowly sinking in its bloody death throes.

"Don't waste time, the angels are impatient! Come on, come on. Soon there won't be enough space for everybody! Hey, fellow, don't yawn. Paradise is not a catchall. Don't yawn. It's not the time for eternal regrets. . . . It's closing time! The latecomers will have to wait a whole eternity, so to speak, to see the doors open again for the innocent. The closing bell is going to ring. Don't push, don't push! You, you and you, but not you! He turned suddenly and pointing a finger at Luambu or at someone behind him: "Not you, the Messiah will only forgive the son of Man!"

"Don't you think that he was more fun the last time?" said Elenga to Luambu. Obviously Elenga was upset and even more so when Luambu said:

"It's not good to listen to a man who is talking to himself."

"Then he must be in great pain, to talk like that," retorted Elenga.

"Our friend is a wonder, his brain can take the hellish fire of his locomotives. Still his mind keeps cool and his heart hasn't hardened."

"In your case, your brain and your heart have been taken by your grandfather back to Senegal, and as for your cock, I see a good case of clap coming on."

"Come on, come on." In chorus: "Let's be serious!"

They joined those who were helping the fishermen pull their nets out of the water. The prophet remained alone to address the angels and the demons. The ebb and flow of the sea jostled him gently. People were swarming, scuffling, and shouting around the fishermen, and the noise was so great that Luambu couldn't hear the prophet any longer. Looking back he saw a naked child sitting on the sandbank, his head propped up in his hands, elbows glued to his knees. He was now the visionary's sole auditor.

"Are you still thinking of what he said?" asked Elenga.

"Stop bugging him, he isn't your grandfather, is he?" intervened Muendo.

"No, he doesn't bother me."

"You two, either you stop or you go on arguing somewhere else. . . ."

"Hey, Pop, we never get angry, even when life is tough."

Nodding in complicity, the three men burst out laughing. Their laugh infected people around them, who started laughing without knowing why.

The prophet had come out of the water and was approaching the fishermen, who looked at him suspiciously. He looked ridiculous with just a strip of cloth between his skinny thighs. The upper part of his body seemed stronger than the lower part, which showed weak calves and bony knees. In his head his protruding eyes were curiously restless. The three men, who in a way owed their meeting to him, examined him closely for the first time. The chief of the fishermen, probably to ward off another of the prophet's crazy impulses, threw him two fish.

"Take that and don't bother anybody."

The man ignored the fish, which fell at his feet. Elenga picked them up to hand them to him, because you throw food to a dog, but you hand food to a man. He didn't hear Luambu say: "Forget it!"

Elenga took the fish, one in each hand, and held them out to the man, who didn't take them but winced with pain. Frightened, Elenga stepped back. But the man, the prophet, instead of attacking him, fled crying and screaming, at the same time protecting his rear end with both hands against imaginary blows. The chief, his fishermen, the crowd, everybody on the beach burst out laughing. Muendo and Luambu controlled themselves out of consideration for Elenga who might have thought that they were laughing at his bold but generous gesture, which had been completely ignored by the madman. They approached him and sang out in chorus: "Let's try to be serious." They roared with laughter, seeming to mock the fishermen, the chief, and the crowd on the beach. They took the fish that the chief had given them and left. Elenga had abandoned on the beach the fish thrown to the madman; nobody touched them, and by the time night fell they were partly nibbled by crabs.

When they parted, each one going home separately, Luambu promised Muendo that he would have ready the next day the letter to his new love. Muendo wanted to give him a few guidelines for the text, but Elenga stopped him: "You don't tell a sorcerer how to lure a woman into infidelity."

"How do you know she is a married woman?"

"Well, well, we'll discuss that tomorrow."

They said good-bye till tomorrow. Elenga took Luambu's share of the fish, because Mazola always prepared Luambu's lunch and brought it to him at the Compagnie Générale du Bas-Congo. Muendo didn't share this secret, which wasn't really a secret. . . . He had fallen under suspicion, or was it for the young man a way to express his admiration? Sorcerer, priest, sage. . . . The finger of the prophet so forcefully pointed at him . . . The last time also, the prophet singled him out. He tried to remember the words that had been said, but none of those he recalled seemed to be the genuine words of the madman, which had made him shudder and which had touched a raw wound deep within him.

"Is it you?"

"Yes, it's me!"

Mazola passed Luambu, who was sitting outside enjoying the cool air; she pushed open the door and entered the house.

He was thinking of streams that were different, because they flowed differently. He was looking down on them, as if from the top of a high mountain. The image was always the same and could not be taken in with one glance. He sees a tangle of mangrove roots, vast stretches of papyrus and of dark, hostile forests thirsting for water, thick streams, wild streams, muddy streams. He had crossed them all, wading, swimming, in a canoe or a boat, walking over a trunk thrown across a stream.

"I can't look, but if I do, I can see that the two of them won't be able to cross at the same time. Their double weight is too much for the trunk, it will break."

The rain falls more heavily than ever, bending everything. Everything is wild. He begs: "Hurry up or we won't be able to cross." He goes first, six steps and he is on the other side. Lightning and thunder prevent him from hearing what she tells him.

Roaring, the stream rushes down. Three more steps, but how can she keep her balance with the terrible wind breaking branches that fall and hit her. A wall of water rises from the river, flooding the riverbed and the banks, sweeping and tearing everything with a shattering noise in which he clearly hears a scream, the scream of victorious death. He closes his eyes. He is paralyzed by the horror of what has happened in spite of him. He closes his eyes over the raw wound. It is as if he had willfully killed her, strangled her. He concentrates on gripping and choking the neck of a woman. He enjoys searching the totally bewildered eyes that fight with a grotesque despair, grasping the fading light, not recognizing the monster in the beloved face. Exulting, he inhales hot air that inflames his lungs. He chokes.

"What's the matter?" asks Mazola.

"Ah, it's you!"

Mazola examines him a moment before explaining why she had come.

"I brought your laundry."

"Thank you."

"You are not feeling well?"

"No, I'm all right."

Mazola isn't convinced. It's obvious that he had to control himself in order not to send her off.

"I can cook some food for you before I leave."

"No, don't bother. You know at night . . ."

Then he burst out: "There is no kitchen here, there is no woman here. I don't want any, Don't . . ."

He calms down.

"You are a good girl, Mazola, you are a nice young woman. Very nice. That's fine. But your uncle, your aunt, and your brother don't know where you are at this late hour. They may be wondering."

"I am not a nice girl. . . . Do you want to see?" And to prove what she has just said, she rushes into the house. Luambu follows her shouting: "Don't be so silly, please!"

"Now look, look all you want. I am a woman, touch me!"

She came closer, took Luambu's hand, and put it on her breast. She was naked. Luambu closed his eyes, freed his hand slowly, and went out. He crossed the courtyard, abandoning Mazola to the frenzy of her desire. He fled. She wanted to show her compassion. He didn't even see the woman in her. Sure, he knows she is a woman. She is rather pretty. She knows it from the glances of the other men, the scoundrels. But him . . . She can't find his eyes. She doesn't want to think of Massengo, even to compare the two men. Whenever she thinks of him, she is even more disgusted with the old jerk whom her uncle and aunt have dug up for her. From where, she wonders.

Her brother Elenga said one day to her: "Bring twice as much food in two separate portions!"

"Why two portions? Who is it for?" her aunt had asked.

"Maybe it's for a friend of Elenga's who doesn't have anybody to take care of him. . . . What do I know!"

"Always your brother . . ." her aunt was going to say, but she held her tongue. Luambu never came to Elenga's house. Once he went as far as the medical supervisor's pavilion. He had accompanied Elenga, who tried to convince him to come in, but he didn't. No. Malonga had seen Elenga in Luambu's company. Who is he? He was suspicious, because of his niece whom men enjoyed looking at, the scoundrels, who wouldn't hesitate to fake friendship with her asshole of a brother!

"I don't want a writer loafing around here!"

"He is a friend. He is fine."

"Why does it make you so proud to be friendly with, with . . . Why do you invite him here? Maybe you want an educated man for your sister. . . . But remember that it's your aunt's responsibility and mine, mine above all, to find a husband for your sister."

Astonished, Elenga had opened his mouth and had closed it with a smile.

"You are surprised and then you smile, watch out my friend!"

He was sputtering with excitement. Elenga had this surprising answer for his uncle: "You are thundering and spouting around here, but it's all for nothing, you want to start sowing seed when it's not yet the season!"

"Right, it's not yet the season, mind my words!"

How unfortunate, it was not yet the season and yet he was giving ideas to those who didn't have any! And when the brother and sister were by themselves, Elenga's words to his sister justified the suspicion of Malonga, the medical supervisor, their uncle, their paternal, not maternal, uncle: "If I could choose my brother-in-law, I'd choose him."

"You see, uncle has reason to be angry."

"Isn't it your uncle's fault, if I am thinking of him?" And he went on speaking enthusiastically of Luambu.

During the whole week when she brought lunch to her brother at the freight station, she saw Luambu every day at noon. She agreed with her brother, but a sense of modesty prevented her from speaking about it. Her feelings were bottled up and when they tried to break through, they tightened her throat and filled her with anxiety and pain. The pain would ease up when she saw him, but it would plague her again as soon as another man by his gaze assumed he had power over her.

Eyes filled with tears, she puts on her clothes. He has humiliated her. She let him humiliate her. No, he didn't want to. His hand was cold. What have I done? She had only tried, in her own way, to foil her uncle's and her aunt's plot and to make him the beneficiary of the situation. . . . She is not ashamed. More than ever she is determined to fight. She is in love with him. His flight is a sign of respect, of love. Wiping her tears, she looks around, checking that everything is in order. The Laris would kill him if he made me pregnant. She puts a bottle of water and an enameled mug on the table. If she can't give herself to him, at least she can give him water. She is calm; she feels that she is calm and that's good. She sprays insect killer around the room. The mosquitoes don't bother her, and she can concentrate on the thought of her body, the body that he can't but have seen.

She goes out. The night is stifling hot. Never mind, she feels lighthearted. There is not another man like him in Pointe-Noire, there are no real men here, only Massengo types.

At the police station located at the end of the Native Village, the militiamen let her pass without any question, since the commander recognizes the medical supervisor's niece. But one of the militiamen couldn't help commenting: "Your uncle shouldn't wait too long to find you a husband."

She shrugged her shoulders and entered the no-man's-land that spreads between the police station and the first houses of the plateau, the Tchinouka zone, which lay in total darkness. Mazola hurried through it, talking to herself at the same time, to fool the evil and malevolent spirits into believing that she was not alone. Luambu walked just a few feet behind her and accompanied her unawares all the way to the hospital.

When she entered the house, Mazola found her aunt Masoni busy scaling fish in the nook that was used as a kitchen. At first, the aunt pretended not to see her, but she didn't sulk very long. Finally she said: "Who is going to scale the fish that your brother brought home?"

Mazola started silently scaling the fish and didn't answer her aunt.

"Why don't you go see if the men want something. You haven't seen your uncle yet tonight, have you?"

The aunt obviously had something on her mind but didn't say anything. Mazola got up.

In the big room she found Massengo sitting next to her uncle and Elenga. They were drinking beer. "Can't we men be left alone?" Mazola doesn't answer, she rummages in the larder and leaves without taking anything. "A schoolteacher, like a priest, opens the minds of children, at least of the intelligent ones. . . ." The uncle is interrupted again by Mazola coming back in. "What's the matter?" Both Massengo and Elenga pat the uncle's hand to quiet him down. Mazola dares to show immodesty and wiggles her hips: "I don't want to deprive him . . . he . . ." "He what?" But he doesn't want to get angry in front of the suitor, so he remains silent for a moment.

"Massengo, my son," the uncle resumes. Elenga can't help smiling. The uncle is no older than the suitor whom he calls "My son. . . ."

The previous day, while the aunt was braiding Mazola's hair, she had praised Massengo unceasingly.

"When a schoolteacher speaks French, the white man says: 'This man is intelligent!' He wouldn't dare call him a baboon. He shook de Gaulle's hand. Do you know anybody who has shaken hands with a general? Moreover with de Gaulle himself! Massengo went to school in Gabon. In his high school, in Brazzaville, many students were not able to follow, black heads, thick heads, but not him."

Elenga had his own opinion of schoolteachers. To hit children on their heads with a ruler, that's their real job. They bark like dogs all the time, so that it's difficult to be attentive and listen when one should. The poor brat is constantly afraid of not doing right, and in the end he can't do right what he's supposed to do. The teacher then hits him again. How can you learn, when you're peeing in your pants out of anxiety? He was full of resentment when he spoke of his own experience, but he spoke also for the man he had chosen and wanted as a brother-in-law.

"Your uncle is now your father and I think, like him, that it might be time for you to get married."

"You are not lacking money or drinks. Elenga is a good provider!"

Her aunt's fingers stopped braiding: "What do you mean?"

"Never mind, I am sorry."

"No, your uncle must hear your words. . . ."

"But you know that when he's cross, he's angry at everybody for days. . . . You have two men in the house; don't I help you too? If I am married, I will have to bring food to my husband as well as to my brother, and if they don't work at the same place, how will I do it?"

She was talking to make her aunt forget her rudeness and her "ingratitude."

"Do you think it's right to get married before one's older brother? I hope you are not angry? . . ."

Massengo was the second suitor. The uncle always picked them from among schoolteachers. The uncle really wanted the happiness of his niece, because the first candidate, also a teacher and a member of their tribe, had been kindly received and rejected without Mazola's interference.

"I'm sorry, but I don't want you to marry my sister. First, I don't like people of your profession; second, being her brother, I must have a good relationship with her husband. I can't get on with you. You want to throw money on the table to get her. She doesn't agree, and I don't either. I am sorry, sir." Elenga got up.

"How do you know that she doesn't agree, and furthermore since when is it you who decide whom your sister should marry?"

To tell the truth, Malonga didn't know how to react to Elenga's outburst. He hadn't behaved properly. One should say: "We acknowledge your proposal. Each party must think it over. We shouldn't hurry." It's not proper to hit someone who is holding out his hand. To apologize for the mishap, the uncle said: "Unfortunately, orphans are often like that."

He tried to smooth things over. Massengo's throat was so tight he felt like choking. His neck was sinking into his body. He was not paying attention to Malonga's words. He stood up, hesitating a moment. He was in the stickiest situation. His lowered eyes were smoldering with a deadly anger brought on by the most bitter affront. Why was he hesitating? Did he still have some kind of hope? He wavered. He was thinking that to get angry with the brother of the woman you wish to marry is not the proper way to proceed. On the other hand, he couldn't simply lose face without showing his displeasure. What he really longed to do was to say to Elenga, that insolent fellow, that if he hadn't learned anything in school, not even good manners, it certainly wasn't his fault or that of the other teachers, since they never expected miraculous results from duds like him!

"Please sit down, my friend! And you sit down!" As he himself was still seated, he got up, and trying to please Massengo, almost begged: "Let's try. Let's think it over. We must talk. Yes, we must talk."

Stubbornness was in Elenga's blood. He was like his father and didn't listen, once his mind was made up. But realizing that he had gone too far, he eagerly joined in to appease Massengo, though he was secretly satisfied to have angered the teacher who, he knew, had expected Elenga, the mechanic, to show deference to him. Elenga now had a sly smile that his uncle pretended not to see, lest he explode. He had not yet made a firm promise to Massengo, they had not yet reached the step of a formal proposal. . . . One should examine whether a marriage proposal was eventually possible. They all had to agree. Still, as the head of the family, he had the last word.

Born sententious, he thought highly of those who give lessons. . . . Teachers give lessons. Her brother, when you consider what he had done for himself, should have appreciated his choice of a suitor. . . . Massengo sits down with affectation, regaining his sense of self-respect and importance, which are strengthened by Malonga's admiring eyes. He sits just long enough to strike a pose and say: "Nothing good comes from heated argument. We should examine this affair calmly. After all, the subject of our discussion is life, not war!"

The flourish of his response was impressive. The uncle then found the right word to soothe miraculously the inflicted pain: "That's right!"

Tuesday, June 20

Massengo repeated: "We must think it over!"

Indeed, Massengo would have been better off if he had gone to a marabout to get the means of making Mazola fall in love with him. As a matter of fact, when you think of his title and his position, it really didn't look good!

"We shall all think it over!"

Massengo stood up, held out his hand to the uncle, who took it eagerly and gratefully. Then he extended his hand to Elenga, who said: "That's right, we shall think it over."

He looked at Massengo's hand, then at his own: "My hand smells of grease. Do you mind?"

"It doesn't matter. Shake hands, do shake hands."

After Massengo's departure, the uncle exploded: "You are in the house of your uncle, the house of your father's brother! You insult the house where you sleep, where you eat, where your sister . . . What the hell is this unjustified pride? You who are just good enough to cover your face with soot, don't insult someone who is highly educated. . . . Shut up. I am speaking. A duck shits where it eats. It's not . . . If you got your manners from the ducks, don't show them off here. Tomorrow, you will go to his house, yes, to his house and you will offer your apologies. Then, he'll come back and your sister will behave like a well-brought-up girl."

"Don't get excited. . . ."

"Listen to that! Now, who do you think you are? Get out. . . . Go and present your excuses. Then come back and ask my forgiveness. In life, one has to think twice!"

He was looking around the empty room for something to throw at his head!

"You thickheaded asshole!"

In the kitchen, Masoni didn't dare interfere. Massengo was the son of her great-uncle, and she had put in her husband's head the possibility of this marriage. Having raised Mazola, almost from birth, she knew how patient and modest she was. As the saying goes: "Don't turn away from what you fear, but face it." Therefore, when men started to linger around their house, she thought that Massengo, well, that he might be a good match for her husband's niece. As the outbursts of her husband became louder and louder, she spoke and behaved in the gentlest manner toward Mazola, in order to appease her and to keep her from openly taking her brother's side. The rage might kill her good husband. And yet she had warned him not to take a drastic decision immediately: "Here he is, dear daughter, the man I have chosen for you; here is, my son, the brother-in-law who is right for you!"

While pounding spices in a mortar, Mazola pretended to be indifferent to her uncle's shouts. Nevertheless, she was deeply hurt by his words. . . . The husband she wanted, chosen by her brother, had fled. He flew into a rage when she offered to prepare his meal. He had been afraid of her. . . . But he had escorted her home, following her at a distance, hidden in the night. Never mind that the uncle in his rage would throw them out. . . . She would cook for her brother and his friend. Masoni complained: "He is going away, without saying good-bye," when she saw Massengo leaving. Poor man! She tried not to listen to her husband. Even in anger, one shouldn't shout things like that in the night. Mazola heard him but pretended to be absorbed in her work. Her pounding was steady and didn't punctuate her uncle's words to Elenga, and to her. Silently, she was urging her brother: "Don't answer, please, let him speak, you know your uncle's fits of temper. Sure, you were right to send away that pretentious fellow, so inflated with his knowledge. . . . But now get out. Do what he tells you: get out. Don't oppose him. You have done the best you could, now, get out." Tears welled up in her eyes.

"Are you crying?"

"No." It's because of the peppers she is crushing. Masoni doesn't believe it. She didn't like her husband's gusts of anger because he was basically an extremely good man. He himself says: "People are crazy to fly into rages!" He has a sense of authority and likes to exercise it. He has a big mouth, but in his heart he considers Elenga and Mazola his children. They are also her children. When they arrived from Brazzaville, Malonga had said to her: "Don't forget, they are your children now. No fuss!" Did she ever make any fuss? Heavens no! Why did the event take a tragic turn? Enough of that. She was getting up when she heard a loud crash. The door banged. . . .

Tuesday, June 20

Elenga came out and said to Mazola: "I am not sleeping here tonight. Tomorrow I'll pick up my things."

"No, no, don't do that. Go for a walk, then come back and apologize. You mustn't do that."

"Do as she says, go for a walk!"

7.
Victorine at the Market

Victorine had finally admitted that her husband, André Sola, was right to try to understand what had happened. He felt that he had a commitment. He had helped a simple guard be promoted to the position of clerk. Of course, he had been thanked for his intervention. . . . Thank the Lord! The Lord be praised. Lord, thy name be honored. Nevertheless, he who generally made friends fast, had not become chummy with the guy. The "guy" was one of her words whose implication was more of puzzlement than of contempt. Now, just think for a moment, if André had succumbed to the temptation, she could be a widow by now. Whatever you say, the Lord is great. Thank the Lord. . . . When I think of it, it would be interesting to know if Elenga and Muendo had both received, like him, a gift from the guy. It seems likely. So the chap started by giving an impressive present . . . you were filled with gratitude and played right into his hands, and then, snap! He . . . he . . . Sola shivered with horror! But he knew what had saved him. He had made a novena, when he had lost his stutter, after receiving Luambu's gift. He had kept the present in his missal, because it was an astoundingly beautifully written Credo, and the priest had blessed it when he had blessed his missal, everything in it, himself, and everything in him. You could understand it this way: he might have been doomed without the novena. He might have become the friend of the guy and that would have been the end of him. Sometimes the devil fakes God's way in doing a good deed (the Credo, the stutter) but then you must ask for the Lord's protection if you want to escape the demon. Yes, that was one way to look at it.

He thought it over: "Don't you think you exaggerate a bit?

Actually, I am at a loss!" The stutter had disappeared, had come back, and finally had gone for good. Victorine's imagination, the intensity of it surprised him. Suspicious imagination. From then on he was afraid of opening his mouth and of resuming his stammer until the end of his life. Tchilala, who was sitting at their table, expressed an idea that intensified the gloom: "We don't know whom we meet nowadays!"

Tchilala's leitmotiv was that "with all the people who came with the construction of the railroad, who followed the railroad, corruption entered our lives and we were contaminated." He was not the only one to say so. They showed their contempt for the newcomers who, they were afraid, would take over. Do we know where the guy came from? Tchilala was Victorine's cousin, and André Sola had also got a job for him at the C.G.B.C.

Wait a minute, I only had him promoted, I should find out who hired him in the first place as a guard. I have always faced my responsibilities in life. Why should the people we meet every day be worse than . . . He wasn't going to say than white men! What a strange story!

Tchilala's comment implied the threat of another, even greater danger. That's why terror was growing with the spread of all kinds of gossip and stories, like those of Victorine, who had reported what she had heard with her own ears and seen with her own eyes at the market. The same event had been witnessed by a lot of people, and they couldn't all be victims of delusion or of collective madness. I swear to God that . . . Oh, you don't have to swear. No, *aya*, let me swear, because what I have to say is so unbelievable that you would wonder if I am telling the truth, had I not taken an oath beforehand. Sola didn't dare open his mouth, and his anxiety was growing. If his wife was in such a frantic state, she must have something terrifying to tell.

"It happened at the market." Véronique, you know, Costodi Mengha's wife, and Sidonie Lilesu are two reliable witnesses and you can check with them. We had been shopping for some time, when we decided to look for fish. Over there, we were told. Indeed, there was a mob scurrying about in that

Victorine at the Market

part of the market. When you buy fish, you inspect it first, guess its weight, and only afterwards do you look at the seller, who is sometimes the fisherman himself and at other times a salesman. You look at him in order to bargain, so you have to know how he looks. Victorine glanced at her husband and wondered: "What's the matter with him? Usually he interrupts me, complaining that I waste time on trivial details!" But the details are most important. He still didn't say a word. Is something wrong? With a gesture he urged her to go on. He must be terribly upset to behave like that.

The market should be divided into different sections for different items. You would go to one place for tomatoes, red peppers, cassava, *saka-saka,* sweet potatoes, to another place for meat, and to still another for fish. Unfortunately, that's not the way it's done; you have to run in all directions to find what you need. The sellers have a bad habit, they always place themselves where there is already a big crowd, so that when somebody shouts, "Fish," everybody rushes in the same direction.

So what happened at the market? André is still silent. He knows why he doesn't dare open his mouth; he is afraid his voice may go to pieces and also expects the worst in this woman's story. Indeed, she'll never learn to tell a story without drawing it out. And today she is making a great effort, passing over particulars, like things seen on her way, the way some man looked at her, or some woman, and so on and so forth. . . . The usual minor problems of a family, the small favors that her good heart urged her to do and so on until you lose the thread of the story.

Where was I? Yes, Véronique and I put our hands at the same time on a pile of fish, of herring. You know that Véronique and I are like two sisters, so we were not going to fight over the same fish. We were still recovering from our surprise when panic broke out around us: "It's him, it's him!" "It's the man in the coma!" we heard. We tried to catch sight of the women who were screaming and of the man they were accusing. They were pointing at the fish seller, a tall man with an open face. At first the two young women were thought to be hysterical. Then the surprise and confusion of those who didn't know what was happening grew when the young women went into convulsions and passed them on to the other women who were trying to calm them down. "Don't buy the fish, don't touch them. These fish are not fish, they are worms, the worms of a corpse, of parts of a corpse." They lift their hands to their throats, as if struggling with someone invisible who is strangling them. They thrash about, strike out with hands and feet, roll over on the ground, scream, foam at the mouth, twist their bodies, roll their eyes. You should have seen the panic that overtook the whole market.

Véronique, Sidonie, and I were crossing ourselves continuously. *Aya*, we were not ashamed to flee. And who could have pointed his finger at us? We were not the only ones to flee and because we believe in God, people were hiding behind us to avoid rolling on the ground and being strangled. Half the market was upside down. Mostly women were under the spell and held their throats, choking, struggling, and screaming. All hell broke loose! Instead of going on crossing myself, I took out my rosary which I had had blessed at Easter and I advanced confidently. Véronique screamed: "Don't move!" But I was not going to let the demon have his way. By God, I am a Christian!

I went forward—yes, I was terrified of course, but faith is salvation. As the Lord is great—if I were in doubt, I would from now on never again go out—a miracle, just as in the middle of the day bats fly off in a cloud, just as suddenly the women who had fallen under a spell, who were possessed by a demon, regained consciousness as if nothing had happened. It was a miracle, I don't know a better word, because in the meantime the fish and the seller had disappeared, completely vanished. We had seen the fish, buckets and buckets of it, then nothing. The women had recognized in the salesman the man in the coma who had tried to strangle them when they unmasked him. Fortunately there were too many of them, he couldn't murder them all; also we kept crossing ourselves and I held my rosary while I was saying one prayer after the other, Hail Mary, Paternoster. That was our salvation and the greatness of God. The devil couldn't multiply himself in order to strangle us all, so he chose to disappear without leaving any trace. No trace of the fish seller or the fish, absolutely nothing.

"Didn't I say that we really don't know whom we meet anymore? What do you think, *aya* André? I just hope we won't be afraid to live."

At last André spoke with a calculated slowness that sent shivers through his listeners, but mainly through himself. When he realized that his voice had not gone to pieces, he regained confidence and smiled. But another danger was slowly emerging, taking possession of his feet, his belly, his shoulders, raising his hair, confusing his mind, tickling his spine, narrowing his eyes, an overwhelming and terrifying danger, the coming of the bad angel, the black angel. A revolting smell comes from the black swamps, from the neighboring Tchinouka swamps, from the Tchisoindji swamps, and from many others which had been drained to build Tchikungula, also known as Pointe-Noire, to be used as the dumping ground for the disgusting rubbish from beyond the Mayombe that was carried by the ebb and flow of the current. Are you shaking? Didn't you know that you were shaking? Perhaps.

Victorine had nothing to add, but she couldn't help giving her conclusion. "I wonder if we can still go to the market without fearing . . . What if the rosary, the sign of the cross weren't effective any longer?"

"I have seen your husband tremble. Have you seen it, yes or no?" He had the tone of a judge.

Victorine didn't want to contradict Tchilala, so she admitted that her husband had trembled, but that it shouldn't be taken as an omen. But what could she say, omen or not?

"Why, why? It started in our office." André looked at Tchilala: "It started in our office, why? He was working for us. What do we know? When your wife puts her hand on a pile of herring that are not herring, fortunately, yes, fortunately, they unmasked him. Your wife is there, the wives of Lilesu and Costodi Mengha also, does it happen often that all our wives find themselves together at the market? Don't you understand that it's because of us. . . . A man gives you a piece of paper that turns out to be magic and chases the spirit that

The Madman and the Medusa

makes you stutter. It was that spirit in you that prevented you from becoming a priest. Doesn't all that open your eyes? All right, our eyes weren't open any wider than yours. I don't explain it very well, what I want to say . . ."

"Now, keep it to yourself. What happens and may happen again isn't something to make speeches about. One shouldn't confuse 'chance' with God's work, if this man is really a man. . . . Well, what I am saying is inspired by what you have said: 'I hope we won't be afraid to live!' Didn't your wife wonder if she can still go to the market? . . . If you give up going to the market, give up eating, give up living, death won't help you live: the fish is not fish, but the void. That's where we are . . . already? That's why you trembled without knowing it yourself, why I saw you tremble, why your wife saw you tremble. We are all going to tremble."

He escaped death. Where is the key to all that? Is it a comedy or a fable?

8.
Wednesday, June 21

It's gone. I have lost all feeling. My heart feels nothing any longer. Julienne, Mazola. Mazola. Julienne. "He has fled. . . ."

Give, give. If you still have a lot after having given, it's because you haven't given anything. You have nothing essential to give. You think that you have given all you have and yet you have given nothing. Did you have feeling in your heart? What is the answer? Julienne. Mazola.

Julienne came back to him. All he could see of her was her hair, her luxuriant hair braided in coils above her oval face. The black lumps shone with the rancid black oil of the burnt buds of the palmetto, whose strong scent was becoming to her. Then he remembered the light and firm steps of her long legs. He could only recall that her legs were long, since her skirt always came down to her ankles . . . ah, her modesty! Because of her modesty, because of the night, he was imagining her more than remembering her. Touching himself at night, he wanted to dissolve into the night, enter its depth, and, jerking, shaking, achieve ultimate ecstasy. Falling into an infinite abyss, without ever touching bottom, he was floating: his body over her body, the body he had possessed and could not define any longer. His memory had retained Julienne's figure but not her size. To whom could he speak of Julienne? His nightmare was to wonder if he wasn't himself the monster he was fleeing, the monster that was chasing him.

Mazola, in offering her nude body, obscured the scene. Pleasure dissolves everything. Desire creates new possibilities. He no longer wanted to flee. Was it possible that he was no more pursued? He wanted to stay. Would the obsession end? He wanted to stay on and to live, to found a family. Mazola.

Julienne. Would the lost feeling come back to his heart? Perhaps it was irretrievable now and forever.

"My blotter! Who took it? I don't like people to take my things!" one of the clerks complained.

"Sh-sh-sh-sh!" ordered the head clerk.

The blotter absorbs ink. The earth absorbs bodies, so does water. How terrifying the whirlpool that sucked Julienne in. Mazola, he resisted her seduction attempt, but he followed her in the darkness to insure her safe return home. Innocence should beware of the night.

The noonday whistle of the C.F.C.O. sounds. Monsieur Martin enters the clerks' office. All activity stops. Thus it happens every day, a strange ritual. Everything on schedule. Monsieur Martin has to go through the clerks' office to enter or leave his own office. He stops, turns toward Luambu, seems to waver, his face twitching as if he can't remember what he had on the tip of his tongue.

"Ah, yes, Luambu, let me not forget, please come to my office this afternoon."

"Yes, sir."

He goes out. Luambu's colleagues watch him. They all seem surprised to see him there and especially surprised that Monsieur Martin wants to see him. The activity resumes. Books are closed, drawers opened. André Sola, the head clerk, wipes his pen in his hair. Donatien Kouba dries his pens with a bit of cloth that he stows away with great affectation. Lilesu Dieudonné checks the tips of his pencils. André Sola stands by the door and lets the clerks out, one by one. His lips move slightly. Is he counting? Luambu in turn goes out and forgets his coworkers, who also forget him.

On the other side of the street, leaning against the gate of the C.F.C.O., in the shade of an almond tree, Mazola waits. She is relaxed. Day drives out night, drives out evening, evening has driven out day. Julienne is an obsession. It is the name of a body he can only see through another body close to his hand, which remains cold even when he touches a glowing breast. He lets two rickshaws struggle past through a throng of bicycles. Then he crosses the street toward Mazola. He knows that in spite of her lowered eyes, she watches him approaching her. Her body doesn't reveal her longing. Is he going towards his lunch box or towards a woman? "You are a very nice young woman!" She says: "Elenga isn't here!" With her chin she points to the railroad station and the C.F.C.O. depot. Indeed, the usual activity is missing. No locomotive maneuvering, no bustling around the boxcars. But that was indeed the noonday whistle of the C.F.C.O. "What's happening, are you worried, why?"

He can speak to her because of her anxiety, which is unrelated to what happened the previous night. "They stopped work. The train engineers have all gathered at Kilometer 4. The office employees have gone out. . . . I'm not sure. Soldiers have been seen. This is war, and nobody is allowed to stop work." Is she aware of what she is saying? She repeats what she has heard, that this could turn bad because this is war.

Yesterday Elenga hadn't mentioned that there were problems. "Lately the trains have been jumping the track all the time. Maybe that's why they have stopped work." What a coward! How would he have handled the situation if there hadn't been this welcome topic of conversation, the work stoppage? Otherwise, what would he have talked about? Could he say that he would explain later, that he would speak of Julienne, of the child, of the tragedy in which she and her child. . . . It's important that she know. No. Or should he simply say: "Maybe tonight you could come and cook my supper." Why maybe? Or else under the pretext of inquiring about Elenga—that is, if he doesn't see Elenga before, because in that case no pretext would exist—but let's imagine the worst, that they don't see each other at night as usual, well then he would go meet her family. Everybody knows the medical supervisor, a man of authority. But he doesn't say anything.

She strolls with him under the almond trees, along fences covered with bougainvillea and hibiscus. The smell of cooking, of roasted meat and fried fish, pervades the air. The sea is not far, you can smell it. The railroad is not far either. You can also smell the steel of the rails and the ashes of the burned coal. The smell of sweat is in the air. The sweat of Ju . . .

Mazola, the sweat of swarthy people. They meet very few people. It's very hot, the light is blinding, and it's not easy to walk with half-closed eyes. Trucks roar by, racing their engines, the frames shaking loose on their wobbly cabs. People cluster in the backs of the trucks rolling toward the harbor. Bicycles and rickshaws move in the opposite direction toward the Native Village, but only to the elegant section of the village, where the natives live in concrete houses with running water and electricity, under red-tiled roofs.

It occurs to him that Elenga is the same age as the town of Pointe-Noire. He wonders if Elenga and Pointe-Noire have the same life, the same story. Where did he tell me he was born? . . . Kinkala? Boko? The same age. Elenga is about two years older. They have the trains in common, they share the same deep commitment to them. Where the train can't take you, the harbor will. He himself knows only the riverboats that are quite different from ocean liners. He closes his eyes remembering the different places on the river where he went by boat. The Congo-Ocean line is a kind of river, but a river that sometimes jumps its track: like the Mayombe which fights abuse, refuses the right of passage and takes its tribute of flesh and blood. The sacrifices are its due, its compensation for the damage and violation suffered through repeated explosions of dynamite. Everything jumps the track—rivers of water and rivers of earth, of forest and mountain, the ocean . . . Abysses open up and engulf human lives. Expiation for man's sin.

"What are you thinking about?" She raises her head to meet his gaze. "Nothing!" "I am going home." The women in his life are all the same. Not one of them is willing to give him a serious dressing down: "Look at me, if you go on like that, I'll leave you. You can go on racking your brains by yourself or you can speak." He is not going to start to speak of himself to himself. "I don't want anything, do the best you can," sighed Julienne. He did the best he could, and now Mazola is holding out his lunch box, without saying: "Do the best you can," though her behavior implies it. No. "Have you eaten?" The question surprises Mazola. She hesitates. "Well then, eat with me." When Elenga is with me, we go to the seaside to eat, otherwise I go there by myself, every day at noon. Afterwards I go back to work. . . . Even when the weather is hot, it's very cool by the sea. There is a breeze. What is the matter with him? Doesn't he have anything else to tell her? Someone is gesturing to him in an insistent way, someone obviously wants to be seen by Luambu in order to build, if necessary, an unimpeachable alibi. What's the name of the fellow? Jean-Pierre Mpita, the guard who succeeded me in my former job. Why is he insisting in this way? "I am going to Kilometer 4, so maybe . . ."

A whistle blows three times. They both listen. It's a train. They run to the grade crossing to watch it pass. Elenga, goggles on his forehead, drives the engine. He shouts to them, but not loudly enough, and his voice is drowned out by the terrible noise of the engine. A group of kids arrives from nowhere, cheering and jostling them. . . . Luambu points with his finger to the beach, the place of their meeting. But Elenga, with a negative gesture, cancels the meeting. He pats the locomotive's side: work has resumed and won't let go of him. Not until five o'clock, as on every other day.

A space opens up around them, and they feel for a moment the weight of the silence dampened by the sea spray and the sweat of their foreheads. The silence seals Mazola's lips in spite of her determined look that surprises Luambu and frightens him to the point of confusion. Suddenly he realizes that if he is put out of countenance, he'll be lost. So he grabs on to the first words that occur to him. "I am hungry, what about you?" The words are so weak that he compensates with exuberant and needless gestures, scratching on the ground two lines parallel to the railroad, then erasing them, while he waits for her answer. She doesn't answer. That's ridiculous, it's really stupid! He feels trapped in his own life. "I'll leave you and you can rack your brains by yourself . . . alone . . . or you can speak. . . ." All alone.

When you pee on sand, on a pile of sand, you don't make a pool. When you speak into the wind, you don't fill the wind with noise. When you take salt from the sea, you don't desalt it. What are you doing? You have done nothing. But once more you are lamenting in the midst of your lamentation. For all eternity the sea will be the sea, wave after wave, wild or calm. Come on, don't give in, if you start, you'll always give in. "Look, am I not a nice girl?" He fled, because in her is the other one whose shadow is more alive than her body. Julienne! . . . The sexual urge that grows in him calls for the absent woman who throws ashes on his desire. He remembers the wrath of the water that spared him because he was glued to the bark of a tree assailed and tossed by the wind. Coward! He sees the water engulf Julienne and her child, throwing her up before swallowing her completely. Coward! What kind of refuge is his heart? Ever since he has this gnawing doubt. Does he have feeling left in his heart or not?

The train that went by comes back. Elenga is amazed to see them both standing on the same spot, they don't seem to have taken a step since he last saw them. What's happening? The train is returning to Kilometer 4. He asks Luambu with a gesture if he is going to eat, or if he has already eaten. Luambu realizes that he hasn't eaten yet and that it will soon be time to go back to the office. "Let's go!" His mouth spells out the words for Elenga to see and hear. The train takes him away. The grade-crossing gates are raised with a steady ringing. They cross the track and stumble along on the white, warm sand. Alone, the sea rages against itself. It is the rage of a stutterer who spits, explodes, sputters, slobbers, foams, rattles and . . . thunders. The sand that was lolling along the sea is devastated, suffocated, by the strong smell of iodine sprayed by the waves. Mazola has difficulty breathing, as she did in her sleep the previous night because of Uncle Malonga's anger at Elenga's rudeness to the visitor.

If he speaks of Julienne now, he will kill her a second time and this time for good. He will be guilty without extenuating circumstances. With premeditation. If she is frightened and disappointed, it's only just, for Christ's sake! Then after the remorse, hope will grow. Mazola breathes like a fish thrown out of water whose gills beat convulsively. When the waves return, they will gain about a foot and a half. There is so much water in the air that you can't see the approaching wave. He guesses from the roar that it will be a big wave that could pull Mazola away and she wouldn't suffocate anymore. He is on the point of asking her: "Do you swim?" On this wild shore, to leap into the water is to leap to your death! Every year an oyster gatherer pays with his life for the recklessness of others as well as his own. He shakes himself as if he had just come out of the water, as if his mind were coming to the surface. He says finally what he should have said earlier under the almond tree: "Thank you for coming, after what happened last night . . . Elenga!" She stood up. "I know what he wants, what he wishes. But what about you? Of course . . ." "We'll discuss it tomorrow. First, I must earn the money for your dowry, don't you think?" Her mouth looks hurt, her smile is strained, her eyes glisten: "I am afraid for Elenga. I had a bad dream last night. I didn't tell it to my aunt, who went to the market without me. My uncle was very angry last night. Elenga told Massengo that he didn't want him as a brother-in-law and that he should look elsewhere for a wife. Elenga didn't behave properly. Uncle screamed the whole evening. Afterwards, I had a bad dream. The whole morning trucks full of soldiers went by. They are going to Kilometer 4, people said. The engineers and all the other workers of the C.F.C.O. refuse to work. The soldiers will kill them. Nobody is allowed to go and see. I was frightened, but I managed anyway to prepare the food. I came hoping that Elenga might not be at Kilometer 4.

It is clear that now she can breathe again, after having told her premonition. Where can you walk when there are threatening signs everywhere? Where can you look without losing your eyesight, blinded by seeing more than is allowed. Moreover how unnecessary this anxiety is! A woman, or a child? He pulls himself together.

The all clear has sounded. Mazola is just a child. And he was going to fall into a trap laid by the brother and the sister. . . . It's really funny! She watched him smile, laugh, laugh more and more heartily until he was convulsed with laughter. She couldn't resist and started laughing herself, performing a few childish pirouettes. She even provides a good reason for their unexpected laughter. But she can't stop laughing, so that he doesn't understand a word of what she is saying. The sea, as if to join in, sends a huge wave; thundering, sprinkling, exploding, it drowns their feet and chases them with the threat of another less gentle one. He feels as childish as she does, invaded by a pleasant coolness. His body is light, he is in a state of levitation, none of his limbs hurt anymore. In his chest his heart is no thicker than a dot of light. He is in the trees. More agile than a lizard, he can descend the steepest slopes head first. There is no abyss for him; when he reaches the bottom, he starts climbing again, holding in his hands a burning coal on a cushion of moss. It's the live coal kept burning during the past migration and exodus of his tribe.

The whistle blows, signaling the return to work. He shudders and stumbles on a rock in the railroad bed as he passes the gradecrossing. The pain is so sharp that he feels it like a stab in his heart. He hears her say: "Here is the husband that my father's son has chosen for me." He shuts his eyes. She watches him go away. At last she leaves also, crossing the immense square in front of the train station. The square is too big for the few people who cross it, too big even for the crowd that arrives with the train every Thursday. Tomorrow he will go to the station for the arrival of the train. It's doubtful that there will be enough people arriving to fill the square. The big crowds come for the parades of July 14, of Joan of Arc's Day, of November 11, for the arrival of the Governor General, of General de Gaulle. They come for the military parades. . . .

André Sola and the other clerks are already sitting at their desks. He meets Jean-Pierre Mpita at the door. The guard greets him with a knowing smile, to which Luambu doesn't pay any attention. They are all conscious of their work, keeping silent, proud of their concentration and diligence. They ignore him. He has never showed any interest in them either. It even surprises him. Who are they? But he thinks no more about it and remembers that Monsieur Martin had "invited" him to come to his office that afternoon. He knocks on the door, waits for the order to come in. Obviously, Monsieur Martin was expecting him. In spite of the many papers spread over his desk, he doesn't seem to have been disturbed in his

Wednesday, June 21

work. Luambu stands and waits. His great calm protects him from suspicion of any kind. He is calm, which means he is ready for anything, ready to submit to anything. Monsieur Martin takes the offensive: "Luambu, is that your real name?" "I don't understand, sir." "Sit down." Luambu knows too well what is allowed and what isn't. So he pretends he hasn't heard and remains standing. Martin rummages through the papers on his desk, looking for something he can't find. Either it's a game or a trap. He has found it or he hasn't found it? "You know, I have never seen account books so well kept." He hasn't found it or he is still looking. "Thank you, sir." "I would like to entrust you with a special task. . . . Do you have a family? Could you come sometimes in the evening to my house, for instance, next week . . . let's see, today is Wednesday, isn't it?"

He could have said all that in front of the others. "Where did you learn to write like that?" "In Gabon, at the Seminary of . . ." "In Gabon!" "Yes, sir." "Well, fine. So okay for next week." I can't believe it, there we are again. "Go back to your work now."

At five o'clock the weather was still stormy. The whirling wind blew up swirls of dust, then dropped down, exhausted. It was strange that Elenga was now waiting for Luambu. At the same place where Mazola had waited for him at noon, he was leaning against the same almond tree. Elenga crosses the street and joins Luambu. Mpita watches them walk toward the Chargeurs Réunis and assumes that they will take the seaside path.

"You're not very cheerful."

"No, I'm a bit tired."

"Do you think it's going to rain tonight?"

"The last whim of the rainy season!"

"How did it go? . . ."

"No, I don't think it will rain tonight. . . ."

"This weather is rather upsetting."

The conversation lags. They both have a lot to tell each

other. The talk about the bad weather and the rain proves that they are anxious, or rather, embarrassed. They are embarrassed out of modesty, because they have to speak about themselves and one doesn't enjoy speaking about oneself. It can be relaxing for a while to speak of others, of their shortcomings, especially at a social gathering, but when you are only two the talk becomes slanderous. You don't make friends by burdening others with your problems, by putting a weight on their shoulders, on their hearts. Muendo, Elenga, and he, are they bound up with one another, bound up with what and for what? If they were really bound up like that, they would not open up to one other and burden one other with the essential pain of being . . . and with what else?

For the second time that day, Luambu burst out laughing for no apparent reason. His laugh was catching, and Elenga responded just as Mazola had, by relapsing into childhood. An adult learns to control the expression on his face, otherwise he could be accused of vain prodigality or of excessive pusillanimity. An adult with a child's face is idiotic or stupid.

They were both laughing, pointing at each other, either because the way they laughed was screamingly funny or because the laughter unveiled in their faces the pure beauty of their souls and you wonder how they could have kept it hidden for so long. The only dance steps that they permitted themselves came from the contortions that their laughter provided. Mazola had danced like a child, stamping lightly and throwing her bewildered head backwards in a sensual display of throat and breast. If she had been there, she would have swept them up in a round.

They looked like two boxers feinting with their heads and protecting the solar plexus with crossed arms. They were holding their sides, choking, convulsed with laughter. The passersby, nonplussed or even scandalized at first, ended up by smiling and hurrying away to avoid being infected with an idiocy that, according to some, was quite common these days. Luambu collapsed on the sand, and while he tried to catch his breath, rubbing his stomach, laughter went on shaking him spasmodically. Elenga recovered sooner and said: "What in the hell made us laugh like that, just like kids?" But he couldn't quite control his face and become serious again. He added: "You know it's good to laugh like that, your eyes can cry as much as they want." "You said: 'Your eyes can cry as much as they want.'" Repeating these words calms Luambu's stomach cramps caused by laughing so much without quite knowing why. One laughs to hide a wish to cry. One laughs out of anger, out of vexation, to relax one's nerves, to release one's anxiety! To reach a level of serenity in one's own heart, when that heart rebels, turns hostile, and shuts off on you. "Yes, that's what I said!" If he knew, good Elenga would not take on this suspicious look. So we have in our eyes the water we need to wash them out. "What are you thinking of?" "The words that you just said are true, indeed, they are so true. Well, how do you feel now? I know your answer, which is also true. You feel good, I feel good. I could even tell you something I didn't have the courage to face. With dirty eyes I couldn't, with clean eyes now I can. Good, so tell me please what has happened at Kilometer 4."

Naturally having laughed so heartily allows him to see the events of the day in a different light, to find their gravity somehow relative. A minor gravity that everyone, strikers as well as management, who had turned the workshops of the C.F.C.O. into a fortress, had vastly overrated. There were more soldiers than strikers. On the spot it looked like a joke. One that wasn't worth telling. He preferred to inquire if Mazola had prepared a good lunch.

Luambu was flabbergasted. His embarrassment was so great that he couldn't easily hide it. Fortunately, Muendo happened to arrive at that moment. "Hello, lazybones, how come bayonets are now necessary to make you work? Good evening, 'Father'! I hope I didn't keep you waiting, because at our place it's the work that doesn't wait. We start a job, we finish it! Is it nice to take an hour break?" (He was apparently imitating the voice of his boss.) "I'll teach you to loaf, you filthy monkeys! Just four gaboon logs in one whole afternoon, what do you say about that?" "Have you finished?" Elenga and Luambu asked at the same time. "Here you are, the engineer

The Madman and the Medusa

and the priest teamed up against the worker, yes, gentlemen, a good man who kills himself cutting lumber to feed his family. Don't laugh. Why the hell are you laughing so much?" "We don't laugh. We are just as serious as you guys who cut wood!" "Father, I respect you, but this guy. . . ." said Muendo, repressing his laughter. Joviality with him was second nature.

"Now, now, let's be serious!"

"At our place the office workers also went on strike out of solidarity. Some of them complain that they are not paid enough for the work they do, which has doubled, tripled, quadrupled. . . ." Elenga was reporting the facts like a witness who keeps aloof from the event. "And why didn't you refuse to stop working?" "Muendo, please, let him talk." "I can also tell. . . ." What he could not tell, because he didn't know, was that the three of them, who had met by the seaside, on the same beach, a little farther off, were all working on the same production line, or sort of: Elenga worked the engines of the train that brought from the Mayombe the logs of gaboon, mahogany, limba, etc., which Muendo cut into planks that were then exported by Luambu, or more precisely by the Compagnie Générale du Bas-Congo. Through the events at the C.F.C.O., he became aware of their bond, of their double bond, their meeting in work, in which Muendo, in spite of an increasing work load, made barely enough to feed his family, though he received quite a lot of sawdust as a bonus, the sawdust that dirtied his hair (even after a good shampoo it looked full of lice), the sawdust that he sold to housewives. A good chap, Muendo!

"You were saying that you could also tell . . . You could tell that you stopped working for an hour, couldn't you?" The tone of his voice was mocking, though Luambu detected deep within it another meaning, which could have been just an impression, of course. Luambu got up: "Let's go! He can tell us about it while we walk!"

The usual crowd wasn't on the beach. You couldn't say that the sun was setting, as it hadn't appeared during the whole day. The beach was almost deserted.

The sea is as calm as a lake. On a day like today the sea

doesn't withdraw more than a few steps at low tide, leaving grooves and here and there small puddles that Elenga examines carefully. He goes from one to another like a dog digging up the shell of a crab, a snail. . . . "Everybody is on edge right now. Not because there is less work, but because there are a lot of accidents."

"What is he talking about? Is he confessing by any chance? Are you confessing?"

Luambu knows that if he keeps silent, he won't be able to control the feeling of uneasiness, the growing anxiety that accelerates his breathing and wrinkles his forehead. Both his friends seem to suffer from the same discomfort that plagues him secretly. All three would like to say what they cannot express, make confidences they don't dare make. They could drown themselves in a flood of words making fun of their uneasiness, their anxiety. . . . No. The words don't come. They sit on the sand which is warm, even though there has been no sun. They are together, a few feet from one other. They had met by chance and remained close, first by sheer habit, then by some strange need.

At the beginning of the week, Elenga had had a surprising, an amazing encounter. Among the women who sold food to the C.F.C.O. workers, fritters known as *mikatis,* grilled almonds, fried fish, and the like, he noticed a young woman whose features seemed familiar to him. He had searched his memory, trying to remember where and when he had seen her. He had passed her two or three times, and when she looked up at him, a name sprang to his lips: Solola, Solola, also known as Marie! The name belongs to a little girl he knew in his childhood, in a faraway village of the Kinkala district. He saw her for the last time in the Lower Congo, about five or six years ago, or it may even have been the year he left Brazzaville. He had ruined any chance of a romance with her when he had persisted in calling her Solola. . . . The joy of seeing each other again had not lasted, and Solola had proved once more that her nature was definitely frivolous. She gave pleasure mixed with desire to those who looked at her, thus confirming her vanity and great coquetry.

"Well, are you going to buy something or not?"

The shrill voice of the past had softened somewhat and clashed with the sly beauty of her face. He said: "Hi, Marie, don't you remember me?" He smiled and bent toward her to say that, beside her parents, he was the only person in the world who knew her under the name of . . . "Ho, ho, ho! Elenga! Elenga! It's you! You are an engineer and work here? And where do you eat? Aren't you going to buy something for your lunch?"

"Generally I eat at noon with a friend over there, at the freight station. It's far. But you see, I live at Kilometer 4, which is nearby."

She was selling fried fish and cassava. Solola, a vender! His smile vanished in the deep emotion he felt when Solola recognized him immediately and in the friendliest way. Being a saleswoman made her more friendly, whereas everything had seemed to destine her for the trade of prostitute. She had been so beautiful, so seductive. She was still beautiful. . . .

Elenga didn't know how to mention to his friends, especially to Luambu, this meeting with Solola, probably because he didn't know how the situation was going to develop. The way he told the story could reveal inner feelings that he didn't have, or about which he wasn't sure himself. But the thought of Solola and her smile made his mind wander at times. Which accounted for his seeming indifference to the events of the day. His hope and his interest lay elsewhere, interfering with one another and upsetting him. A song rising within him was his undoing, causing him to lose his sense of composure.

Muendo also has a worry that he can't define. He keeps repeating: "I could also tell you something," and then he doesn't tell anything. Luambu is listening, but he knows that if Luambu is like him he won't listen carefully to what he could tell him.

There is a kind of unspoken pact between them. They would never be so shameless as to pour out to each other what was troubling their hearts, heads, and bodies. They would not even speak of the slightest injury, not even for the satisfaction of pretending it didn't hurt, that it had been rather silly to mention it.

Wednesday, June 21

Souls!

Lost souls!

Souls in reserve or life in its initial stage without any past history to contend with. Muendo is the only one who has his own family. He looks at Luambu, but avoids his eyes. You know that from birth: "You don't look into the eyes of someone any more than you look into his nose." Can you look into his body? You would have to open it, in other words, to kill it. Who is going to kill him? Death will creep into his body and devastate everything. Maybe *it* is already entering his body. He may suffer from wounds he doesn't feel yet, of which he is not aware! Then he says to himself: "Hey, Muendo, how can you have such ideas?" This is not his usual mood, so he feels compelled to get out of it. "I don't feel good today." Elenga joins in: "Yeah, I don't feel good today! If we changed the day, perhaps we would feel more cheerful?"

Luambu remains silent. Muendo tries to break his silence: "Did you hear what he just said? That we should change the day! You must learn, young fellow, that days change by themselves and that you have to accept each day as it comes. The priest will confirm that."

Muendo tried to start a conversation, teasing Elenga, provoking Luambu, who finally said: "Well, if we have nothing to say. . . ." The routine of the day had left a void; the beach was almost deserted, without fishermen, without the gangs of kids, without the madman. The slack surf didn't provide any excitement and didn't engender in their minds the calm and peace so necessary after work. Daily routine induces gestures one is unwilling to execute, keeps your arms glued to your body, throws loose words into your mind so that you don't know which ones to use and when, for they don't come spontaneously! Routine has broken down. As far as Elenga was concerned, that was what brought on his arrogance and the lack of respect for his uncle Malonga, who had replaced his dead father. What a shit that teacher is! The meal that Solola had offered him was also on his mind. She had not taken it out of her stall, but had prepared it especially for him. "I thought, maybe you'd come at noon." She had been very considerate.

In the future, Mazola will only bring food for Luambu. She will marry him, and he'll marry Solola, Marie. Was she already married? He hadn't dared ask. Routine has broken down. What else was going to break down? His life, no doubt. Would he dare convince himself of it? If Solola . . . If with the teacher . . . he shouldn't have . . . To hell with the teacher! Tomorrow he'll find out if Solola is married. He will ask: "Where does your husband work?" Then he'll know: "He is an engineer, don't you see yourself?" Heavens, yes, he saw himself already the engineer of the Brazzaville–Pointe-Noire Express. Tomorrow . . . But in the meantime tonight he will have to face the uncle who usually remains angry for a long time and whose anger keeps coming like hiccups.

"Shall we go?"

Luambu notices the speed with which Elenga and Muendo both responded to his suggestion. Obviously things were not right today, but not to the point of wanting to change the day. He still had to live the best day of his life! The best or the most beautiful? One should be able to tell oneself: "Look, I'll make this day the most beautiful day of my life." He had done it already, so why think any more about it? Let the day take its course. Twice today he had nearly choked laughing, first with the sister, then with the brother. That was his way of breaking down daily routine. Mazola doesn't realize that she demands that he bury his past, uproot himself and grow new roots, when he already feels that his arms are covered with moss. When already at night he yawns in vain, sleep is failing him, and the endless night weighs on a body that can't make any movement whatever and a flank that is flabby! "Why ask what we are doing together? Doing nothing is not worse than doing silly things together! We haven't yet discovered sin!"

"Really, Muendo, you said it!"

"And why do you say that?"

"Just look at our faces!"

"How do you want me to look at my face, do you have a mirror?"

"Hey, priest, don't you think he should be serious for a change?"

"Well then, let's try . . ."

But Luambu and Muendo are not in the mood. Elenga doesn't finish the sentence that had always been the key to their good spirits and even adds with a gesture of annoyance: "All right, then, keep your funereal looks."

"We are not the only ones. . . ." Luambu doesn't finish his sentence either. What he was going to say frightened him. Muendo did not live alone. He was married, had two, maybe three, kids. His house and his brother's shared the same courtyard. His brother also had children, but by two wives, whose constant fights enlivened the household. Other relatives, among them their mother and a younger brother, lived with one family or the other. At Elenga's, the medical supervisor, who was childless, had raised the two orphaned children of his older brother, keeping them on a short leash and how! He had already found a suitor for Mazola, and probably had his eyes on some bride for Elenga whom Elenga didn't know about. Going home, Muendo and Elenga will find . . . and he will find himself stuck with the ridiculous promise he had ended up making to Mazola, the promise to raise money for her dowry. He hadn't had enough money to obtain Julienne's hand and he had therefore been forced into shady business, instead of having the guts to face life and go home on a bicycle by the plateau road like André Sola and all his colleagues.

"Let's put if off until tomorrow?" This silence had to be broken somehow. The effect was impressive. Elenga added immediately and mysteriously: "Well, what do you expect? The days follow one another, they're bound to be somewhat alike!"

"Put off what?"

"The strike, right after the arrival of the train from Brazzaville!"

"Well, if that's what you want!" said Muendo.

"We had a warning today with the one-hour break."

"The soldiers. . . ."

"What about the soldiers? They haven't killed anybody: a strike doesn't turn us into Germans."

"I thought that it wasn't. . . ."

Luambu remembered Mazola's fright that had come mainly from her bad dream. . . . Certainly there was no reason to shoot at the railroad workers simply because they were protesting their workload and the low pay. . . .

"Solidarity, you know what it means?"

"Sure!"

Obviously Muendo had no argument against solidarity.

9.
André's Fear and That of the Others

My wife told me a strange story about what happened at the market! My wife also told me a story, the same, I suppose. And he? Yes, mine also. And likewise the wives of Douli, Zonzi, Lilesu, Mpassi, all of them. Together they looked toward the desk of the "guy," to use Victorine's favorite expression. On his way to work, André Sola had stopped at the church because he was making a novena again. He had brought back with him a bottle of holy water wrapped up in kraft paper. With a bough he had sprinkled the guy's place, which in fact didn't look more ominous than any other place in the office. André Sola sprinkled it twice, reciting: *Libera, domine, animam ejus, sicut liberasti tres pueros de camino ignis ardentis et de manu regis iniqui. Amen!*

Good heavens, they all have gloomy faces, thought Monsieur Martin when he entered the bookkeeping department. He answered with a nod the greetings of the employees. Sometimes he would just grumble slightly before entering his office. "Still absent, still comatose?" Sola wondered if perhaps he was right there but could not be seen. If he is a bad spirit, the holy water must have sent him straight to hell. But he said: "When I went to the hospital Monday morning he was there, when I left he had disap . . . he had left the hospital. . . ." "That was yesterday?" "Yes, Monsieur Martin. "So he left, but where did he go, he can't be in a coma any longer?" "Well, yes and no, it's difficult to know exactly!" "To know what exactly, if he is still in a coma or if he is not?" "Yes, that's right, Monsieur Martin." "What kind of mystery is it?" "It's a real mystery, Monsieur Martin, a very dangerous one." "Has anyone gone to his place to check on him?" "Wherever

The Madman and the Medusa

he was supposed to live, he hadn't been for a long time, Monsieur M . . ." "So none of you knows where he lives?"

They all looked at one another. Mpita, the guard, who had just brought in some documents, heard Monsieur Martin's question and said: "I know!" Everybody turned toward him. At least one of them knew something. "And where does he live?"

"The cemetery is his garden, he lives on the other side of it." Suddenly they all looked terrible. Astonishment and terror gave them the appearance of badly preserved mummies that had suffered from exposure and from the violation of their sanctuary. Unruffled, Monsieur Martin resumed his interrogation of the guard: "On the other side of what? Have you been to see him there?" "No, sir, but I know that's where he lives!" Sola thought the time had come for him to intervene. "Sir, the man who worked here, was not quite, not quite . . . a man!" Monsieur Martin slicked his hair back and looked carefully at André Sola and his coworkers: "Would you mind saying that again?" Sola repeated his words. "Does that mean that he was a great sorcerer, a zombie?" (None of them knew the word.) How can you explain to a white man what was happening? He would say that it was the superstition of the natives. He can't understand. This is just the time to say: blacken a white man's head as much as you want, he'll never be black! The reverse of what they say about us. This thought occurred to Sola and Mpita, though probably not to the other employees, who were frozen in their fear of the absent man.

"André, if he comes back, send him to me."

André was about to stutter again: "Yes, yes, sir." But doubtful, he hesitated. Obviously, you don't expect the return of someone who lives on the other side of the cemetery where not a living soul would venture, and whose pleasure garden is the cemetery. It was clear that this guy, this thing, his coma, his presence in this office, his attempt to attract him, André Sola, his power over two wretched fellows whose death he had disguised, hoping that the other workers would rebel and risk their lives, meant one thing: that death was present right here in this office. Good Lord! *De profondis clamavi ad te domine:*

André's Fear and That of the Others

Domine exaudi vocem meam. Fiant aures tuae intendentes in vocem deprecationis meae! Good Lord! Tchilala was right when he said that we don't know any longer whom we meet. We live close to death. We inhabit the house of death. Where is life? Lord, *Domine, clamavi ad te.* Why did he choose to go sell fish in the market, on the very day his wife and his friends' wives were all together in the market? André, André, you'd better watch out!

It was maddening. Fortunately, his intuition had not failed him. He was going to torment them all, his coworkers, Tchilala . . . the others, the neighbors, perhaps even the families of the dead men. He thought of Muendo, of his wife who had just had a baby, of the baby that had dropped from his mother's womb. "As if to take her mind away from her husband's death," Victorine had sighed. One couldn't just hide one's eyes: the omen was there. It invaded his nostrils like the smell of muck. He felt nauseated. But nobody could say that he hadn't been careful, even if his suspicion was late being roused. How could he guess that trivial facts would suddenly over-power his good conscience? It was not the Lord who was on their trail.

He had planned to get at them through their wives at the market. Was he going to accept this setback, or was he going to try again? Who knows?

10.
Thursday, June 22

Noon. Luambu follows his coworkers out of the office. Mazola is not there waiting for him under the almond tree on the other side of the street. People in groups of two or three walk by. There is no sun. The sky is overcast and gray. It is muggy, terribly muggy. Stormy weather. The wind seems to stutter; first choked to silence, then exploding with a gush, it sweeps up dust, dead leaves, trash, loincloths, helmets that were badly fastened and of the wrong size anyhow. Shouts seemed to repeat themselves, as if echoing. It is Thursday noon with its usual confusion at the arrival of the train from Brazzaville. The passenger station is close by, a few steps away. At the office they had discussed the work stoppage of the previous day. One hour all together. Luambu didn't take part in the conversation and didn't offer his opinion, which nobody requested anyhow. Of course, they know that one of the engineers is his friend. They had spoken of the railway workers, but they are more interested in the office workers, who are friends or relatives, who don't go home at night covered from head to toe with soot and grease and who don't go home on foot or packed in the back of a truck that shakes the devil out of them. They disagree; each one has a different opinion, which is that of a friend or a relative pro or con, but they all agree that the situation is serious and could get worse.

Actually, Elenga doesn't fear work—he has to be as sick as a dog to be kept away from his beloved locomotives! But the situation had become unbearable. Every day the work increases tenfold. One passenger train a week, but from three to six trains a day! All kinds, low- or high-speed trains and freight trains. There are heavy loads of rock going to the harbor, and trains loaded with logs for the ships waiting in the port, not to mention the logs cut by Muendo, who is always covered with sawdust, so that . . . It's all too heavy for the track, which is damaged in the process. The teams maintaining the equipment and the tracks are always hard at work. And to think, there is only one track! Every God-given day there is ten times more work than the day before. Fatigue spoils the quality of the work, there are accidents. Men, machinery, the track itself—everything breaks down, collapses— if it doesn't die from exhaustion.

They don't share Elenga's point of view nor that of the administrative employees who were fed up after stopping for just one hour. They hold forth emphatically: It's war! The front is everywhere. They would rather be at the front over there with de Gaulle. Unfortunately, you have to be a French citizen to fight under de Gaulle, otherwise you trail along with the Mboulou Mboulou wearing a red chechia instead of a helmet with the cross of Lorraine. They feel so frustrated that they are ready to take the side of those who are fed up. You can't say that they don't know why. They do know, they know that life is hard when you are so overworked that your back aches all the time. And then what about all those accidents, those derailments . . .

There is the usual crowd at the station. A lot of people come to enjoy the walk. Luambu comes to loaf about. He likes to hang around the station the day the train arrives. Observing the passengers, he has noticed often that when they arrive they look dazed from the trip, as if they had just wakened from a long sleep. They stare at you, their voices unsteady, either too soft or too strong, because they are not sure they are understood even by their acquaintances. They are insecure, they don't know if the language they speak is the right one. They wonder if they have arrived at the right station, though it is difficult to get anywhere else but Pointe-Noire on the train from Brazzaville . . . unless you get off absentmindedly in the middle of the forest, believing that the sea is right there, hidden behind the trees and waiting for you. There is only one platform, and the train doors don't open on the side where the sand reaches the track. One feels out of place, since one travels with one's illusions. The travelers hesitate to get off the train, to leave their element and everything else. The friends who meet them have the same dazed expressions mixed with worried looks that explain the awkward and embarrassed greetings. How strange! Here is a passenger who looks with bewilderment in all directions, rolling his eyes, while his ears remain blocked. He answers automatically, obviously missing the point. The new arrivals bring preconceived ideas, their eyes check the surroundings before accepting them.

Three roads, three streets lead to and from the station. The road that connects the harbor with the militia camp crosses the square in front of the station, which is like a lake, a lake of concrete. Here is a woman investigating how to get to the house where she is expected, and she wants to know furthermore what the house is like. "It's far. . . ." As soon as you arrive, you have to start again for another destination, check your luggage, be careful, even suspicious, since the last thing you need now is to lose something. The family members sent to welcome the traveler are introduced, but the latter confuses the names and the degrees of the relationship. So to help him out of his embarrassment, they ask: "Are you sure you haven't forgotten something in the train?" They find excuses for him of one sort or another. "Did you leave on time?" "Who took you to the train?" "Hey, don't push. Some people are so rude!" "Sorry, excuse me," Luambu said. What's come over him? In the middle of the noise he recognized a voice. Where did it come from? To whom did it belong? Since he heard it so clearly, it must not be far away. He searches with his eyes, strains his ears. "No, he hasn't grown!" She is referring to a child. He is losing his mind; it can't be an illusion. He sees her finally. She is holding the hand of a child drowned in the crowd. He elbows his way through the crowd to reach them, but loses sight of them. Unexpectedly, he stumbles over Mpita, who asks: "Did you lose them? Is it your wife and your child?" He is so dumbfounded by the question that Mpita feels embarrassed. So Mpita had seen him then with a woman and a child, with his wife and his child! "No, he hasn't grown," whispers the voice in his head. This fellow is definitely not talkative, thought Mpita, as Luambu left him abruptly. What if everybody had illusions like his? He certainly has no desire to stroll about any longer. He thought he had heard a voice, or rather he thought he had recognized the voice he heard. . . . Later, when Mpita recalled the meeting at the station, he asserted that Luambu looked like somebody who had just woken up in some unknown place where he didn't remember having gone to sleep. He was looking for something without knowing what it was, and when I asked him: "Are you looking for the woman and the child who were with you?" he looked dumbfounded and turned away abruptly. Then he forced his way through the crowd, staring at faces here and there, jostling people without even bothering to apologize.

If Julienne and the child he thought had drowned, been swept away, been swallowed up by the whirlpool of the swollen river, if they . . . This thought, instead of reviving his hope, struck him full in the face and straight in the heart with the shame of his cowardice. The voice he had heard became progressively distorted and resembled Julienne's less and less. It could have been Mazola's voice just as well or any other woman's, provided that voice was not shrill and harsh . . . Julienne, even when she screamed . . . but had he ever heard her scream? Lately the memory of her had returned to him with the memory of the cowardice that had pinned him to a tree and had kept him from going to help them. He had fled, he has fled. Forced to ponder on, to chew on, to guzzle on, his remorse, he had hidden from his heinous crime, had shriveled up in his own skin, had obliterated himself. . . . There were two options: either he threw himself into the wild waters and saved his wife and child, overcoming the wild storm and thus gaining precedence over everything, or else he drowned with them. Which had been his final decision? Or he might have drowned while Julienne and the child were miraculously saved, alive, thanks to their innocence. Then they would have blamed him for having exposed them to deadly danger and thanked the Lord for having saved them!

Thursday, June 22

In the end Luambu was cursed, with no hope of forgiveness. To expiate your sin you must accept the judge's verdict: Mazola? God creates the coward, the good and just man, the wicked and bad man. Why does he punish the innocent? Love can also be hell. But there is also the other hell. Which of the two is worse? But the question of redemption might not be asked in that form, especially if one's faith is so weak, like a thread that one cannot draw on too tightly for fear it will break.

The timbre of the voice he believed he had recognized because he thought he still remembered it was fading away and was taking on Mazola's intonation. He makes a despairing gesture. The crowd has thinned out. He hadn't seen the face of the woman, only her bearing was similar to Julienne's. Furthermore, Julienne didn't use to dress as women do nowadays. The rayon and cotton of the modern skirt doesn't compare with the smoothness of the traditional wax-print pagne and vest that gave a woman a different figure. He imagines Mazola dressed in a long skirt with a tight waist, a waist to be grasped. His state of alert persists. He looks toward the station. He walks under the arcades. Only the railroad employees remain there, not knowing what to do, lost in their idleness. Dejected, he leaves, realizing that he is nearly alone in the square. He doesn't feel strange or lost in the vastness of this large square. But the mugginess of the stormy weather weighs on his bones. The threat of rain has sent everybody home in a hurry.

Having overcome his shock, Luambu falls into his usual routine and goes to the deserted beach as he is accustomed to do. The beach is empty, which is to be expected at this time of day. At the grade crossing the scene of the previous day comes to his mind: Elenga, in his locomotive, Mazola and he planted on the ground like two anthills. The turmoil of the waves has no soothing effect on the pain of his torn soul. Still there is the pungent smell of iodine. His path was thick with brambles, while fissures opened in the ground. The wounds of the body don't leave the soul free of scars. But there is iodine! A long time ago, in his past, one part of his life didn't connect properly with another. . . . Where is his heart? Where is it? Sing, you who sing, eat, you who eat. Isn't it funny that the mouth

The Madman and the Medusa

serves several purposes, including saying yes to time that flies by, to the great detriment of hope, to the total contempt of hope. Hope dies with a sigh that sticks in the throat. The sea roars, the sea grates. What confidence can we have in anything except in what finally leads to routine. Like the rage of the sea, your rage won't overcome resentment. Pass on, fragile shadow. If your heart is open or if you are deprived of heart, it won't be any easier to brave the storm, be it of salt, of sand, or of sun. What did he do with his life? Where is it gone? The sea is more real here than in the bay. The jellyfish can't pass the bar, whereas the water of the bay is thick with jellyfish. They are unreal, barely visible in the water and will sting the diver who doesn't look out for them. That voice, that figure—could they have been hers after so many months, so many years!

The afternoon drags by. 5 P.M.? No, it's not yet over. . . . His blotter is covered with ink. Why is his pen scratching so badly? The pen isn't steady in his fingers. He has a cramp at the base of his thumb. He coughs discreetly. Nobody minds his cough or his fretting. The ruler slips from his hands and falls with an exasperating noise. His hands are so feverish that his palms are sticky. He wipes them on the legs of his shorts. He urges his thumb, his forefinger, and his middle finger to hold the pen firmly. . . . Again a cramp is threatening. He rubs the base of his thumb. The half-moons of both his thumbs are very big, and he can't believe his eyes. He can't quite remember what it means. He turns around to ask if one of them remembers what . . . but are they in the least aware of his presence, do they hear him? He strains his ears. It cannot be five o'clock every minute. There is no clock in the office. Nobody wears a watch. It's forbidden. One has to work and one shouldn't look at the time while working. Nobody moves. Suddenly several whistles blow at the same time. . . . A ship is perhaps mooring or leaving. . . . What a relief, it's over! Such afternoons are deadly. He regains his composure in order to be the last to leave, quietly.

The empty beach looks as if the world had come to an end. The sand is dull and unblemished by human footsteps. Luambu looks back, sees footprints, and convinces himself that they are his. He fights the overwhelming feeling that the end of the world is close and that his ultimate torture will be, as the last one remaining, to see the earth open up wide and engulf the sea in wild whirlpools, pulling him down, farther and farther, to the bottom of the earth. What could he hang on to? To this shell, a huge mussel, that he picks up? To this piece of black wood that he picks up, grinds feverishly, breaks, and throws at the foaming crest of a wave that threatens to cross over the limit where man keeps his feet dry and his soul free? Nothing, there is nothing to hang on to. Man is reduced to the self, which tracks him down, throws him out of the world, and confines him to solitude. He crumbles more easily than sand in the wind. Out at sea the ships make eyes at one another. Morse code. They speak to one another, but not to him. They ignore him because he is alone on an empty beach, as if it were the end of the world. The beach is bare. He comes near the waves, risking being swept away by the undertow. He looks for a sign announcing tragedy. He knows in his heart that there is this premonition of tragedy: the panic at the station, the urge to rake up his past that overwhelmed him suddenly. What he had ascertained doesn't exist, but he is assailed by vague, fleeting doubts that take shape in a strong overwhelming manner, before at last slipping away, without excuses, but accusing him, forcing him to flee, and assuming the right to brand him a coward. A wave breaks, splashing him and compelling him to walk on the dry sand that renders his step unsteady and challenges his sobriety. His sobriety. His premonition. Where is everybody, Elenga, Muendo? . . . What if Muendo hadn't come? Maybe he is also striking! So are the fishermen, the strollers, even the children are on a mischief-strike! The soldiers on strike around Elenga, who is striking, perhaps because he welcomes the chance to stay longer with his beloved engine, whose firebox's door he opens under the slightest pretext, as if he were incurably chilly. Often Elenga looks up to him, as a son to his father. But he doesn't dwell on Elenga's glance, because suddenly he sees the wild waters rushing away with Julienne and the child on her back. . . . At the railroad station *she* held a little boy by the hand! The whirlpool of the crowd whisked her away while his interest was stirred by what might have been only an illusion! "Is it morning or evening?" Is it a forbidden place, abandoned, eternal? He searches for a trace of life around him, beside the slow and weary motion of the waves, but his attention slackens. . . . Perhaps the world has come to an end and he alone survives the anxiety of the world. What earned him such a privilege? To find again the pain of living, to accept Mazola's nudity, to stop fleeing, to stop living like an outcast.

"What's going on? Where are the others? I didn't see you come!"

"Well then, maybe you are not the sorcerer he said you were!"

Muendo was more than ever covered with sawdust.

"We got them too!"

"What?"

"The soldiers. The boss called them to watch us take a little rest!"

"Do you really think that's funny?"

"Oh, come on! What a face! You wouldn't look worse if my funeral had just been announced!"

Again, as earlier in his office, Luambu felt his palms sweating. He clenched his fists, but felt no strength in them. He wanted to say something but Muendo didn't hear any words come out and looked at him with concern. Luambu's silence spurred him on to talk faster and faster, as if to drown it. They arrived quickly at four o'clock like a flight of sparrows. Then they were picked up—we had started sawing again—and they were gone. Did you hear that, whistles blowing all the time? We didn't know if they came from the harbor or from the railroad; it was as if there were several ships or several trains, we couldn't make out. Then suddenly the soldiers left.

"Yes, I heard them, at the C.F.C.O. and in the harbor. Maybe."

"What do you mean?"

"Nothing." If they think . . . if everybody . . . A vague smile hovered over the painful expression on Luambu's face. Muendo looked at him as if for the first time. A face is the clothing of the soul. From a face's change of clothing you know if a soul is rejoicing or mourning. Is there a face without its mood? Be it white canvas, khaki, or black, the cut is the same; it's the color that declares itself.

"Look, over. there, someone is waving; do you think it's Elenga?"

"No . . . no, that's not Elenga."

"Are you okay?"

"And you, how many mahogany logs, ten?"

"Are you joking or what?"

"No, I am not joking."

He had heard correctly. They had also stopped work for an hour. They had also had to offer the soldiers the spectacle of their provocative idleness. They had also . . .

"No, I am not joking. . . ." It had become more blasphemous than laughable, what did it mean? There were two possibilities, either Muendo got some sort of kudos from carrying around all that sawdust, or he proclaimed his lack of constraint and his refusal to grant any dignity to his job of sawyer. There was no dignity in being a slave to his work. He worked, received his pay, but seemed to say: "Look at me, don't I glitter in my abject poverty?" Luambu didn't ride a bicycle on the plateau road to reach the Native Village like his colleagues, the other white-collar workers. On the contrary, as soon as he left Djindji he took off his espadrilles and his white socks and became a common man, though not completely. On the seaside path, the beach, among the fishermen, with Elenga and Muendo, he looked less ragged, but then he wasn't showing off the importance (if there is any!) of being a clerk. He felt quite as naked as that beach where tonight he was out of place, impious, unwanted.

"So you stopped working yesterday for an hour like the railroad workers?"

"Yes."

"Hm. . . ."

"You are right, that fellow isn't Elenga, but to whom is he waving?"

"He isn't waving to anybody, he's dancing."

"You're damned right! He must be drunk or crazy, dancing all by himself like that."

"Look over there, there is someone watching him."

A child, clad only in a loincloth, was sitting off to one side on a sand dune, his elbows on his knees, his fists propped against his chin. He was impassively watching the dancer, who turned out to be none other than the madman whom Luambu, Muendo, and Elenga knew well, since he had blessed their first meeting.

Within a circle made of herbs, seaweed, debris, fish heads, and fish bones, he was executing a dance inspired neither by the devil nor by demons. He was hopping very slowly on one foot, wavering and controlling his balance with his arms extended in opposite directions. The raised hand formed a conch holding an imaginary volume, while the lowered hand rested on an equally imaginary support. At the same time, he tried with the big toe of his other foot to trace a circle parallel to the circle of herbs and seaweed. . . .

"What kind of dance is it?"

Muendo copies Luambu's behavior. He is circumspect, without a gesture of mockery or any indication of irreverence, without the sceptical smile of the unbeliever, but with the composure of a postulant aspiring to asceticism. The dancer wears a red loincloth. The air he breathes in and out makes as much noise in his chest as in an empty snail shell. His bones poke out so against his skin that Muendo wonders how he could have escaped total dislocation from the fishermen's beating. He hadn't noticed his eyes right away . . . they were turned inward. The madman was looking inside his own head! Slimy and yellowish white specks appeared between his opened eyelids. What was Luambu trying to prove by staring so fixedly at this dance, which was perhaps not a dance at all? A madman playing the buffoon! Muendo made up his mind to break the spell. He got up without worrying about a possible protest from Luambu, took a few steps toward the dancer, changed his mind, and turned to the child. He offered him a coin, "Hey, kid, take this and give it to him." But the child didn't move. He patted his shoulder to urge him on a little, but the child fell backward, like a statuette, frozen in the same sitting position. . . . Muendo stepped back, shook his head, and thought he heard rain falling from it. All the sawdust flew off, scattered over the sand, and disappeared. He could not imagine himself without his sawdust, no one would recognize him without his smell of precious and rare wood. What woman's nose would not become bold and flirtatious when he happened to walk by? . . . They would smell him coming, they would gaze at him while he strutted by, basking in his humility. But why had he come to this beach? To watch a madman dance a senseless dance that doesn't stir up one's desire to dance or one's desire for anything? It's a dance that makes you shiver. He called to Luambu for help, but Luambu didn't answer. It was up to him to find a solution. He put the child back on his seat. Then giving way to anger or to the fear of being the willing victim of a spell, he shouted: "You stay with the madman if you wish, but I am going away. Why don't you come?" Why did he beg the child? This scene, which he didn't want to laugh about, had dumped on his shoulders the weight of the whole exhausting day. He had hesitated to go out on the beach when he had seen it was empty. He had never before found the beach completely empty, because it was a good place for fishing and a few fishermen lived right there. Where had they all gone? Perhaps it wasn't Luambu who had come! But a ghost in full daylight? Actually the day was drawing to a close. And evil spirits don't care if it's night or day. . . . The dancer wasn't the madman, the real madman spoke like a priest. This one was mute: he driveled at the mouth and didn't have the eyes of a living man. Don't turn around, Muendo, and go away as fast as you can, if you care to stay alive! Luambu couldn't catch up with him. Of course, with night coming on it is difficult to see who is walking ahead of you.

To calm Muendo, Luambu kept him company all the way to his door. He apologized for not coming in, but he had something to take care of, nothing mysterious, no, nothing mysterious—so long, I'll see you tomorrow. The Muendo he left felt uneasy and shook his shoulders nervously. See you to-morrow, God willing. Certainly every word either one of them said didn't seem to be the right word under the circumstances. What had God's will to do with the decision of two men in perfectly good health to go home to eat and sleep, and see each other the next day or not? See you tomorrow. It had been ridiculous of him to take such an interest in the madman dancing alone on the deserted beach. The buffoonery of a madman. The strangeness was in the setting. Soldiers had lit fires before the Tchinouka ford opposite the Mission School and the telegraph station.

He and Muendo had turned around to gaze at the fires, by the light of which the soldiers seemed to be wearing masks on their faces. Muendo kept strangely silent and walked in an obstinate way, concentrating on getting home as fast as pos-sible. At the end of their stroll on the beach, he had been an-noyed by the way Luambu had been drawn to the dancer's strange performance. Luambu failed to explain that he needed to relax at any possible, even trivial, opportunity, although the dance hadn't been trivial at all. Nothing happens by chance. One has to see to understand.

Muendo thought perhaps that the walkout and its conse-quences didn't concern him. He should have tried to convince him of the contrary. He understood, and he could have told him that he understood, that it was not a game. Of course, in his work, he didn't risk breaking his neck or leg, at the very most a fingernail, probably the nail of his little finger, which he let grow and which looked like the broken beak of a par-rot. . . . But he had the leisure to examine his thumbs and dis-cover that the half-moons were taking up half his nails and he had wondered what it meant. Well, he should have asked Muendo, who was Senegalese and Vili and who therefore would have probably given him two different meanings and left him as puzzled as before. If he didn't know, if he could not remember the prediction concerning such half-moons, it was precisely because there was more than one interpretation, more then one possibility. They were intertwined like Siamese twins, one couldn't exist without the other, one didn't make sense without the other. The agony of one who sits between two chairs and whose bottom aches from such an awkward position! A life that is not a real life. . . . Pigs, of course, are at home in the mud. Sometimes, according to circumstances, you have come from one place and from another also. But under the present circumstances when he imagines what he sees, what he hears, when his memory is so ashamed of him that it takes flight . . . (Awful day!) He wasn't going to cut off his thumbs in any case. For the Laris, like Elenga, the premonition . . . unless perhaps the half-moons don't have a meaning. What do the Yakomas, the Bochis, and the Tékés believe? . . . And all the men and women who are on the decks or in the holds of ships? And those who in third- and fourth-class train carriages came to work, to live and to die in Pointe-Noire? Good heavens, it's not that important! Even after he had made up his mind that it wasn't so important after all, he still felt uneasy and totally puzzled. He was losing his foothold. A terrible day. Somehow he had to control the uproar within him that prevented him from understanding the people he met. Women and children were going to and from the main water pump located in the middle of the square at the entrance of the Native Village. There was a lot of noise, gossiping arguments turned sour, and scuffling around the four taps from which water would flow miraculously at certain hours. Tears for a broken bottle, laments for a demijohn! Was all this activity reassuring? He listened to find out. The so-called easy water was sparingly dispensed at three fountains for the entire town of four thousand souls. With all the laborers' camps around about, and not counting the white population, there were really about six or seven thousand people living in Pointe-Noire. Fewer than two hundred whites lived there.

Fires were also burning at the entrance of the Native Village. The soldiers . . . Naturally, after all these walkouts . . . Soldiers don't like to leave their barracks, and when they are sent to bivouac, they immediately behave as if they were facing Germans. And since they are aiming their guns at men who are not from the same ethnic group, they are inevitably from a hostile tribe. It's war, for sure. Soldier Elenga, soldier

Muendo, soldier Luambu! "Allons enfants . . ." If he was tired, it was not because he had cut five logs of gaboon and three logs of mahogany like Muendo. Nervous irritation is debilitating and leads to nervous exhaustion.

As he pulled a lounge chair onto the porch, he thought that he might stroll toward the hospital. . . . He would whistle and Elenga would recognize his whistle and come out. But what could they do together at such a late hour, because it would be later than 8 P.M. by the time he got there? See you tomorrow! He hears Muendo adding, "God willing," but he knows that it's not God's business. His appetite is such that he won't die of starvation, he likes to say. Those used to be Julienne's words. And if it had been her at the railroad station . . . He eats sweet cassava and grilled peanuts. He doesn't like to eat a lot at night, especially during the rainy season. The heat slows down the digestion. Or was it Mazola who said that . . . " an appetite" . . . Maybe, I don't remember. Listen, oil is expensive he thinks, and lowers the wick of the hurricane lamp. Only three or four houses in the Native Village had electricity. Perhaps a few more. He had noticed an electric bulb in the living-room of Muendo's brother-in-law, who is one of those French citizen Vilis; Tchi-ngnali is his name! As you see, he hasn't frenchified his name. He places the lamp at his feet and tries to lie down comfortably on the wooden slats of the lounge chair. He forces himself not to think of the events of the day, when he hears a noise inside, which means, he assumes, that a stranger is in his house, presumably in the bedroom, the only place where he hadn't been since he returned home. . . . Someone had coughed and snorted. Who? "You are not very well known around here!"

"Muendo, is that you?"

"I've been looking for you . . . when you think that we have known each other for so long and then it's at night that I have to find your house. Yes, get up. They have killed Elenga! Somebody came to tell us. I went to the hospital. It's true. It's true. Nobody was supposed to know."

"How did it happen, how?" Was there anything more reasonable and less silly than to ask, "How?" How does one die?

Thursday, June 22

Is it death itself or the manner, the way, the reason for death. What is important? The irretrievable loss.

"You say they have killed Elenga?"

"Yes, around five o'clock!"

At five o'clock the beach had been empty, without a living soul, without Elenga. Now and forever.

"Nobody heard the soldiers shoot, they must have shot when all the locomotives started blowing their whistles together, when . . ."

His fingers had difficulty holding his pen. It's nerve-racking to wait for the whistle announcing the end of work. When the hour finally strikes, Elenga is not there waiting for him. Sometimes, when he finishes his work at Kilometer 4, he goes directly home. The distance between the workshop of the C.F.C.O. and the hospital is shorter than their usual roundabout way by the seaside, where they meet Muendo.

"I understand now why I was on edge when you wanted to linger and watch the guy do his crazy act." The parody of a dance, the madman! What was he saying? "Who will comfort your sister?" Luambu repeats the sentence aloud. . . . Muendo stares wide-eyed. The words stab him in the chest. He has difficulty acknowledging the obvious, "Is that what he said? And what else did he say? Tonight he said something else, did he? He might have said something you didn't hear. I don't . . ." Luambu turned his back on him and entered the house to find out what he wanted to know. He saw nothing, nobody. Somebody had coughed, somebody who wasn't there.

Death was coming and he didn't see it. He was sounding the alarm with amused nonchalance, and his eyes screwed up by his smile didn't catch the light that was as delicate as a flower, which he would gladly have put in the corner of his mouth or in his hair had he intended to attract the loose women never tired of hopping into bed. Ah, disgusting life! What can he promise all those who look at him with suspicion, paradise for an angel's fart? Why don't they gorge themselves on the seaweed offered by the sea. Are they complaining of the rash the medusa gives them? They should walk away from the ocean whose deeps are in turmoil, suffering from God knows what kind of weariness of living. He is also assailed by the image of the savanna, where as a child he was already nurturing the dark wish to reach the mirages, the waters of which would not extinguish his thirst for revenge! The extreme heat of the firebox inflames his eyes and burns the side of his body on which his arm pulls the whistle. Did he see Luambu making a vague gesture of retreat from Mazola who wants to bite into the jujubes of the tree on each side of his body. Muendo is a plank that is going to be cut. He shouts to him: Hey, Muendo! Don't let your flesh be confused with wood for the doors of houses that have no thresholds. . . . Death was coming, but stubborn like all the men of his tribe, he didn't care: pulling the cord of the alarm with all his weight, the weight of his past, he roared with mocking laughter to the point of damaging the pearly sheen of his teeth, the teeth of a weed-eating, weed-killing, chicken-killing handsome young man. He catches in his line of sight a miserable skunk who laughs at the laugh of Solola, also known as Marie who had called him, Elenga, a "so-ouassi," a savage. The childhood friend is now an affected young woman, inflated with a bad whiff of stagnant air from a cove of the Djoué that spread all over the Lower Congo when the wretched Solola came by! From the whistle comes as much steam as noise and that penetrates his flesh as if it were tolling the knell. Here he is caught in the crossfire, or between joy and gloom; having wished for one, he falls victim to the other. What a strange situation! What is Luambu's understanding of the medusa and the incoherent and uncontrolled speech of the madman who, you know, might not have been so mad, who was in fact speaking of you, yes, sure, and now of me, and don't hide behind your silence! "Will you comfort my sister?" He can't take the extended hand of Massengo, he loathes doing it. Even if he could, he wouldn't take his hand, because the brute holds in the other hand a whip or a brass-edged ruler that he hides behind his back, the nasty cheat! Obviously he will never like teachers who, the more they hit their students, the less affection they give their wives. And Uncle Malonga surely isn't aware of all that! He shouldn't have let himself be overwhelmed by his

Thursday, June 22

terrible anger, whereas with more circumspection . . . he . . . he . . .

On the sly the soldiers were ordered to shoot. In the deafening, far-reaching noise of the sirens, nobody could hear the crackle of the bullets. Four shots drew a horizontal dotted line on Elenga's chest just under his collarbone. One last shot cut out the chain from which he hung with the hand that had clenched it after the impact of the first bullets. When he fell, he didn't fall toward the open firebox. His body, therefore, was only covered with blood and was not charred, which would have happened if he had fallen in the direction of the firebox! "The late-comers will have, if I may say so, all of eternity to see the gates of paradise open for those who are innocent." He remembers that sentence coming from the mouth of the madman.

It was half past four in the afternoon when the train engines became silent one after the other. The strikers on the picket line couldn't figure out why the other strikers whose duty was to make known how dangerous the situation was at the C.F.C.O. had cut short the demonstration before the agreed time. But as we know, one rarely stops one's ears without also closing one's eyes, they saw nothing. Perhaps the thick cloud of steam from the engines had hidden the smoke of the deadly volleys that had injured, mutilated, wounded, and killed their comrades. Later it would be said that Elenga had died more for his passion than for money. The irony was, as one could also say, that it was true.

> It was the death of a child, not a man!
> It was the death of a child, not a man!
> It was the death of a child, not a man!

Of a little orphan who thought he was a man! He is a child, ho! He is a child, ho! It's an iron bullet that killed the child, ho! It's the bullet, ho! He's a child, ho!

Was it death or dead Elenga? Masoni was crying over the horrible, unforeseen, irretrievable death and not over dead Elenga! "*Elenga-hé! Miana mama, nié ké sé! Na léli yo-o,*

moana mama, nié ké sé! Elenga zongà to bonguisa zoto!" (O
Elenga, your mother's son! O my little one! I am crying over
you, your mother's son! Come back to us, we want to lull you
to sleep!") It's the death of a child, not of a man! A child I rock
in my arms, hm, hm, la, la, la, la, la, la, la, la. Oh, I have found
a louse! And you have a chigger! Take care of your feet, your
sleep was restless again, you must take good care of your bed,
I told you so. . . . I told you . . . These are the wounds of a
child. . . . *Elenga-héhé, moana mama, na léla yé yé yé yé! Na
sala pé boni?* (O Elenga, your mother's son, I cry over you,
what else should I do?)

The virtuosity of the mourners lies in the best use of the
trivial, of everyday happenings sung with humor and play-
fulness. Is death something to be debased? A child, not a man!
Not yet a man, that is. That is to say, that is to say, ho! What
revenge death takes on life in this case, before life could give
life. Elenga, a child, if not, where is the proof, where is his
widow, where is . . . where are his children? That is what I am
saying, ho! He leaves a sister behind, not a widow.

They carried home Elenga's broken body, his chest bleeding
with more wounds than Christ. When he fell, he was holding
the handle and a piece of the chain that activates the whistle of
the engine. Either a bullet cut the chain or it broke with the
weight of his dead body. . . . Though his body was quite light,
this body of a young man just past adolescence!

Malonga, the medical supervisor, had easily taken possession of the body, in spite of the fear of some people that it
might be used to foster more disturbances, for there are those
who are always looking for a martyr, in order. . . . No, they
had expected him to die like his father, who was also an engineer and who had died in an accident when his train went off
the track. Elenga also died in an accident, in a derailment. It
was to be expected, it was to be expected! . . . But when it
happens, it's always too soon. This explanation wasn't satisfying. Malonga asked the chief physician, Doctor Grosgendrin,
for help; he gave his word of honor that one could trust Malonga and that the body would not be used for any other purpose than a quiet and proper funeral. Of course, doctor, yes,

Thursday, June 22

doctor. The body was released, but as a precaution the Native Village was completely surrounded by the militia, just to be on the safe side! Yes, doctor, the wake will take place in the village, not at the hospital. We'll weep within our hearts. Yes, doctor, we'll weep within our hearts.

Old Loubaki offered his house for the wake and respected very reluctantly the stipulations made by Malonga. That they should not cry. That they watch the body in silence. A silence that would mean that they had died with him. That would be as appropriate as the usual tears. They would control their grief so that it would mark them with the sign of their wounded fate. The wake would be silent. Their tears would be silent; there would be no lamentation.

When the heart breaks, no wound gapes in the flesh of the chest. And if tears drown the eyes? For what purpose is life so arrogant? Death turns around in Malonga's mind, and he uses words that don't seem to glorify the pain. Speak, speak, how else can you choke your sobbing? Choke your words, your cries, your sobs. It has to be that way, because life doesn't dare face itself, doesn't dare face a smiling man without firing a shot! . . . Was it really because the father wanted his son to be like him even in death? So be it!

At night the body was carried from the morgue, where thanks to the doctor it had been kept. The only consideration Elenga ever received was for his dead body. At any other place he wouldn't have been safe from his fellow strikers who had claimed his body, since he had died for their common cause, and their request was understandable. Unfortunately they were all hotheads who, if they were given the opportunity . . . He wasn't taken on a stretcher to the house of old Loubaki, but carried on the shoulders of his uncle Malonga. That was his cross, his shameful and humiliating glory. A strange way of keeping a secret, a strange secret that was out in no time. People found out where the wake was taking place, but they complied with the rule of silence. Strange customs, strange times, where are we headed? "We'll weep within our hearts." So they found eyes in their hearts to mourn silently the death of the child, ho!

The Madman and the Medusa

They came from everywhere. The night was alive with shadows, swarming like bugs, like ants, with jack-o'lanterns, djinns, *mami-ouatas,* ghosts, bats, zombies, some with one head, some with three bellies, some walking on their rear ends, some who have always preferred night to day, some limping, others who in broad daylight still carry night deep in their eyes, and also the neighbors of neighbors, all those who are ashamed or frightened to sleep next to Elenga's body, black from the blood oozing from his chest wounds! They all stumbled in the night that was as smooth as nauseating slime. The strange wake overflowed the house, the courtyard, the street of the old chief Loubaki who was trapped by this death, which had extended his authority beyond his age limit and the prerogatives granted by the administration, because they knew he was able to apply the rules and have them respected without explanation.

Suddenly Malonga was struck by a cruel thought that shook his teeth and his body. Who was this nephew of his whose death affected more people than the town had inhabitants? What would he have me do, throw him out? Useless and silent protest! Wasn't it his decision that the wake be held in silence? Many more people are confined to silence than those who still suffer from the weakness of speaking at random of what they are or are not, of what they eat or don't eat, or what they drink or don't drink, that nothing will ever be satisfying if they are consumed with hunger and thirst. . . .

The intensity of the mourning frightened the night, which feared that it would never again be offered such a grievous death, full of the fresh scent of iodine, and that life would ultimately triumph with boldness and joy over pusillanimous existence. Bodies for sale! Night was receiving more than it had ever wanted. There is a darker night in the depth of the night that awaits him who goes alone to the ford. How wretched we are! And if man's heart is the lie that lives within him? He comes and goes! Only his shadow dies, for his flesh returns to the dust from which he came, ephemeral, dry and crumbly as soon as water is lacking!

The dead have all come back and are among the living, who

believe they will never rot, even though already one has bad breath, another an incurable wound in his belly or in his hand. What are these gashes in the body, in the mouth, the eyes, the nostrils, the ears? . . . Dare we pollute those ears by mentioning the rest? They exhale the nauseating smell of the arrogance of Elenga who wanted to take part in this dangerous game that breaks backs, even those wearing a rope with seven knots. Who slams the door in the face of whom? A door of straw, a door of loose-fitting planks, because the wooden planks had been badly cut and didn't join or the straw had been badly plaited, ho!

They all came. There was Luambu and Muendo and also the madman who didn't know he was present, he who prophesied their agony while he scooped up in his hands the medusa from a sea in turmoil. . . . "Why was he weary of living?" One will know one day that if he didn't obey the law of men, it's because he obeyed the night, his mistress, his mother, the mother who attends all of us with delicious exhalations of macerated animals, herbs, and unspeakable minerals. Sulfur, kaolin, and blood. Laugh, sulfur, kaolin, and blood! Weep, blood and laterite. There was a silence such as had happened only once in the mists of time, when night went to the wedding of the sun with the moon who promised each other, instead of meat and wine, the tender flesh and sweet blood of their children, the stars of the night, the stars of the day. A feast of gluttons! Ho, ho, ho! Is there a human mother more dissolute than the moon? Perhaps it was eyeing Elenga's remains to appease its morbid hunger. . . . Morbid hunger! The ogresses of old legends seem so restrained compared to the moon, though they only liked the flesh of the sun's sons.

His nails' half-moons! *Elenga-hé moana Mama Nié-ké-sé!* (O Elenga, son of your mother, O little one!) Mazola devastated by grief, shook her head like a lizard, nodding tirelessly while she stuffed her mouth with handfuls of ashes that tasted bitter: she accepted their bitterness! If you can't see the tears, if you can't hear the sobs, then whom are they mourning?

There came also the creatures of the swamps who are considered bastard children by the sons of the day and by the stars of the night with the red moon! They didn't have far to go. Those who were already there had spread out from the house, the courtyard, the street of Chief Loubaki and were spilling over the square around the public fountain at the entrance of the Native Village. They—the frogs and toads of all ages—scorned the orders for a silent wake. They started croaking with such sadness that their funereal song could have killed a second time and many times more Elenga whose soul could be seen on the alert close to the open wounds of his destroyed chest. It seemed that on each side of the road to the plateau there were two choirs of batrachians and of reptiles, their cousins, who showed the dead and the living how to mourn a child, ho! A child, not a man, oh! The roaming dogs also joined in and howled. So did the mosquitos.

Because of the order not to weep, people were watching one another by the light of the resin torches, to check if anyone was overcome by the sadness of the strange mourning song. More than one, the next day, felt a brotherly or sisterly feeling for the frogs and the dogs who had shown more compassion than the human beings. It's a man who killed the son of man, not a frog, not a dog. The soldiers guarding the access to the European city had tears in their eyes and gloom in their hearts from the pain that one of them had inflicted. Since the streets spread out in a fan from their post, they could see their many spots of light quiver in the black night!

Luambu thought that he had never felt so humiliated. Why is it so difficult to revolt against the unfairness of death? It's unfair to kill, unfair to be killed. It's unfair to be there without crying, to choke in silence, to be trapped in silence, tormented by all the gestures that are forbidden, all the harsh words that cannot be said. Elenga, Elenga! What could he tell him now? Are you blaming me for being here, for not having told you the whole truth? I wanted to speak to you of Julienne, of Mazola, and not just answer: "No flaw, why?" . . . I should have spoken of Julienne and the child. . . . A coward cannot be an honest man!

Thursday, June 22

Muendo was exhausted from the events of the day. He was devastated by grief. He started to doze off, then pulled himself together and stared wide-eyed, opening and closing his hands as if to say, "Good Lord, what does all this mean?" Luambu patted his hairy forearms covered with sawdust to show his compassion. He was getting up when the frogs and toads burst into their song and the dogs started howling, here, there, everywhere! It happened so suddenly that everybody was startled. It was a deafening lament of grief that no human heart could have ever expressed. A sort of wonder. Everybody instinctively looked up at the sky that remained dark and silent.

After his anger and his sense of humiliation, Luambu felt a kind of relief that estranged him from the wake and deadened his emotion.

Mazola seemed to beat out a sort of mea culpa with her head, shaking it from left to right with a jerky movement like a tit or a woodpecker that doesn't know where to look and what to expect. Muendo uttered the only words that were to be heard during the entire wake, "Let's go." But it wasn't easy to leave, the courtyard was filled with people and the street also, how could one leave? There seemed to be no way out. There was no room to advance or to step back. The frogs' croaking and the dogs' howling broke like the waves of a wild sea. You could imagine you were on the beach, except that the smell of resin torches had replaced the smell of iodine. Was it a wake or a waking nightmare? And how could one get out of it?

Muendo clung to Luambu, who he thought was steadier on his feet, but Luambu wasn't steadier, he felt swept away by the billowing waves! Perhaps after all it wasn't Muendo who was clinging to him, but the other way round. Muendo had just time to ask, "What's the matter with you?" before another wild outbreak of the croaking and the howling. The torches flickered and died out. With rare violence, wind, lightning, thunderclaps, cloudbursts swept the night.

II.
The Consultation

In the office there was a kind of conspiracy against André. He had finally agreed to another gathering at his house. J. P. Mpita had not been invited, because then why not invite all the employees of the C.G.B.C.? It was important to clarify the situation among those who shared the same office. Tchilala thought that Mpita should have been invited also because he knew "things," but he didn't insist: "Good, let's not waste time." In addition to those from the office, there was André's guest, whom all examined gravely. He had the neck of a vulture and the slit eyes of a snake, which were intimidating.

André put down in front of each person a kola nut, a few pepper corns, and a lump of ginger root. The guest received a double share of everything. The guest had asked the participants to wear white loincloths. The mat spread on the ground was also covered with a white loincloth. The guest got up and went to a bundle of raphia he had left in one corner of the room. He took out wooden bells and a resin torch, which he lit while mumbling incomprehensible words. Then he went around the circle of spectators, spreading the acrid smoke over them!

Each one of them spoke in turn. André was the first.

He had appeared at the market. The women through their vigilance had foiled his attempt to hurt innocent people. When they had exposed him, he had vanished into thin air. Still his disappearance didn't make them feel secure. Each one of them sought to discover how he personally could have harmed this man. It was difficult to speak of a man. This bad spirit had entered the body of a man and had mingled with them. He had studied them to find their weak point, to coil up at their core. Lentils are good, but don't gulp them down greedily, beware of the little stones that get caught in your teeth. Oh, disaster!

Tchilala started to tell how last night . . . but he couldn't go on. Which seer should one consult who could explain what to do to protect oneself?

The whole night. The whole night. A wild running of hooves around the house. Growlings in the courtyard. It seems that somebody was tearing off the tin sheets of the roof. . . . Cold sweeps through the house. Silence. Growlings again. The howling of animals being skinned alive. He hears this uproar, but doesn't know what to do. Get up? He can't. His wife also can't move. Can he talk? No, he can't. His throat is frozen. Suddenly, silence again. . . . He is finally going to be able to get to sleep. But now he hears voices in the courtyard, people who are talking. Well yes, but neither he nor his wife understands a word of what they say.

Lilesu had not witnessed what had happened in his house in his absence. When his wife came home after a visit to the hospital where her sister had just given birth to a baby, the children told her that there was a man in the house. "Who?" They had never seen him before. "What does he look like? Did you let him in?" "No, mama, and he is dressed like daddy on Sundays." She had concluded that it must be a friend of her husband, but how come he doesn't work? She enters the house and sees a man in the living room. She greets him; he doesn't answer. She gives him a glass of water, but he doesn't touch it. He doesn't look at her. "Are you waiting for my husband?" He doesn't answer, but since she has work to do, she leaves the man alone without any further questions.

She begs the children not to be noisy. She is going to be busy in the kitchen, because she had promised Victorine to make some peanut butter for her. She starts working and forgets the man waiting in the living room. In the evening, when I arrived home, the children shouted, "Dad, there is a friend of yours in the living room!" I asked my wife who it was. She didn't know, she had never seen him before. When you are exhausted, you don't ask too many questions. In the house, no-

body. "He didn't wait for you. I gave him a glass of water."
But where is the glass? No glass of water. Shrugging my shoulders, I paid no more attention to the event, though I should
have been suspicious. Weariness or something else took over
my mind. That happened the day before yesterday. Last night,
the same story again. Nobody saw him come. He was there.
Nobody saw him leave. My wife and the children saw him in
the house. Dressed in his Sunday best, he sat on a chair with
his legs crossed, saying nothing, looking at no one. What does
he look like? Nobody can tell. You know, you can't stare at
people. And you can't always foresee the consequences, not to
mention the trouble. You know how we are. We come, we go.
You go home and find somebody sitting in your living room,
you say hello. Maybe he just needs to sit down for a while,
or maybe he came for a visit, but has nothing to say or to
ask. . . . Well, it happens sometimes. . . . A man in his Sunday
best? . . . But what was really extraordinary was to see him
sitting at the foot of our bed, in the middle of the night. . . .
One is asleep, one feels the presence of a stranger, one wakes
up . . . my wife and I both wake up. My wife turns on the
light, or rather turns up the wick of the lamp, and there he is. I
see him and she sees him also. With a glance she indicates that
it's him. By the time I managed to open my mouth, he had
disappeared. I rub my eyes. In order to control her hysterical
fit, I am compelled to beat my wife, who accuses me of witch-
craft. . . . And what do you think I hear in the middle of her
screams? . . . Distinctly the crowing of a cock, as if it was just
behind our house. . . .

"Good Lord!" said André Sola.

The man he had invited agreed that something had to be
done, otherwise nobody would have any peace. But was it
really a question of peace? He was waging war, and he had to
be prevented from winning that war. Obviously, these words
didn't set their minds at ease. To be on one's guard wasn't
enough anymore. The guest promised to visit each one of their
houses. The enemy was dangerous, but the real problem was
that he could not be found anywhere. He is elusive. This
name, Lufwa Lumbu Luambu, is not a name. If it was a name,

the man who went by it was not a human being of flesh and blood. Does anyone possess an object that belonged to him and that he had touched? We should find something in one of the drawers of his desk.

Are you sure? If we can't find anywhere the body he is using, where are we going to find something he has touched? André remembered the handwritten prayer. And the others were gazing steadily at him. . . . He said, "I don't think so." There could not be any trace of the devil on the sheet of paper that had been blessed by a priest. But the devil often adopts God's ways, when the demon of disobedience has entered the body of man. The others couldn't understand André's reticence. Anyhow, the guest would be a better judge, and he settled the question: "There is nothing in this house that can be useful." "The Lord is watching over me!" sighed André gratefully.

In the void that was invading his head, André, elbows on the table and chin on the palms of his hands, was trying to find a harbor of peace for his tormented mind.

Victorine found her husband in that position, which could only bring disaster down on them. He sat in near total darkness, the three blinds of the room still closed, since he hadn't bothered to open them after the departure of Tchilala and the others. She knew what the smell of torches and the stale smell of chewed kola nuts and pepper corns meant. At dusk a wet and cold fog spread from the Tchinouka to the houses of the residential district.

He had not spared himself any effort, going places, listening, begging, consulting, and spending most of his salary to find out how to avoid the worst in the progression of this tragedy. He didn't look at her. She dragged a chair across the concrete floor to wake him up, to pull him out of this posture that would seal their fate. As far as she was concerned, she had quickly recovered from the shock of her adventure at the market. She didn't even listen any longer to the gossip still going on about that *guy* and that *event*. She spent all her time at Rosalie's or in the field that she farmed near the Protestant Mission, beyond Vounvou, in the midst of the coffee plantation of Ya Zéphirin Mpoaty.

She begged him to get up, but didn't ask how he felt. God knows what came over her to ask him if he had had news at the office of . . . She bit her tongue, embarrassed to be so thoughtless, to appear indifferent to his . . . "torment" and said the word only to herself. He acted as if he had just then noticed her presence: "Oh, you are back!" He got up and dragged himself to the threshold with the slow shuffling steps of a man recovering from a serious illness.

She asked him: "Are you eating here tonight?" in a tone of voice designed to cut off any inclination he might have to go out. Her voice was firm and calm and indicated that she was suddenly feeling pity for her husband, to whom she had been united before God, before her father and mother. "Perhaps I could pay a visit to Ya Ndindu." Ndindu was Muendo's widow, whom she was seeing regularly to help her get over the horrible death of her husband. It just happened that one of her plots was adjacent to the plot of Ndindu, which was just a small one with a few cassava plants. She herself was growing sweet potatoes.

André didn't answer. He remained standing on the threshold, his back turned to his wife.

The neighbors' children were competing in a counting-out game. They kicked a rag ball about, counting out: "101, 102, 103." "Winner, winner," shouted the youngest kids, excited by the performance of the champion.

The electric lights of the street that separated the elegant district from the rest of the Native Village always attracted crowds of children. Victorine sat down on the threshold next to her husband, who was still standing.

He knew what decision he had to take, he had to flee his office. If he had one chance to escape doom, that's what he had to do, to flee. Then peace would be assured. But this decision had not been generated by the group consultation he had just had.

Victorine was relieved when she heard her husband complain of the noise made by the children, who had gathered at the foot of the street lamp at the entrance to their yard.

She got up, took the prepared food out of the larder, and put on the table a dish of fried herring and sardines and a loaf of pounded plantain. "The food is on the table." "Thanks! Are you going to Ndindu's? Don't stay out late."

Ya Anglade, probably coming from the plateau on his bicycle, stopped when he saw André standing at his door. "Hey, André, come to my place in a little while." André agreed to

The Consultation

come by. Anglade was one of the rare half-breeds (his mother was Vili) who lived in the elegant part of the Native Village, five plots away from André. He was a civil servant and worked at the Otino Hotel, which, with the railroad, brought prestige to the town of Pointe-Noire.

What André heard at Anglade's impressed him, but not unduly. One can guess why. He was still so tense from his own worries that he didn't grasp the importance of what he had just been told. At the origin of the strike there was one white man who was promoting disorder so as to counteract the good will of France. If the authorities had felt compelled to deport a few people, it had been in order to avoid riots that would have endangered everybody. All who had a deported relative should be confident that they would see him back soon. Isn't Etienne Ling'si one of your relatives, André?

André was dumbfounded. "The good will did express itself, among other ways, by the fact that our colony was the only one to have a governor general who was a black man like us." Furthermore, a young civil servant had just arrived who was black like us. Anglade had been at his wedding, which was held at the church of Pointe-Noire on the day of his arrival. André knew about the civil servant and his wedding, since they had talked about it in the office, and Tchilala had observed, "That's fine, a black like us, but why not one of us?" André had silently blamed him, because he thought that such comment would bring more harm than good. Another proof of good will is that soon we are going to be told, "Vote for one of your own people, and he will be your representative. This is what we foresee after the end of the war." André had only listened with one ear. When Anglade had taken him aside, he had been nonplussed by his sibylline admonition explaining that he, André, should not forget that though Léon Anglade's father was French (Had he even known him?), his mother was Vili and lived under his roof and that if someone should be named . . . voted for . . . André had simply answered: "Yes, of course *aya,* I understand *aya!*" And then he had gone home. He knew what was in store for him, but of that Anglade had no idea. What exactly did Anglade mean? "That we shouldn't move? That we should let ourselves die? That we shouldn't interfere with the plans of the authorities?" But how should one behave, if one decided to protect himself from evil?

Before going to bed, he told Victorine that he would soon be forced to stay at home for a few days.

Victorine was not content simply to withdraw in silence to protest her husband's decision; she blew out the lamp and pummeled her eyes in the dark to make light within herself.

Life is like a suit that has to be always new, clean, well-pressed, and fitted to the body. "And before?" "Before what?" "What do you mean before what?" "Didn't we go naked ear-lier?" "That's right, life comes afterwards. . . ." "After what?" "Are you kidding?" "Come on, don't get mad! Anger won't solve anything." "Right, but why is he making a fool of me? I like to understand, to explain things, but not to be ridiculed." "Why me, me?" "But look at him, I don't know if I can con-trol myself. If I couldn't. . . ." "Well then, control yourself and explain." "Never mind, I don't think it's worth the trouble to try to explain anything. I know the game. You use up all your saliva trying to explain things to no avail, because they look at you with eyes getting smaller and smaller, so that you wonder if you are going to be held responsible for their blindness, on top of everything. It's too bad if some of you can't understand that first of all life must be loved, otherwise it's nothing more than a bag of shit on a man's back or something just as ridicu-lous. Life has a value, one should not make fun of it. One should laugh and joke *in life but not about life.* I stress *in* not *about!*" "Ah! that's it, in and not about." "You got it, buddy, in but not about." "You mean that we must laugh and joke in life but not about life." "Right, man, now you're with it." "Isn't that something—in but not about!"

André closed his eyes and remembered that for a long time afterwards his nickname had been, "In-but-not-about." When somebody addressed him, he straightened his gait, pulling at the crease in his white canvas trousers, lifting his chin and throwing out his chest. He recalled his nickname, but nobody else did, except perhaps Victorine or Tchilala, who at the time had drawn his attention to Victorine. Back then he was already stiff. His stutter didn't allow him to adorn his conversation with details that were beside the main point. However, such a big idea of life makes you conscious of the particulars, in which he was absorbed and lost, and from which he escaped, bursting and exploding:

If . . . if earlier it was . . . it had been the same.

Bu longu bu yenda toto-lô siba bula nien!

There is light at the ultimate borders of the world!

Since life comes from it, how can we not conclude that life is light. Night is not the mystery; light is the mystery. Light began with God, is God, exists because of God. Through God's light, life reveals itself as the greatest mystery of all. So don't mess it up, or, more precisely, don't make life unbearable to body and soul.

The reason why André didn't live in exaltation anymore but in confusion was because the reign of excellence had been disturbed and was nearing its end. Because no-light had been mixed with light. From now on one had to hide in the night, as one had lost the dignity of living in broad daylight, in the great mystery of life.

Disgusting wonder. And now: "Flies speak to men." What will men do? Will they have to wander over the wounds of mankind? The world is one big wound: "*Bazinzi baka tuba y batu*" (Flies speak to men). Tchilala, who had sung these words, was triumphant. And André would not be able any longer to have him behave more cautiously, to moderate and dampen his lachrymose xenophobia. What he thought life had been in the past had now become threatening. The Christian in him said, "I have not seen my brother." The pagan said likewise: "*Ndotchi*, sorcerer, evil being." In what do I believe more? In the calamity that has hit me or in hope? He knew and didn't know. Not because he, André, had not qualified for the priesthood, but because he knew what he had to fear most. God had not taken all the light out of darkness. God is all light, that is why the light he gave us is a mystery. If he had given us all of light, we couldn't bear it. But was he, André, going to find his way out of the night?

He will resign his job. He will leave his office. . . . Victorine had not said anything. Terror prevented him from being overwhelmed by his wife's silence. If he could protect himself, he would also protect her. He prayed until dawn.

12.
Friday, June 23

When Muendo woke up, he ate the meal that had been prepared for him the previous night and decided to make a few
important calls on his way to work. He lingered for what
seemed an awfully long time. He wanted to shout to his wife,
who was busy in the kitchen washing the dishes from the
previous day: "*Ho amua!* ("My friend!") I have finished eating! . . . Come now! I don't hear the children, they are not yet
awake." They already had three sons. His wife was pregnant
and would give birth in a few weeks, or even sooner. "Give us
a girl this time!" Why was he complaining? It's a blessing to
have sons, it means more working hands in the family. Now
people say it assures the continuity of the name.

Three sons, three boys who were growing up in good health.
Maybe a daughter next time. Later. He couldn't make up his
mind to leave, to walk to a forest of boles, of trunks that lay
wounded and hostile. For thousands of days they had stood
upright, defying the sun, a sanctuary to ancient gods in ancient times. . . . He had to go toward that truncated life, toward the scent of wood, that hard wooden flesh that had survived so many hurricanes! He made a gesture that provoked
an amused rebuff from his wife. When he stroked her belly,
she said: "What are you doing?" His wife, his children, his
home, his brother, his family, they all belonged to him. They
were his life. "I am going," he said. His behavior astonished
his wife, as he had always been ready to leave as soon as he
got up. She heard him call in the enclosed courtyard of the
Senegalese house left by their deceased father to his brother
Sow, who lived there with his family: "Hey! I'm leaving for
work!" That wasn't the way he usually was. She thought he

must be upset by the death of his friend and by the wake from which he had returned soaking wet. The rain had been threatening for a long time, this last rain of the rainy season. The rain had turned the backwater of the Tchinouka into a wild river intent on drowning everything in its path. Part of the dam, over which the muddy road went, had collapsed. Children, naked or covered with rags, gazed at the whirlpools of muddy water that were swallowing up all kinds of vegetation, ferns, and grasses. . . .

The dam withstood the rain thanks to the clumps of Chinese bamboo planted along the side. This was Elenga's rain. The roaring wild water of Elenga's rain. He thought that it was difficult to imagine him dead and therefore to weep for him. . . . The heavens had taken care of the weeping. The heavens knew that Elenga had to die, the heavens knew when he died, but we, we were in doubt. The heavens let us doubt and then they burst into furious tears, weeping in our place. We end up first with hardened hearts and then we don't believe what we are told. That is life. He still didn't quite believe in this death and wondered how Elenga's uncle would receive him. He imagined his astonishment. . . . Not his astonishment, but his indignation, because he was not the kind of man to accept the gruesome offer of having a coffin made for someone who was still alive! Perhaps he would call him a rotten Vili drunk! How could he be a rotten drunk when he had not drunk a drop of wine? . . . He saw grief on the face of the woman who said she was the wife of Malonga, the medical supervisor: "Yes, he is here, wait a moment!" Her expression was confirmation that . . . O Lord, who are we? Repressed tears tightened his throat. The woman sitting on the ground, leaning against the wall, her arms, shoulders, and face covered with ashes, silent and exhausted, must be Elenga's sister, he thought. Malonga appears at the door wearing a black armband pinned to the sleeve of his khaki jacket. How illusory was this doubt! Muendo spoke quickly: "Elenga was our brother. I will cut the planks. You don't have to worry about the planks. Laurent Sow is my brother," he added to give weight to his offer. Who didn't know him? "If somebody comes by, he will find me at the Scieries Réunies, next to the village of the Popo fishermen." "Fine, fine. I'll come, I'll come." And Muendo left more confused and moved than he had been at the wake the night before. "Well, now I have forgotten to ask when the funeral will take place, today or tomorrow?" He was already beyond Antonetti Stadium and too far away to go back. "I'll ask the old man when he comes by." And now he was indeed going to saw the planks . . . for poor Elenga! Luambu was not going to tease him, and Elenga wouldn't tease him any longer. What did he used to say to tease me? If only I could find the son-of-a-bitch who shot him, I would make him fuck his mother till he died and then I would shit on his corpse! By God, I would, Elenga! Really, even if you were my brother, I couldn't grieve more.

He stared at the people he passed, at the people who walked next to him, in front of him, behind him to check if their faces showed grief for Elenga's death! Did they know that he had died? He went on, walking right into the puddles. Well, they wash your feet, but the problem is that you don't know what you are stepping on. The pools made by Elenga's rain. The rainy season had waited for Elenga's death to depart. How did it know, when we didn't know anything? He teased me about the letters I had asked Luambu to write. But they were not really for women, it was just a way of talking . . . talking . . . to give myself a kind of reputation . . . so that he could tease me! . . .

In spite of having gone out of his way to the hospital, he arrived at work well ahead of time. He thought for a moment that he could ask for a leave of absence because of the death of his brother, no, his friend, he corrected himself superstitiously though his boss might not agree, and furthermore, how could he leave now that he had promised planks for the coffin. What would old Malonga think, even if he went by the hospital to let him know that really he couldn't saw wood with this weight on his heart, because it was unbelievable to die like that? He was greeted with exaggerated deference, he thought. He even noticed astonishment on the faces of a few who felt it was indecent of him to come and work when . . . Of course, he hadn't come to work but to cut the planks for Elenga's coffin! The bell rang as at school. The engines started droning. A huge log was already in place. The big wheel of the saw became invisible through the dizzying speed of its spin, lifting a cloud of sawdust. Muendo heard himself say with Luambu's voice: "Let's go." An endless screeching rose through the air with the splitting of the mahogany log.

Luambu missed Muendo by a few minutes. A pregnant woman told him that he had left not long before. He thanked her and left. He also went by the hospital, glanced at the medical supervisor's quarters, but didn't go in and continued on by the plateau road, which was all mud where it had not yet been paved. At the Mission, he got on a truck crowded with workmen of the Chargeurs Réunis and got off near the Harbor Hotel, which, it was said, had belonged to old Portella. He was a black, a Vili, who had died extremely rich. More unbelievable than a legend. The movie house of the harbor had belonged to him, so actually he owned half of Djindji. The truck went on and he walked back to the C.G.B.C. where he arrived at almost the same time as his colleagues. As he had expected, Elenga's death (though he was not mentioned by name), the strike, and the people wounded in the strike were the subjects of their conversation. They added to the accounts they had given Wednesday or Thursday afternoon, Wednesday rather, the day of the first walkout by the workers of the C.F.C.O. It seemed that there had also been tentative strikes at the harbor. Mengha, who was well informed, said that the authorities believed that this was a rebellion of the blacks, who had taken advantage of the fact that France was deeply in trouble to revolt . . . to revolt and sink back into savagery. . . . There were ringleaders, agitators, criminals! But the authorities were watching. The proof was what had happened at the C.F.C.O. Sola said: "Ho, ho, ho!" with an offended expression, not because he didn't believe what Mengha was reporting, but . . . : "Good Lord, some people are unconscious, really unconscious! Also at the harbor!" Luambu was waiting for one of them to say that the death had been justified, which would make the others stop and think. Tchilala was the one who started the horrible tale. . . . The dead man was a young Lari, wasn't he? Those people are headless and proud of being headless. They are like sardines in a can! He was the nephew of Malonga, the medical supervisor. André Sola stammered out again: "Ho, ho, is it true? My God, my God, poor old Malonga!" Tchilala didn't feel sorry for anyone: "It's all right, minds will . . ." "What do you mean minds, first they must have brains. . . ." "No, *aya,* minds will calm down, a death makes you think." "You forget that he was a Lari, and from those people, headless as they are, I fear the worst!" "No, no, you are mistaken, there are not so many of them around here, we are in Pointe-Noire after all and not in the Lower Congo. If it had happened over there, I might agree!" "That's not my opinion." "And why is it not your opinion?" "I am going to tell you. . . ." Luambu got up and left. He couldn't listen any longer.

They had begun to relax. They were splashing in the mud of their consciences. Their lives were mud. You wouldn't find a drop of clear water in them. The desire to live beyond routine, beyond carelessness was one more reason to be choked. Someone was whispering in his ear: "Stillborn, stillborn."

He tried to remember the story in which one is surrounded by invisible walls and cannot imagine coming out of the nightmare! Throwing oneself against the void, the invisible wall, one bounces back, while the heart jumps and the blood curdles. In order to sleep, you go into a deep forest where lianas wind round your neck, your feet, and bind you. How did you sleep? I find it difficult to say all I want to say. But who says everything that is in his mind? There are things, words that are stuck in the head, which grow stale and rot in the heart. The heart doesn't need mold, only clear blood, but all these words smell bad while they rot in one's head, because they are too difficult to express and anyhow never at the right time. How do you want . . . What did you want to say? What he wanted to say was how disgusted he was by their attitude, by Sola's words and those of the others.

When Monsieur Martin entered the office, Luambu sat down again. He sighed, grateful for the relief. If only they would shut up. They immediately covered their faces with masks of allegiance, of silent submission, and followed with devoted eyes the few steps that Monsieur Martin took in the office. "Sola, are the inventory lists ready?" "Yes, Monsieur Martin." "When you have finished with the books, you will bring them to me." "Yes, Monsieur Martin." Monsieur Martin gave Luambu a bundle of sheets that he held in his hand: "I want you to transcribe these documents and put them in order by noon. Follow the directions carefully."

The silence that followed Monsieur Martin's exit was soon broken by Lilesu, who was eager to hear Mengha's opinion. "My opinion? Well, you know . . . The wake took place at old Loubaki's, André, that's not very far from your home. . . . When? Last night!" "There you are, you caught on right away." Silence. Silence. Lilesu and all the others, André included, who pretended he had understood, did not grasp what Mengha was alluding to. He shrugged his shoulders and became silent. At last they all became silent. If only they would remain silent for good. He decided to block his ears. In any case he wasn't interested in what they had to say and would say. Who was the fellow who died? Which walkout was it all about? Who were the people behind the names that he recalled . . . Julienne, Mazola, Muendo . . . Elenga. I don't know any of them. And these men, mere shadows in this office, why was it less boring to live with them than to tramp in the foul mud of the Tchinouka swamps? Why was he still sleeping when he should have woken up and gone to work? In spite of the fog, a new day had begun. His legs are weak and don't support him, especially in the mud, which is getting blacker and slimier. But, of course, he can stand, he is in the dry grass on the seaside, on top of a dune. It makes you dizzy to look at the sea from a height. But he can't stop looking at it. The ebbing sea has left a strip of sand, which disappears in the waves. The water is clear. He sees the fish swimming playfully and lazily about. If he extended his hand, he could catch them.

Friday, June 23

But from where he is, his arm would have to be a long pole. He can't go down, he wouldn't be able to land on the strip of sand, and would be carried along into the waves; and being as heavy as a rock, he wouldn't float. The thought of it chokes him. Air, air. He has the gills of a tuna, on his back is the fin of a shark, why is he afraid of drowning? It has never happened in such clear water. Look, over there the beach becomes wider. Damn it, it still goes down abruptly. What is that fellow doing there? I am too high to see what he looks like. What is he trying to hide? Now, why do you pretend that you can't see that this man is trying to hide the body of another man under a heap of rubbish made of bits of wood, grass, seaweed, sand, and rocks? It's certainly not a place I would try to hide a body and conceal my crime. Hey, can't you see that the sea won't allow you to bury and dirty this body with all the trash you are throwing on it; the sea will unearth the corpse and wash it. You are not at the end of your troubles. Look right and left, there are two more bodies that the sea has already disinterred. There, and over there, in the water! They are so black in the clear water that you can't miss them!

There you are! Claim your innocence. Don't shout! Don't shout! Luambu woke up from his nightmare, hypnotized by the images still vivid in his eyes that were coming back like scraps of a song whose true words have been forgotten and which would have given a less tragic meaning to the tune that he keeps humming insidiously within himself!

He was hiding in the darkest folds of his dark soul and was not able to use both his arms and his heart to save his brothers who were in mortal danger. When fear left him, he washed his eyes, but he didn't see that the day had replaced the night and that it was time to face life and free himself from remorse.

Someone patted his shoulder: "Hey have you finished the work that Monsieur Martin gave you?" Don't scream, don't scream! André Sola gave a start. Why, did you hear me scream? Did I scream? Sorry, sorry! All right, and your work? . . . I haven't start . . . What, and what is this? So, there you are, it's done. . . . Yes, it's finished. Luambu got up and took his work to Monsieur Martin. Behind his back André Sola tapped his temple with his forefinger to draw the attention of all the employees. It is as if I had awakened him from a deep sleep.

It's impossible to be the friend of a fellow who is always absent.

He stood aside to let his coworkers pass, and went out last. He opened his arms, inhaled deeply, and gulped down a few mouthfuls of air with a grin of extreme delight. Then he froze. An engine in the distance made a noise: Vo, vo! Who is booing me? he thought. Whistling away, hands in his pockets, he crossed the street, made a feint with a pebble and shot it toward the railroad. Then he shook the hands of the people gathered under the almond tree, some sitting down, others leaning against the railing of the freight station. "Oh, Mazola, there you are! Come, you have never seen Julienne? Well, here is Julienne; Julienne, this is Mazola. Mazola is the sister of Elenga, whom you see there. I didn't think I was going to see him today. I was told that he suffered from a weak chest. He is better, that's fine. It's fine! Ah! . . . Come on Muendo, it's not the moment to pretend to be shy. Don't look as if . . . Oh, what was I going to say? Well, my friends, I thank you for having come promptly to help me out! Nowadays work is the bed on which we die! But I am not accepting that. For heaven's sake, don't laugh like that! You are going to be thirsty and will only swallow dust. Shut up, don't laugh like . . . Come on! Come on, let's be serious! Look, you make me feel like grinding my teeth! But I am not going to give you that pleasure!"

He left abruptly while everybody was writhing with laughter and found another pebble with which to dribble. Never had the workers of the C.F.C.O. seen a clerk as funny and as cheerful as he was. They would have laughed even more if they had witnessed the encounter of Luambu's head with the knotty trunk of one of the almond trees planted along the harbor road, the last one in the direction of the harbor, or in the other direction, the last one close to the station.

Friday, June 23

His expression was that of a good man hurt in his dignity. He woke up and probably understood that the world is cruel to those who think that if one doesn't face life, he is free of the duty of modesty and good behavior.

He remembered everything. Everything. Elenga's death! He was overwhelmed by a violent urge to sob, to rebel. But to rebel against whom? A leaf from the tree against which he had bumped fell on his shoulder, then at his feet. He looked at it and picked it up. It was bigger than one of his hands. It was speckled with spots of rust and coral. The leaf was answering his question: his life was smaller than this leaf and would fall one day on the shoulder of someone, then at his feet.

One day he or someone else will crush it under his foot inadvertently or mistakenly. . . . Elenga should be buried deep in the ground so that if one day somebody walks over his grave, he won't step on the dust of his bones!

He remained for some time leaning against the trunk that had knocked him awake, breathing with difficulty. A woman, probably one of those who sell food to the workers at the freight station, stopped in front of him and asked: "You are not feeling well?"

He hadn't even noticed his nosebleed. He said: Oh, thank you. "Do you want something to eat?" There was compassion in the woman's voice and not the obsequiousness of a saleswoman who wants to attract a customer. The return of his appetite chased the gloomy thoughts and made him aware of his empty stomach. His first reaction was to refuse the food offered by the saleswoman, since Mazola was going to bring his lunch soon. He looked in the direction of the C.G.B.C. while fumbling in his pockets. The woman placed the white enamel bowl on the ground, squatted down, and using a leaf as a cone filled it with a few morsels of fried fish, added some red pepper and two dumplings of *foufou*. But as soon as he had paid the woman and taken the food, his hunger vanished. He handed the food back to the seller, who looked annoyed. He said to her: "Keep the money." Then he turned his back and left: "Hey, why? Hey, why?" shouted the woman. As if he knew! . . .

The Madman and the Medusa

Doctor Grosgendrin said to Malonga: "Take care of your nephew's funeral." He took 200 francs out of his pocket. Malonga thanked him.

Had Muendo come back two hours after his visit, he would have found the young woman still sitting at the same place, powerless and stunned, with traces of tears running down the ashes that covered her face. But as long as he lived, Muendo was not destined to visit a second time the quarters of the medical supervisor. . . .

If you don't want to sink in the loose sand, you have to walk fast. Out of breath, Luambu collapsed on the sand. When he faced the sea, he realized how ridiculous his internal turmoil was. In the same manner the sand remains calm opposite the sea that moves endlessly, hurls itself, pants, growls, bites, nibbles, laps, sucks, drivels, rattles, and loses patience because it cannot achieve the orgasm sought by its tortured guts. Has there ever been a woman whose thigh, hip, or belly had the softness of the wave that approaches slowly and voluptuously with an iridescent crest, rolls itself up before throwing itself at the pleasure that dissolves it. Very well! I am now a dying old man who is revived by the view of a young virgin! He gets up. If he can chase death, life will survive. Peeing in the sand, he draws a woman's vagina and fills up the bottom of the central slit with his urine. There is now a large hole in the sand that looks like the entrance of a crab's dwelling. He admires his work. He sits down again on the look-out and watches the sea. Iodine has the sour smell of a vagina that has matured in lust! The flesh of so many people has melted into the earth! Good-bye Elenga! Good-bye Elenga! Poor kid! He gets up. Impatiently he unbuttons his shirt. . . . He wants to be naked to face the wave that fascinates and seduces him. "Hey, why?" He turns around. The saleswoman is there. She holds the bowl on her head with one hand, and with the other she offers him the cone of food for which he had paid. Disconcerted, he buttons up his shirt and doesn't seem to understand what the woman wants. She watches the eyes of the man or she tries to understand what is going on in his head. "I am not a beggar." She bends down, sticks the cone of food in the sand, and leaves.

Masoni asks: "Are you going away?" Malonga answers: "Yes, to get the coffin." Masoni says: "I'll go there." Before leaving for his appointment with Muendo, Malonga approaches Mazola. Masoni looks at him, because she knows that he won't know how to talk to her. So she anticipates his thought: "Come on, you don't want someone else to wash the feet of your brother. You will cut his nails. Come, my dear child." Malonga scratches his head, because he would never have thought of saying that. On the threshold he met Massengo, who greeted him in the old traditional way, one hand holding the wrist of the hand extended for the greeting. Malonga was moved and thought: when common sense again prevails, God knows what His will shall be. . . . "Thank you for coming." Massengo didn't allude in any way to the quarrel of the past Wednesday. He who has never been young may blame the pranks of youth! He who returns to the place of his crime denounces himself. Since he has come back, it means that he is innocent of Elenga's death. Still he won't avoid the gossip of the people who happen to know of his rejection by the late Elenga or prevent their insinuations. If he intended to scold the brat, he certainly had not wanted it that way, God is my witness! What a pity, my Lord, what a pity. "His wretched sister has been speechless, headless, faceless ever since." "It's a calamity that robs one of speech." Malonga repeated Massengo's words. "It's a calamity that robs one of speech. I am mourning my brother a second time."

He raised his head at the noise of the rattling of planks. Somebody hailed him: "*Ta* Malonga, I am bringing the planks. *Ta* Muendo asked me to do it." He had wanted to spare him the trouble of going there himself. A friend of Elenga's gave us the planks for the coffin; some people are really generous! "Yes, yes." Many people came and made donations. Many.

Massengo remembered that he had also brought his contribution. "Excuse me, I had nearly forgotten." Thank you, thank you for him. It's very generous. No, not at all, not at all. The planks had been brought on a rickshaw. Do you know where Chief Loubaki lives? Yes, pop. Take them there. There is no reason for me to bother him now. I'll go there later. Now I must find a carpenter.

Luambu glanced at the people who were sitting under the almond tree below which Mazola and Elenga used to wait for him. He wavered slightly, rubbed his eyes to convince himself . . . and looked a second time. Their eyes followed him with a smile that ended in wonder. This man was not the halfwit who previously had taken them for God knows who, Julienne, Mazola, Elenga, Muendo. . . . Do you think he is the same? How can we be sure? This one is very stand-offish. You can't joke with him. . . . He didn't have the gait of a drunk who looks around senselessly. He didn't seem to be concerned by the obscene joke hurled at him in order to challenge him. But what really shocked him was to see people standing at the place where only Mazola had the right to be in order not to miss him when he left the office. Mazola or Elenga. She would not have been content to wait among these bums who he had mistakenly assumed were workers of the C.F.C.O., those wretched people drawn to the city who willingly followed their natural tendency to laziness. He was speaking now like someone he had heard . . . who was it? A European, of course. But who? Perhaps Monsieur Martin when he was bullying the niggers who were swarming at the door of the warehouse.

Malonga changed his mind. He could see Muendo first and thank him and then go to Chief Loubaki. Massengo was willing to keep him company, as he wasn't tied up until the afternoon. When tragedy strikes, most other duties lose their importance. Malonga talked about his family, about the direct line from which he is descended like his older brother, the father of Elenga and of your . . . of Mazola, as well as two married sisters who lived in Brazzaville and who had been the first to take care of the orphans of their older brother. Our entire family is from Kinkala. As the Vilis say: I am a real *Tchilanda Laï*, I have followed the railroad here. And I have seen all kinds of deaths. . . . Each death upsets you in a different way. The living will never get accustomed to the idea of death. . . . Perhaps there is an old belief referring to men and women who never lost their lives! But old beliefs have nothing to do with civilization. He said that for the teacher, who, like him, was closer to civilization. To learn to read and to make money were steps toward civilization and progress. His brother who drove the express train also wanted progress. (So did Elenga; if he hadn't ridiculed the teacher, you could say that he was also for progress.) No, it isn't true that progress kills people, it's what remains of the old primitive beliefs. He had to go on talking because nothing is worse than to keep silent when suddenly your heart couldn't care less about civilization and your head turns to the beginnings of time and the roots of the family from which you have descended. And when they have all heard you promise that they would cry only in their hearts, but he didn't know what to do now that they wanted a big funeral in which all his coworkers would take part. How could he face the fact that it was, not the living, but the dead who had wept over Elenga? It had been the most terrible night for anyone to live through. The man, the uncle, the medical supervisor, were all speaking through one mouth. Words formed on his quivering lips, others drowned in him not without bitterness, and still others vanished, mocking him and calling him all the names under the sun. But he shrugged his shoulders because in the end only the medical supervisor was right, though in a truly shocking way! The saying, Cursed be the bearer of evil tidings, did not concern him, and was not fitting in this case. Of course, Elenga was going to be buried, but where? They knew where, but the price to be paid was enormous (it is hard to hold back one's tears, just as hard as preventing the Tchinouka from overflowing and drowning everything in its path after the rain—the heavens wept along with

the dead—one can't, but then one could, one could). He had
succeeded in turning the body over so that the nails could be
clipped, the hair cut, and even if the living didn't mourn it, but
who hasn't mourned . . . in silence? The teacher kept silent
out of respect for the grief of the uncle of the young woman he
wanted to marry, out of respect also for the pain, or rather the
sadness, that was invading him and numbing his tongue.

Malonga changed his mind a second time. Perhaps it was
better to take care of the coffin now, since he didn't want to
leave all the burden to Chief Loubaki again! On the whole,
the wake went very well and without mishap, but if Elenga's
friends were going to leave their work to be at the funeral, it
wouldn't be possible to avoid incidents. . . . He concealed a
triumphant smile, which he owed to his resourceful mind:
Elenga would be buried Sunday morning, at the time or just before the mass for the dead when the workers of the C.F.C.O.
would be in church. He didn't share with Massengo the poor
invention of his mind, which seemed a concession, a tribute,
to progress. For what the authorities wanted to avoid and
what he himself was afraid of was to have the railroad workers turn the funeral into a massive demonstration. "May he go
peacefully to his last resting place, accompanied by the grief of
his relatives and not by wrath: wrath is madness." They
turned back.

It happened so quickly they couldn't tell exactly how. All of
a sudden, they saw the body collapse and fall right there. He
had been busy with a log, putting it into place. They don't
know if he had come too close to the saw. When the big saw is
working, you have to hold on firmly, even if you are two yards
away, you have to be careful. . . . No, no, I didn't see what
happened. I was over there, far away. Only afterwards I saw
the pieces of the body and the blood splashing over everything. Brr! . . . Your stomach has to be pretty strong in cases
like that. One of the apprentices lost control and rolled around
in the sawdust; you could hear his screams in spite of the
whistling of the saw. . . . He was cut and thrown up in the
air. . . . I saw the body fall. . . . Someone, I don't know who,
had the presence of mind to turn the saw off, too late, how-

---

ever; . . . it could have gone on running. . . . The faces of all the workmen had turned grey and were frozen with horror and terror under the usual layer of sawdust. The boss's white face seemed even whiter in spite of the tan he had acquired during his many years in the colonies. The planks that had been cut and piled up that morning were splashed with blood. Nobody could speak without shivering or having his face twitch. Work had stopped of its own accord at four o'clock because of the madness, the revulsion, the terror, the anger, and the horror that had overcome everyone.

The foreman could not understand how his best machine operator could have been the unfortunate victim of this accident. The pitiful victim. He was aware of all the risks and knew all the security rules to be observed. It was fate. What else can you say? The line beyond which one should not go when the saw was in action was clearly marked on the floor: a death's-head with crossbones and those who were literate like him could read "*Kebe ku fua*" ("danger of death")! His face was intact, still expressing his firmness and eagerness to work. He never stopped. He had worked like a locomotive today, from the beginning, nonstop! From the boss's pinched lips came a single word: "Shit!" Going round in a circle, he beat the palm of one hand with the fist of the other. They expected a fit of rage from him because obviously the rule of security had not been observed. Bad luck, bad luck. What is bad luck, did he believe in it? Has one notified . . . the family must be notified. . . . Nobody had ever died, nobody had ever had a fatal accident. There had been squashed feet, one crushed leg, but now this sudden death and blood splashed everywhere . . . but the worst was . . . he didn't want to think of the worst . . . because superstitious as they are . . . there had already been a death at the C.F.C.O. and now Muendo. He belonged to one of the civilized families, didn't he? He would go himself and bring the news to the family!

Luambu heard of Muendo's death much sooner than he had heard of Elenga's death, which had occurred at about the same time the previous day. He was told by Jean-Pierre Mpita, who brought the news to André Sola, a neighbor of the family: "Have you heard? The brother of Laurent Sow died at the Scieries Réunies." While Mpita gave details of the accident as if he had witnessed it, André Sola was shattered and visibly shaken: "Good Lord, good Lord! Ho, ho, ho!" What else could he say? It's unbelievable. . . . And he added without quite realizing what he was saying: "It is a very serious occurrence!" Deep emotion always reveals itself in convention and conventional words. Luambu was listening, listening, listening, and what he was hearing became progressively imperceptible, inaudible, dissolving into an infinite landscape of languid beauty shading into the dull colors of a doomed twilight. Little by little the landscape changed, turning into the head of a poor old man who smiles at his misery, then into the still warm breast of a dying young mother whose lover's eyes fill with nostalgia knowing that they may caress but cannot save the victim of murderous fate. "How can you find your path in the night?" He had always known, but one day he is fated not to know! Muendo, the journey. Perhaps *Muendo* means that just as *Elengi* means joy. Perhaps Elenga means joy! Luambu got up. It must have been half past four. He left the office without saying a word to anyone. His back was stiff, his mouth shut, his eyes . . . But who has ever seen his eyes?

In the sky the moon was full and white. The fog covering the swamp fell heavily over the beach, almost at the end of the path followed by the night traveler, where three women spit huge flames as if to remonstrate with the moon. Sleeplessness had come to the land of night reached only by beings with multiple bodies. This traveler lost in the insalubrious areas of the night was Luambu and yet someone else at the same time. He thought he saw a fire with three flames, which was slightly strange, then a sensation of heat and cold flowed through his hair and the numbness in his legs prevented him from walking fast. Julienne falls into the water in which she flounders, and when she opens her mouth, water rushes into it and no sound comes from it, whereas she had opened her mouth to cry for help. But why does he pay attention to the cries of a woman when he has been called elsewhere to a threatening fire.

He had been warned: "Never take this path, especially not under a full moon." But he had the faith of a nonbeliever. It was pleasant to see the shape of his mouth when he was joking. (Only Mazola remembered precisely the shape of his mouth.) A snail married to a millepede accepted the blame of thinking he was shrewder than the others. One knew, everybody knew that sorcerers exist and many night travelers had been their victims, one losing a leg, another his eyesight, and still another his potency. There were things one could not do with impunity. There were doubts one could not allow oneself. As a challenge even. . . . It was not as a challenge that he had taken the road to Massabi that night, among those creatures that were crawling, brushing against him, sticking to him, whispering, whining, whining right under his skin.

Should he wait until the next day? It was not in his character to put things off until the next day. He was rather stubborn, sometimes in a terribly exaggerated way, this time as if he wanted to fall into the trap awaiting him. Nobody that night was going where he had been called. He was alone now and had only his legs and the weight of his body to rely on for his dark trip. He didn't turn around. Is it possible to wander at night without the company of evil? No! That was also one of the things one should not do. He knew it. He knew he was courageous, but not to the point of confronting the sun that dries you out, pulls your tongue, makes your eyes bleed with the abundance of light in front of you, with the illusion of water ahead for which you swoon, but it is bad for the heart to jump ahead fast and lose your breath. So he had to go at night, not to answer a challenge, but out of convenience. The dangers and the fear are nothing compared with the coolness the night lets fall on whoever dares to confront it, and to concentrate on what to expect at the end of the trip. All these lakes, these streams, these swamps, were inhabited and formed an inextricable labyrinth. It is the land of the past, belonging to those who exist no longer, who live there scorning their former hearts! The place is only attended by those whose bodies are not burdened by unnecessary flesh and bones.

He heard a laugh, not a laugh at a tall story but a laugh full of irony, that of Julienne, Mazola, Elenga, or Muendo? No, maybe it had been his own laugh? It was very much his kind of laugh, a controlled laugh with stiff lips to avoid showing the inside of his mouth. His tongue was forked, and nobody could see it without being hurt. He knew that people couldn't stand his exceptionally white teeth. Nobody thought that such a set of teeth was genuine, and because of his love of the night, he could read on the faces of people assumptions that annoyed him. Later, he suspected that somebody was laughing behind his back. Although he strained his ears, he couldn't hear clearly, and when he relaxed his body, he didn't hear the whispered words of a quarrel, but the loud shouts of a scuffle! Thick voices. Should he turn around? No! His imagination was playing dirty tricks on him. They were silly to think that he was going to fall into their trap. He was jostled, somebody pushed him in the back as if to hurry him up. He stumbled. The moon was motionless, close and interested—not lively, but interested. He looked at the moon, which felt his glance. Why suddenly this shameful rattle? Was the moon an accomplice in the plot against him? It didn't seem to be a bad sort. It spread a light so clear that one could not think otherwise. It could have been broad daylight, if there had not been this false silence and a coolness so pleasant that one wanted to share it with someone.

For the first time he remembered with sadness the reason for his trip. Was he going to arrive in time to be helpful? He thought that he should not be overtaken by doubt. He will find the strength to go on walking. He will be on his way the whole night. But where is the night? In spite of his longing he didn't examine his path to check if he could see the blades of grass. It might have been possible, but he refrained from checking, just as he refrained from finding out at which point of his journey he had arrived. It was more important to arrive on time. There was only one road, which he had to follow on foot. What an expression! However, he felt that he wasn't guiding his own steps. His destination carried him but not as fast as it might have. And why wasn't he walking himself? At this moment the road branched off and disappeared in fog. He felt it on his ankles. He pinched the legs of his trousers at the knee in order to lift them. He was astonished by his gesture and let his trousers fall again. He resumed his walk. His feet were following the path that was naturally wet from the fog. The fog now reached his waistline. Again, his reflexes tricked him and he walked with swinging steps, as if he were tramping through water. These gestures that he felt he made were unbearable. He stopped. He looked in front of him, but didn't turn around—you lose sight of where you want to go. It slows your progress down, so you shouldn't do it. He saw nothing but the fog curling around him. Suddenly the moon hurried away in the sky so fast that he felt dizzy and breathless. Fortunately. But he felt relieved only for a short time. The moon didn't get lost in the sky. Its light did not fade, but on the contrary threw the landscape into relief. The tufts of papyrus could be seen clearly, though they seemed to be transparent. Their fibers were whistling in the wind. The moon wavered, not knowing if it should go back, so fragile suddenly that it looked listless and feverish. It seemed embarrassed to be there so useless. Luambu begged it not to leave him to his despair. Why was he thinking now of ashes? Because he had confronted the night? Had he enjoyed doing it? For the sake of offending, death passes through ashes. Death offends, salt wards off. He was unable to lift one foot in front of the other. He was caught in the fog and paralyzed from the knees down. Only the upper part of his body was still alive. Exhausted, his eyes wanted to leave him. The moon turned around him, hiding from time to time in the clouds, still trying to make a fool of him. To placate it, he executed the dances of his distant childhood, but it defied him even more. His heart remained calm. The racket was entirely in his head, where waves of shrieks, laughs, laments, and tears succeeded one another. He was inhabited by an entire population that was searching him out and insulting him. His eyes couldn't see any of that, because they were turned toward another, more external, sight. The moon was reduced to a whitish and slimy pulp, beside a wide stretch of whitish and slimy mixture of mist and fog that looked like the vomit of a newborn. Sometimes Luambu's body felt bigger, sometimes thinner, but he clenched his teeth, caught his breath, and kept the nine orifices of his body shut tight.

In front of him, gliding like a shuttle against the warp of some material, he saw a small craft that was neither a canoe nor a boat but about as long as a body, without a stempost and cut straight down at both ends. In spite of its back-and-forth movement, the object was approaching him. If Julienne was on board, she had to be lying on her back or on her stomach. Maybe it was a trick from Muendo, who was disparaging his own death by spreading wood chips on all the traces of light still to be seen on his body.

A sudden fire set aflame the whole landscape with crackling noises, but for a moment it seemed that the moon and the boat were going to escape the blaze. When the first flames hit the moon full in the face, there arose from the boat a yell so horrible that the whole batrachian brood that until then had seemed drugged and overwhelmed by an infinite stupor, awoke with a lugubrious clamor. The sky became darker as the moon was progressively and entirely consumed by the fire with the resignation of a female salamander sacrificed to the flames of a blazing ordeal.

Paralyzed by astonishment, Luambu couldn't move. He was unable to help Muendo, who died silently in the huge splashes of blood-red flame. The thick layer of fog, as sticky as blood, still held him at the waistline stuck in hopeless immobility. A moment later the thick layer of fog again changed color. The caked blood had darkened entirely, but had remained rust-colored around the traveler, as harmless as an abandoned ant-hill that only bothers the plowman.

He stood motionless in the wind. A host of dark clouds were moving rapidly toward the sea. Wide horizontal stripes of indigo and purple spread over the eastern sky.

Lufwa Lumbu woke up. His neck and back were stiff. He was hot. It was still dark. He heard somewhere a tom-tom beating rhythmically like the heartbeat in his body. Doom, doom, doom! Then a pause and doom, doom, doom again, bringing the threat of an irregular heartbeat. His waking up in the middle of the night worried him. He felt that he was in a precarious and fragile state of health. The darkness weighed on his open eyes. But he didn't want to pay too much attention to his feelings. He strained his ears, but didn't hear anything like the beating of a tom-tom. He didn't have a clue to the meaning of his dream. Did he dream he was going to Massabi? His whole family came from there! Was it the goal of his trip to be the powerless witness of a delirious moon setting ablaze a man and burning him down to his blood and bones, when this man was joyful and generous? If he was powerless now, to whom could he extend his hand?

13.
Resignation

When on the morning of June 30, Monsieur Martin entered the clerks' office, he noticed immediately a change in the behavior of his employees. The usual competition by which each one of them tried to be the most deferential (or even obsequious) had been replaced by a simple politeness that he preferred. With a glance he examined the office and ventured a question about the absent employee. Had they had news of him, had he been found, and was he still in a coma?

"Precisely, Monsieur Martin . . . precisely." André couldn't find the right words.

"Precisely what, André?"

"There will be more calamities in our families, if we go on working . . . in this office."

"What?"

"He was a ghost. . . ."

André knew and had warned the others that it would be difficult to convince a white man of this fact. They had answered that they'd rather be considered uncivilized, no better than monkeys, and stay alive than risk their lives; all the sorcerers that André himself had consulted had given the same warning and had recommended that he act fast!

"That's the best yet, a ghost story now!" Fine, but the inventory cannot be postponed, and, moreover, he had no understanding of ghosts.

"Please, Monsieur Martin, let us go! We are sorry, yes, we are sorry, sorry. . . ."

Each clerk repeated: "Yes, we are sorry."

Martin turned around, feeling concerned by this "Yes, we are sorry" that underlined the request of their spokesman and supervisor.

"Now, go back to work, enough of this joke!" and he left the clerks with their ghost.

Alone in his office, he didn't have a fit of rage, but he burst out laughing. It beats everything, Luambu a ghost! He was sorry he hadn't asked them what evil the ghost would bring them.

Tchilala was the first to go back to work. The others followed his example. Once more André sprayed the room with holy water, said a prayer, and threw under Luambu's desk what would temporarily fend off the devil.

The concern of the boss for his absent employee was understandable. André was not in any way responsible for the work that Monsieur Martin gave directly to Luambu, who didn't receive it through the guard and who had to give it back himself. Luambu's talent for calligraphy had been discovered by André himself. Out of loyalty to the company in which he was employed, he had done something quite natural in drawing the attention of Monsieur Martin to Luambu's talent. This act had made André aware of the extent of his loyalty. So he deserved his new position and the "trust" they had placed in him. From stockkeeper he had been promoted to supervisor. Therefore, it wasn't a sign of mistrust if Monsieur Martin had chosen Luambu to work directly with him. It was while telling himself this that the gossip whispered once long ago came back to his mind: "This man used to work for a white man named Martin." This disclosure had been whispered, and he couldn't understand why it was surging now from the depth of his memory. He wrinkled his forehead, screwed up his eyes, his heart beat faster, and he started sweating.

Which Martin was it? He had known Monsieur Martin for years. Even before he joined the C.G.B.C. Monsieur Martin had already been working there. His mind was jumping from one idea to another, gathering information here and there. He recalled entering Monsieur Martin's office holding in his hand a sample of Luambu's handwriting. He recalled Monsieur Martin's gesture toward the bell. He saw Luambu again enter the office, which Monsieur Martin asked him to leave rather abruptly. Just as abruptly Luambu was promoted to the position of clerk. André himself had envied his handwriting. "He was involved with a white man . . . his name was Martin!" Monsieur Martin had not even seemed astonished that a simple guard . . . If Monsieur Martin wasn't astonished, he must have been the same one. . . . Had he heard what was emerging from the depths of his memory? Was he the same one? The boss is this same Martin? What had first been whispered became a loud clamor that threw him into confusion, made his pulse beat faster and his blood race madly through his head and body.

At the seminary, André had known a brother called Martin. That's why he had mentioned more than once, "Funny that the boss is also named Martin!" He even decided that one day he would tell Monsieur Martin that at the seminary he had known a brother Martin who "might have been a relative of Monsieur Martin." Either because he never saw Monsieur Martin on Sunday at the high mass to which all the Europeans came, or because he never had the opportunity to tell his boss of the coincidence, he had forgotten it. Now it was all coming back to him because of the words he had heard God knows where and when. But these remarks were upsetting his mind that was already confused. He was frightened, all the more so when he heard Monsieur Martin's demoniacal laugh coming from his office. Monsieur Martin was laughing at him because he wanted to escape the devil, and his laugh was triumphant.

His coworkers looked at him when, suddenly flabbergasted, he shouted: "Unbelievable, unbelievable!" Stunned and terrified, he stared at Monsieur Martin's door. All his colleagues moved toward him, ready to help him, though they didn't know what kind of danger was threatening him and themselves. Ah, how thoughtless they all were!

Could he explain himself? He was shaking his head to say no to the silent and anxious question of his colleagues. He opened his mouth, but his tongue was paralyzed, and he couldn't express with words the terrifying and unbelievable discovery he had just made. There was no hesitation in the tone of his voice, but astonishment! He saw himself the prisoner of a circle of white magic drawn around him by Monsieur Martin and Luambu. Monsieur Martin and Luambu were accomplices, confederates!

Resignation

They were going to destroy him because he had not given in to Luambu's friendliness. Both Luambu and Monsieur Martin were bad spirits in borrowed bodies that had survived the departure of their souls. Like crabs in snail shells. God knows how long the real body of Luambu had not been alive, and it could have been the same for the body of Monsieur Martin.

His forehead was covered with sweat, his hands were wet, the muscles of his jaw clenched, his legs weak. Monsieur Martin's laugh had created an uproar in his head, in which a nagging and wild lashing, whipping, and pummeling went on. Instead of giving in to Luambu, he had made novenas, placing God between the Devil and himself. But the Devil easily circumvented the obstacle.

"Please, let us go, Monsieur Martin." And Martin had laughed at them: they had been done in! How could they escape the trap? A trap? He saw in front of him the opening of a bottomless abyss, from which sulfur fumes rose. Hell. He hung on to his desk with the last of his strength, invoking the spirits of the departed who are under our feet and our Father in Heaven. "Ah, *Zambi Abkulu!*"

What did he want to say that couldn't come from his mouth? "André, André! What's happening, my brother?" Lilesu, who had a basic knowledge of "hospital medicine," said: "This is not an attack of malaria! We must tell the boss that he must be taken home!" The mixture of astonishment and pity gives a broken voice to the one who tries to control himself and to suppress his deep emotion. Tchilala, the pervert, always ready to attack, was losing his voice, and his courage to confront the braggart who is actually, as has always been known, a coward. Tchilala lost his loud mouth and for once started to shake when he saw André collapse. He couldn't understand the situation. The turn of events had branded him with infamy, and like a ship tossed about in the storm, he had become one of those nitwits who are afraid of the shadow of their wooden sword and who don't understand that to have lice is a sign of a lack of personal hygiene and not a stroke of fate. Unthinkable! But is it the right time to look for lice?

"Luambu lies comatose in his bed, but you blink once and he is not in his bed any longer." What kind of delusion is it?

The Madman and the Medusa

Could Luambu be a brother? Why didn't he look him straight in the face? "Where is your brother?" "Am I my brother's keeper?" A credo is like a set of jewelry, but the soul is like a banished daughter once the flesh of the body falls apart. Which fumes, which incense does she need to give the illusion that she is the daughter of the original fire? She is the daughter of the original fire. She is the daughter of the original fire and doesn't need a credo-passport to join the father. These words, "Am I my brother's keeper?" are the words of the flesh facing insanity. Did he recognize this brother? This brother could have been Luambu, whom he accuses in order to justify himself, who knows?

Indeed, André was not responsible for anybody else nor for the poor son of Ngoma-Luambu, called Tchiti-thi (by his mother who wanted to stress the fragility of the creature she had borne). Why not Ngoma N'kuanga, to imply that this son had been granted joy for the length of his life?

What is the delusion? It is said: "Face life and it will watch you live; if you don't face life, it will not take care of you!" Had he forgotten that? He could also say it in Christian terms. Without your guardian angel, death will push you and your steps will lead to the threshold of the abyss. In the language of the past the guardian angel is replaced by manna.

André! André! *Aya!* You are not faking, you are not hearing me, are you? Tchilala is already finding solace in the fact that Victorine is childless. He thinks that he might comfort her. Why is he already thinking that André has reached the last hour of his life and is therefore so confused and is going to be lost? The death knell obstructs André's hairy ear, and his eyes that were so vivacious a moment ago are now glazed.

He had been entrusted by all of them with presenting their resignations. . . .

Who invokes all the saints misjudges the Devil and brings much ugliness to the face of God.

And the Devil is behind the door at which André stares with an intensity that exhausts him. So they were accomplices. This discovery proved that it was not an invention of his insane mind if he knew that he was condemned.

Resignation

Why did he not call the soldiers to punish them instead of making fun of them and laughing at them? He was laughing at him, André. He was the only one to be concerned by Monsieur Martin's laugh. The others had resumed their work, though they had asked permission to resign. Now they were submissive at the risk of their own lives and those of their families. There you are, the Devil's sarcasms were only for him. The Devil doesn't need the help of the soldiers. He simply shows his victim that he can't escape from the trap and that he must die.

And there you are, Tchilala used to protest the invasion of their land by a crowd of people arriving from who knows where and who don't mind the evil deeds of the Prince of Darkness. Because it is easy to attack the *Bilanda Laï* but not the Devil when he appears in the body of a white man. Tchilala's gaze is aghast and pitiful. Oh, he knows he has fallen in the trap like me, like all of us. "Don't touch me! Don't touch me!"

Ah, they are all dumbfounded! And guns or saws had not been necessary.

14.
Saturday, June 24

Saturday morning Luambu got up, washed, dressed, chewed a kola nut, and started toward Djindji to go to work, but he didn't go beyond the hospital. He realized that he was pacing up and down in front of Malonga's quarters. The blinds had been pulled down. Going back and forth, his gait didn't show indecision, still less determination. There are automatic gestures that don't express anything: restiveness, exhaustion, anger. Nothing. Unconsciously, he retraced his steps and started toward Muendo's house. The fog of the dry season spread everywhere with a moldy or muddy smell. The raindrops of Thursday night had already been swallowed up by the dust.

Victorine, Sola's wife, saw him go by, but she didn't know that the man who walked with his head bent was a colleague of her husband's and precisely the one who had given her a chicken and a prayer in Gothic script as if from a missal. . . . She wondered who he was, a relative, a friend of the Sows who was bringing his condolences to the bereaved family? She pricked up her ears to check with what kind of voice the man was going to greet her. But the man went by without a word. The man seemed strange, and she felt disturbed. She would have been just as upset if she had seen a ghost. One could use a shortcut between her fence and the property of Février (a European in exile at the Native Village because he lived with a native woman) to go to the Sows, and this Saturday morning, since she was going there herself "as a neighbor visiting mourning neighbors," she watched all the people going by in order to know who they were.

As her husband had said: "It's more and more difficult to

understand what is going on," it was necessary to keep eyes and ears open. He had said that about the fatal accident that had ended poor Muendo's life. Then in the middle of this tragedy a child was born in "the desolation of the family's mourning." To be born under such circumstances! . . . André Sola had also quoted a sentence that referred adequately to the situation: "There are people who weep and people who laugh." It was cruel and sad. Put yourself in the mother's place . . . it's the worst thing that can happen to a woman. The people Victorine saw go by were all in deep mourning. . . . The man she had just seen must not have been informed of what was awaiting him where he was going. . . . Though it was unbelievable that anyone did not know of Muendo's death. Nobody had ever died like him! Perhaps nobody could die like him.

Luambu didn't join the group of people who went streaming from Muendo's house across to his brother's house. He heard nothing, he saw nothing, and let himself be jostled by the crowd. He had come there last night and yesterday morning. Yesterday morning it had not been for the same reason. "Muendo has just left for his work." At night: "Muendo has just died." What can one make of it? If the day before yesterday he had gone to the hospital in the morning, he would have been told: "Elenga has just gone to his work," and if he had returned at night: "He has just died." What is this refrain? Is it going to be a popular tune and be in every heart, on everyone's lips? It is too pitiful to become popular. What is absurd all the time isn't absurd anymore. And yet. Nobody greeted him, nobody exclaimed to him: "It's unbelievable, isn't it?" "Yes, quite unbelievable." And this diversion from the sorrow? What can one make of it? "Is it a boy or a girl?" "A girl, no a boy." "It's his refusal." "It's his refusal." "If I had been told that my eyes would see such wonders!" We have wept over women who died in childbirth, but who has ever wept for a man . . . a man! . . . What wonders will the child born into double grief grow up to witness? Luambu followed the funeral procession at a distance. After Muendo was lowered into his grave, his mother refused to go back home. She ran off, threw herself on the tomb, scratched the dirt with her hands, muddied her face: "No, I won't leave you here. They have abandoned you now, and they want your mother to abandon you also!" The women of the family held her hands and wept with her in a last farewell.

The badly planted graveyard was not well kept. The concrete markers were painted white and surrounded by weeds. The poorest graves were simple heaps of dirt and reminded you of the fields that used to be plowed and were now abandoned to the weeds. The ground where they dug Muendo's grave had been recently weeded. Prints of shoes and bare feet covered the ground with a blurred design like an illegible epitaph. The flowers looked dirty on the freshly turned soil and didn't suit the overall disorder of the place. Ridiculous. Luambu's glance lingered on this disorder to avoid the confusion that was invading him and would rob him of the control of his feelings. If he were to die in this town, this would be his final resting place. The place of ultimate passage. The earth was black and still wet from Elenga's rain, but thin. He looked for the place where Elenga was to be buried. He had lingered in front of his house, then near Loubaki's in order to find out the day and time of his funeral. But he came back from both places without the information he had sought. He was wandering like a blind man who doesn't need a dog. With the instinct of a sleepwalker, he had gone from Loubaki's to Muendo's and at last had followed the mourners who were carrying Muendo to his grave. His grave was a hillock of black or rather grey, dirt, loose because it was sandy. The black foliage of the mango trees, the ash-colored trunks and branches of the silk-cotton trees cast a gloom over the landscape that was accentuated by the cawing of the crows. He took a handful of dirt from Muendo's tomb and squeezed it. He was getting ready to throw the dirt far away, far from this miserable grave, hoping it would spread in the air, but he controlled himself, examined it, and stuffed it in the pocket of his shorts. He left then, abandoning Muendo to the wasteland that would be burnt over in the dry season, because there is no better way to clear the land.

He had nearly arrived at the market, when he remembered

that after all he hadn't seen where they had dug Elenga's grave. He wondered if he should go back. But it was too late when he finally made up his mind to return to the graveyard. At his back a crowd of people prevented him from going back. He was pushed to the center of the market among strong, spicy, and irritating smells, surrounded by women crying, calling, boosting their wares, jostling, joking: "*Aoua! Aoua! Ya peté-peté!*" What is there that isn't "sweet and tender?" The fritters, the coconuts, the eggplants, the flour of cassava, the *gari*, the smoked fish, the smoked meat, the dried sardines, everything was "soft as silk"! Cheap: half a franc for the whole bunch. The plantains: "soft as silk"! Take everything and give me one franc. The dry pepper: "soft as silk"! "You won't cry when you eat it." Worms in the cassava? Where? Oh, that! Well, either you take them out or you eat them with the flour and save on meat. Meat is expensive, even bones aren't cheap. . . . "Buy, mama, don't let the children starve! . . . Weevils in the beans? Where do you see them? It is sprouting! Sprouting? If you can't afford it, forget it! . . . These are French beans: *Ya soua, ya peté-peté.* If you are black, you buy black beans, these are for women, the white beans for women! Show them, mama, that your husband makes a lot of money. Expensive, no! Come close, closer! Look, this bowl and that one are already empty. Here are the last ones . . . there won't be enough for everybody. . . ." Luambu bought some kola nuts, some ginger, and a stock of licorice from a Senegalese woman wearing a turban. The crowd pushed him toward odors of salt: "Save on salt! You won't have to borrow salt from your neighbor for this fish, the salt is already in it. The good taste is in it! Don't add oil. The oil is in it." "Salted fish from the Portuguese! Cheap, cheap! Chicken from the Mayombe. Batéké chickens. Live. A hen? This one is going to lay an egg. . . ." He sticks a finger in the hen's anus. There is an egg. He makes an obscene joke to provoke laughter. The bystanders laugh. He is delighted. Indeed the egg is in there, bigger than my two eyes together! He sniffs his forefinger in appreciation and blinks excitedly at the spectators. Ah, life! "There is an egg! There is an egg! Give me three francs. . . .

Saturday, June 24

All right two and a half francs! Just because you are beautiful, my lovely!"

People watch the performance of a young boy in charge of catching the chickens and the hens in the bamboo coop on top of which is a smaller cage in which a rooster struts about. Each time the boy catches a bird, the rooster crows, twice gaily if it's a hen, once sadly if it's a chicken, obeying a sign from the merchant. The trick of the man and his rooster comes as a bonus for the bargaining. Here the slogan, "*Ya soua, ya peté-peté*," is not in use. Further on, there is a joyful bustle among the customers, who are mainly children, but the seller is offering something strange, astonishing. Luambu is startled when he recognizes the seller. He is the prophet, as Elenga calls him, or did. Luambu feels sick when he sees what he is offering his hilarious young customers, a basin of water in which jellyfish are swimming over a bed of seaweed. He starts the bidding himself. I say: "Five francs!" A bouillon out of that and you will never again have a bellyache and you will never itch in your entire life! Come on: "Five francs!" "Six francs!" shouts a half-naked brat! "I know you don't have the money, I offer seven francs!" Flabbergasted, Luambu watches the bidding. "Eight francs!" cries a little girl jumping with joy. . . . No, no! Take it, I am giving it to you for nothing! A bevy of eyes, popping out with laughter from the children's heads, converges on Luambu, who shudders. "He saved my life. . . . So I am giving them to him. Money brings death. He knows it. Ask him."

He took the jellyfish from the water and lay them on the ground. First, he separated the jellyfish into three piles; "There were three," he said, and then he changed his mind and made two piles. . . . "There were two, then . . ." He thought again: "No, he should have the whole lot. Of the three who saved me from the hands of the fishermen, he is the only one left! I am going to save your life." Then he made the children roar with laughter when he put a foot in the basin and started a dance that Luambu recognized as the one Muendo had not let him see the end of. He examined the crowd of children to see if one of them, like a statue of driftwood, had his eyes fixed on the

The Madman and the Medusa

dancer. It was unbearable, his ears were invaded by silence, as if he had become deaf, and the silence exhausted him as it emptied him. The children, whose cries he no longer heard, made faces of horror rather than joy. He could hear only one voice, echoing Muendo's, almost grieving and coming from behind his neck, where silence had not yet taken over.

"Don't listen to such nonsense, you can stay with the madman if you want, but I am leaving. Are you coming?" "Hey, hey! Are you coming?" Two little hands had taken hold of his hand and were pulling him. "Come, come!" The call was made by a weak voice blurred with the echo of another voice that could not be Muendo's, or Mazola's, or Elenga's, or even his own voice begging, pleading, on the verge of tears, tearful. The silence became less deafening. A violent "NO" escaped from his chest, scraping his lungs as it passed and bursting forth like an explosion that engulfed the laughter.

The dancer had tripped and fallen head first into the mass of jellyfish. Luambu saw the slimy, yellowish, and upturned eyes. He saw a hand with fingers similar to the claws of a bird of prey extended to him, grazing the air and trying to catch him, and though he was far from the harmless madman, the prophet, according to Elenga, his face was scratched by an unexpected gesture of the madman. He turned his eyes away, and as soon as he raised them he saw Elenga, his chest splattered with purple; he saw Muendo, who was losing half of his body like a badly split log. . . . He saw them mimicking the laughter of the children. . . . "Come!" He was pulled by the two little hands hooked to his hand and the hand extended to him by the prophet: ". . . will come out of it . . . life . . . take . . . save . . . life." The joy of the children was almost delirious. . . . He saw the burning eyes of the prophet. He closed and opened his eyes three times in a row and very fast to make sure that the insane raving that made the children laugh uproariously was not a product of his imagination.

He glanced behind him. He saw a little boy who was pulling his hand. "Come, come!" He might have been six or seven years old. He wore shorts with suspenders crossed in the back and made of the same khaki material as his collarless shirt. He was pointing his finger toward the chicken sellers. He let the child lead him, making one final effort not to turn around. Conscious and unconscious at one and the same time of what was going on, he was obedient like a man in a dream who doesn't mind dreaming twice the same dream or starting his strange dream all over again, because, conscious or unconscious, every bit of him wants its share. Therefore he acquiesced and followed the child he had never seen before, but every particle of whose skin he knew when he touched it, whose every pore was at the same time sweetish and harsh under the tongue with an aftertaste of baby's vomit and placenta. "He still smells of his mother's womb." His skin still had the natural odor of skin. With his thumb he felt the back of the child's hand. . . . He hadn't looked at the half-moons of his thumbs. . . . What else could they say that had not already been said? Indeed, what has been said cannot be gainsaid! One has to follow one's fate. . . . Luambu, hey, hey, hey! . . . "It isn't far!" No, the voice doesn't remind him of anything. It is clear, like the umbrella of the medusa. What does all that mean? Who took him to this market? What did he do the whole morning? If he is at the market, perhaps he is not working? "Money brings death!" Where did he hear that? "Hey, little one, what do you want from me?" "Come and see mommy." "You want me to see your mother?" "Yes." "And why?" "Mommy said: Go and tell the man over there to come!" "Ah, ah, if your mother said so . . . well, let's go."

The child was still holding his hand, but he advanced so hesitantly that he slowed Luambu, whose step was big even compared to Elenga's and Muendo's, so it was difficult in the swarming crowd for him to keep up with a child who wasn't very tall. "Don't you want me to carry you?" "No!" (The answer was categorical, the child knew what he wanted!) "What is your mother selling?" "She is a buyer." "Ah, of what?" He didn't hear the child's answer and didn't ask him to repeat it. Then suddenly the silence invaded his ears again. People's gestures and faces were expressing anger and threats. The only humming he noticed came from what he was holding. He tried to understand with his eyes what was going on around

The Madman and the Medusa

him. Women seemed to want to throw in his face fritters, cassava, coconuts, salt, eggplant. They were only pretending to throw and he raised an arm to protect his face and his eyes. He had a weight in the other hand which hung from his arm, which hung from his shoulder, which hung from his body, and his body threatened to collapse. Then again his ears opened up to the noise. He saw a child offering his hand, a child he had never seen before, but whom he knew he was not seeing for the first time. He had already seen him, where, when, under what circumstances? "Who is your father?" "It's not my father we are going to see, but my mother!" "All right, but who is your father?" "My mother isn't sure that he is still alive." "Ah, ah. . . . then let's go."

The child stopped. He looked all around. "Well, now!" "She was here." The child at last let go of Luambu's hand. His hand felt numb. He rubbed his wrist, then the back of the palm of his hand, and finally his fingers one by one. The crowd went on swarming around him. He was planted in the middle like a rock in the middle of a flooded river, in the middle of troubled waters swirling, surrounding, and jostling him. He fought off the dizziness as much as he could. "She was here, I am going to look for her, the flood took the child away, engulfed him, perhaps his mother also. What kind of story is that?" "I am the madman." His statement made him smile and burst out laughing. People looked at him with uneasiness. They even kept away from him, so that he found himself in the middle of an empty circle that the passersby avoided. The scatterbrained, those who walk without paying any attention to where they are going would suddenly stop just before the invisible circle and look around bewildered. It seemed that he was himself bewitched and could not take another step. In which country was he? How deferentially they all behaved! Had he been suddenly elevated to the position of sovereign, king of the misery, the hunger, the thirst, the laughter, and the sadness of the world?

The circle widened progressively as his kingdom thrived on scarcity and destitution, as his subjects withdrew on tiptoe while making great demonstrations of allegiance and submission. The smile on his lips was triumphant music. Nodding, he showed his contentment. "Indeed, the earth is heavenly." He imagines himself challenging Monsieur Martin. "No, this voucher is not in my handwriting." He didn't copy anything. Nothing at all. There is no reason to suspect him because he is black. Oh, oh! What a face. "Yes, it is your handwriting and not mine!" Cornered! Only two hundred francs for the dowry, a bigger stopper! "And here, Monsieur Martin, why do we have only fifteen kilos of gold instead of sixteen? Is that my handwriting? Cornered! Cornered! He rules. He corners them. It was M's. . . . The kingdom is less and less populated. He waits for total depopulation before taking a step toward the exit. What poorly educated people: he withdraws while turning his back on his prince!"Out at full speed, macaques! Gibbons, sapajous, orang-outangs, baboons! Get out!" He is unbeatable. A fly writes with its legs dipped in India ink, or in blue ink, or in violet ink. He writes like . . . and it is an exact copy. "Get out!" "I'll kill you. Admit your guilt, admit it, admit it." "Not at all."

He would rather die than admit his guilt and accuse himself of a crime he hadn't committed. He disappeared and was not seen again.

Monsieur Martin's books showed bookkeeping errors, and they were all in his handwriting . . . his. Luambu copies Monsieur Martin's writing. . . . And everything was lost in the whirlpool: Julienne, the child, the treasure gained with such dexterity, everything. . . . Soon the slack expression he had adopted, his heavy gait were all going to disappear.

When you try to dance on one foot, you fall on your face. That is not what he wanted to say, but he also wanted to say it. "Money brings death." He was not going to correct himself at every word. He woke up completely and understood all the words uttered by the prophet when he stood in the middle of the waves. But the dance had a special meaning that he hadn't had time to understand. Muendo hadn't given him the time. He looked around. Yes, indeed, he was at the market. The market was empty. So it must have been later than half past twelve. He knew that the impression of having seen the prophet dancing his strange dance was not really an impression, but the details escaped him. He was sweating, he was feverish. He wondered if he had a chill, if he was shivering. He thought that he didn't have a fever, but that he was shivering and cold. Perhaps that was the reason he didn't go to the office. He assumed that he had planned to go to the outpatient clinic, but he didn't know, he couldn't remember what he had done.

At that moment Mazola entered Luambu's house to see him and do what Elenga had begged her to do in her dream: "Start a fire in his house, wait for him, the wind will thunder, he will come back. He will take care of you, while I'll take care of Julienne. . . . Who is Julienne? . . . Just start a fire. . . ." Mazola entered the house and did what Elenga had told her to do in her dream.

In the street leading to his house, a woman and a child walked in front of him. The skirt, the vest, and the madras of her turban were of the same textile printed in green. The child wore khaki pants and a collarless shirt of the same khaki color. The woman walked slowly so that the child who was trotting along beside her didn't have to run. The young boy was about six or seven years old. He wasn't sure if he had seen that morning a child dressed like him. He realized that he was walking faster, then slowed down again.

There was nothing special about the woman's gait and the swinging of her arms, but they caught his eye. He wrinkled his forehead and racked his memory to find the reason why he was in a state of alert and why he felt compelled to stare at that woman's back and at the way she held her head. Where was she going? Who was she? People coming out of a yard came between her and him, and he lost sight of the woman and the child.

It was Saturday afternoon and in a few hours it would be Saturday night, and Saturday night belongs to everybody, as it says in the song. A group of very small men came out of a cross street. The leader was beating a *patingué* with a quick hand. Another made screeching sounds with a transparent sheet of paper stuck to his mouth. Still another one was beating a bottle with a thin sheet of iron. Two more men had made maracas out of two cylindrical tin cans pierced with small holes and filled with pebbles. The leader was snuffling between two sighs. They were practicing for Saturday night. Luambu moved aside to let them pass. He smiled at their stern appearance. The woman and the child had disappeared. Luambu didn't think of them anymore. And he was in a hurry to reach the clinic. Since he was cold and shivering, it was better to go to the clinic. Perhaps he was going for no reason. The consultations are generally in the morning. He could, if necessary, go to the hospital. . . . The blinds of the outpatient clinic were raised, and there was a crowd on the porch, mainly women, some with babies. He didn't know any of these women. . . .

The clinic has a red tile roof like its twin building, the school, which was the first concrete school of the Native Village. Both buildings were the first concrete houses there. Now you can't even count all the concrete houses. There is the Vounvou school, which by itself . . . then there are all the new houses of the residential district. Certainly, if he remembers all these details, it means that he must be better. He enters the clinic more as an observer than a patient. The male nurse has a strange way of treating his patients. He examines them from behind his window. Of course, the smell of antiseptic is so strong that it makes you sick. He looked at Luambu as if to size him up. Luambu also squinted, trying to identify and place the nurse. . . . "You are Jean Tati, the nurse?" "Yes, I am." "And you?" "You don't recognize me, of course?" "Why, of course?" "No, no, never mind."

Jean Tati was puzzled and clearly didn't like riddles, especially when they proved his memory deficient. Those who were close to him knew that he liked to boast about his good memory. "You had a cousin . . . wait a minute! Prosper Mpoba." "He is still my cousin." "And one of your relatives was Ndehlou Damien, whom I took to Diosso in the ambulance." "Well, it all happened a long time ago!" "Fifteen years maybe. That's right, that's right. It doesn't make us any younger." He repeated: "It doesn't make us any younger." He utters with real pleasure a sentence that he likes to utter. . . . "You see, in spite of my good memory I might not have remembered you." "But wait a minute, I have seen you lately, I have seen you lately!" "Right, yesterday. Poor Muendo. Last night. What a horrible death! Horrible, horrible. Good Lord. Even I who am accustomed to blood, I couldn't, I couldn't, I couldn't. Who can understand such a death? Oh, my Lord!"

Oh, hey! What are you doing? Come back. Catch that man, tell him to come back. Hey, hey! Luambu didn't turn around, didn't come back. Yes, that's the fellow, he is not sick. Is he insane or what? You had to wonder. The patients made a few comments that pleased the male nurse and his good common sense.

You can't take a step without hearing about death. . . . Do they enjoy it or what? Let's speak of something else. No more discussion about it. It's over, over. We won't mention it again. When we were together, did we ever mention it! That was a time! . . . I said to you: "One has to be careful, because one always ends by doing what one says." "You say: I am going to eat and you eat. I am going to sleep and you sleep." "You don't say, I am not going to die and you don't die." But who nowadays takes advice?

We are insane. We must speak to each other. People talk to one another. That is normal. Yes, it's normal. The opposite isn't normal. Otherwise one would lose one's sanity.

He was smiling as he talked to himself, full of the obstinate and unshakeable conviction that he had an appointment with life. Flirtatious, life resisted slightly . . . just the proper length of time before giving in and making a soft bed on which the body could rest. He couldn't understand the faces of the passersby.

Whatever their reasons are, they are suspect. They know how to twist you around, watch out, Luambu. They might decide that you are responsible if everything doesn't go right. I know what I am doing. I have my secret. You wouldn't know by looking at me.

Saturday, June 24

As he went by, people turned around and stared at him. He didn't answer any of their greetings, didn't nod to anybody. "What a bastard, that nurse! He really thought I was an idiot! I can't be ridiculed that easily." Watch out!

He saw running toward him the little boy from the market whom he had seen later walking by the side of a woman in his street when he was going to the outpatient clinic. "Why didn't you wait?" "But I waited!" "You should have waited longer!" "Are you scolding me?" "Don't you know that my mother scolded me because of you?" "But where is your mother?" "She is waiting for you at home." "Well, let's go then!" "What are you smiling at?" "Am I smiling?" "All right, let's not waste time!"

Mazola was sitting in Luambu's house. She didn't lose patience. She had been waiting since the beginning of the afternoon. Soon it would be night. Did it matter? The night is no stronger than the word of a dead man. Now that she was in mourning, she had all the time in the world to wait. And he would have the respite he needed so much. It is not easy to earn the money for a dowry. This promise was Elenga's legacy.

He didn't wonder why the night was falling so fast. He didn't wonder when he saw that the fires had been started in the village yards. He didn't wonder why he felt a chill, it was the season, after all. He didn't wonder either why his house seemed so far. It was not astonishing because he was taking small steps like the child who walked with him. He didn't wonder either why the fire had already been started in the yard of his own house. It was understandable because that's where the mother of the child was awaiting him. But he didn't understand why the child now said: "No, no, it's not here, she isn't here. Look . . . it's over there."

Luambu turned around so fast the he lost his balance very oddly and fell. His head hit something soft, recently upturned earth that had a little more consistency than a pile of medusas, but though it was rather acid, it didn't give one a rash. . . .

Before he fell into a coma, he heard a voice that he recognized without any doubt. It was the voice of Julienne, who said: "He who looks life straight in the eyes will not lose face. . . . Love life."

Caraf Books
Caribbean and African Literature
Translated from French

Serious writing in French in the Caribbean and Africa has developed unique characteristics in this century. Colonialism was its crucible; African independence in the 1960s its liberating force. The struggles of nation-building and even the constraints of neocolonialism have marked the coming of age of literatures that now gradually distance themselves from the common matrix.

CARAF BOOKS is a collection of novels, plays, poetry, and essays from the regions of the Caribbean and the African continent that have shared this linguistic, cultural, and political heritage while working out their new identity against a background of conflict.

An original feature of the CARAF BOOKS collection is the substantial critical introduction in which a scholar who knows the literature well sets each book in its cultural context and makes it accessible to the student and the general reader.

Most of the books selected for the CARAF collection are being published in English for the first time; some are important books that have been out of print in English or were first issued in editions with a limited distribution. In all cases CARAF BOOKS offers the discerning reader new wine in new bottles.